Mad
about the
Hatter

Dakota Chase

Mad About the Hatter

bu Dakota Chase

Evil Plot Bunny, LLC

PO Box 722

Loughman, FL 33837

Copyright © 2015

Cover by Paul Richmond

Published with permission

ISBN: 978-1-951777-01-2

www.evilplotbunny.com

First Printing: November 2015

Second Edition: August 2019

Printed in the USA

Chapter One

Hatter's eyes remained closed, but he was awake. Indeed, he hadn't slept a wink in what felt like forever, even though it couldn't possibly have been more than a mere quarter of eternity that had passed. He heard the lock rattle and the cell door creak open, just before a large hand pulled him roughly from the bunk to the floor, where what felt sure to be a booted foot connected with his ribs. His body instinctively curled into the fetal position, as if that alone would protect him should the owner of said foot decide a full stomping rather than a single kick was necessary. Pain shot through him like lightning, his nerves screaming. Cracking open one eye, he looked up at the Red Guard looming over him and felt a bit of relief. For once, perhaps, luck was, if not on his side, at least not galloping full-out in the opposite direction.

His quick glimpse told Hatter this Guard was getting a bit long in the tooth to administer full-on stompings. Proper stompings required a great deal of energetic stamping, as well as vigorous browbeating, enthusiastic kicking, and spirited name-calling. There was a decidedly pink cast to this Guard, as if he'd spent far too many years outside patrolling the Queen's borders, his color slowly bleaching out under the brutal kiss of the Wonderland sun. He looked tired and worn, and Hatter noticed a crack in the armor on his left knee. Hatter almost smiled, deciding full-on, proper stompings were quite beyond this Guard's capacity. Hatter wondered what happened to all the younger, stouter, more crimson guards the Queen usually sent to administer the royal stompings.

Perhaps they had somehow all fallen out of favor with the Queen. Now, there was a lovely thought that cheered him considerably despite the ache in his ribs. He wondered if the other Guards' red heads were still attached to their red bodies, or gracing a series of pikes decorating the Queen's croquet lawn.

His money was on the pikes.

After all, it never took much offense for the Queen to call for the Axe. Her temper was so quick he wouldn't be surprised if this faded old Red Guard was all she had left at her command.

Nah. Hatter wasn't that lucky.

Still, it was nice to dream.

"Get up, you."

Another kick, albeit not as powerful as the first, sent Hatter scrambling to his feet. He was as quick, at least, as the pain in his ribs would allow.

The Guard nodded toward the cell door. "You been summoned right and proper, you has."

"A right and proper Summons? Oh, dear. That won't do. Not at all. Look at me!" He brushed futilely at the filth clinging to his cutaway coat and pant legs. Two fingers came away covered in a particularly gruesome spiderweb studded with tiny fly corpses. He grimaced and shook it away. "I'm not dressed for a proper Summons. No, indeed. You simply must go back and ask Her Majesty for a right and improper Summons instead." He sat on the edge of the bunk, and crossed his legs. He tugged on his rather soiled, slightly frayed, fingerless gray gloves, and tamped his top hat down on his head. "Don't worry about me. I'll wait right here."

For a long moment, the Red Guard looked confused. It was almost painful to watch as his expression morphed through several degrees of uncertainty as he obviously tried to muddle his way to understanding. Confusion, befuddlement, mystification, and bewilderment progressed each in their turn to puzzlement and stupefaction, which followed one another in quick succession before finally culminating in total disbelief, which, after an all too brief moment, deepened into intense irritability. A beefy hand reached down and plucked Hatter off the bunk as if he weighed no more than a Dormouse, depositing him none-too-gently on his feet.

The Red Guard might be faded, but he was still as strong as any Hatter knew. He wondered for a brief moment if guards were chosen for their strength, or if they were somehow infused with it when they took the job. He wouldn't be surprised if it was the latter. The Queen's physicians had a boggling array of medicinal remedies at their disposal.

"None of your word games, Hatter. Get on with you, I say! The Queen is waiting, she is." The Red Guard gave Hatter a shove toward the door.

He rolled his eyes. Wonderful. The very person waiting for him was the first person he wished dead—preferably beaten about the head and neck with her own damnable croquet mallet—and the first person who wished *him* dead, no doubt in a most discomforting manner probably involving hot oil and pikes. Having the Red Queen waiting for him made things oh, so very entertaining.

If one were easily entertained by things like unfathomable pain and eventual decapitation, that is..

His cane tapped against the flagstones as he followed along the twisting walkways of the Red Castle. He actually had no trouble whatsoever walking; the cane was more an affectation, an accessory, not a medical necessity. When given his choice, he went nowhere without it. It was a handsome cane as such things went, carved from some unknown exotic, darkly oiled wood. It was as twisted and knotted as both his soul and sense of humor, and topped by a smooth cobalt blue diamond the size of a goose egg. Quite striking, indeed. Good *for* striking as well, which he proved when he suddenly spun on his heel and cracked the Red Guard atop the head with it.

The Red Guard dropped like an ill-baked soufflé. Hatter sidestepped the body, pausing just long enough to bend over and straighten the Red Guard's epaulettes—tidiness was a virtue after all, and since Hatter possessed so very few of them himself, he felt inclined to practice those rare merits he did have—before taking off at a brisk pace.

He skirted the Royal Topiary, keeping his head low so the Red Gardeners, always armed with terribly sharp shears and remarkably short tempers, wouldn't see him, then turned and hurried down a very narrow alley between the Royal Stables and the Royal Tannery. The reek of manure from the former and the stench of the vats from the latter forced him to hold his breath until he cleared both buildings. By the time he left the alley, his eyes streamed tears and his lungs burned for oxygen. He stopped, bent at the waist, wiped his eyes with his sleeves, and gulped greedy, noisy mouthfuls of blessedly sweet air.

Which, alas, was his mistake.

"You there! Hatter! Stop!" Another Red Guard, this one decades younger and shades redder than the last, called out from a nearby garden patio. "Seize him!"

Hatter didn't need to turn around to see the dozen or so Red Guards swiftly approaching him from behind—he could hear them tramping across the patio like a herd of stampeding elephants in tap shoes. When they rushed him and pinned him to the ground, they *felt* like a herd of elephants as well. Porkers, each and every one of them. They really needed to lay off the tarts.

To add insult to injury, one of the fat bastards farted on him.

After enough time passed—he assumed they were hoping that with time, the pressure of their combined weight would squeeze him into a diamond, and trusted they were thoroughly disappointed when he remained uncooperatively fleshy—the weight lifted away, and he was yanked to his feet.

His ribs, sore from his earlier stomping, ached anew, although he refused to let the Guard see his pain. Stubborn pride wasn't exactly a virtue, but it was close enough that he counted it as such, especially since he had so very few authentic ones. He brushed his lapels, hoping his indignation showed half as well as the bruises he knew must be blooming on his face. "My hat and cane, if you please."

His answer was the diamond knob of his cane pushing into his stomach hard enough to force the breath from his lungs… again. Gasping for air, he glared at the Red Guard who held his beloved cane. "I feel obliged to warn you about the curse."

The Guard harrumphed, but a shadow of unease flickered in his eyes, just as Hatter hoped it would. The Red Guards were notoriously superstitious, after all, as was anyone who served the Queen for any length of time. They spent the majority of their day crossing their fingers, knocking on wood, spitting into their palms, and tossing large portions of their wages into fountains, wishing wells, and other small bodies of water in hopes of catching enough luck to avoid her displeasure one more day, and keep their red heads attached to their red shoulders. "C-Curse?"

"Heavens, yes. That cane holds a curse most foul. Look what's happened to me since I've had it! Trapped in an unending tea party, then locked away in the Queen's dungeon for so long, forgotten and forlorn, enduring stompings at regular intervals, only to be dragged into her presence for what I can only assume to be a beheading, and with little hope at all that it might not be my own neck meeting the Axe." He tugged at his collar for good measure.

The Guard's eyes widened. "Oh, yeah. It's to be a beheading all right. Saw the Axe at the whetstone this morning. I'll wager you're right about it being your neck on the block, as well." He tossed the cane to another Guard. "I don't want it. You take it."

That Guard immediately threw it to another. "Not me! I don't want to be cursed!"

"I have enough trouble! I'll not borrow more." The third Guard flung it at a fourth, who quickly chucked it back to the first.

Hatter watched this odd little game of hot potato for a while, but soon grew bored as there seemed to be no hope of a clear winner until three of the four Red Guards dropped dead of old age. Since he really didn't want to wait that long, he reached out and plucked the cane from midair between tosses. "Fine. Being the kind-hearted soul that I am, I'll take one for the team, as it were."

"Thank you!" The Red Guards' faces held identical expressions of relief and gratitude. "You're a gentleman, you are, Hatter."

"Indeed. All I ask for this great sacrifice is the return of my hat. I fear my hair will catch cold without it."

"Oh, of course! Please, take it." The first Red Guard produced Hatter's top hat, slightly dented and a bit scuffed but otherwise unharmed. He rubbed a spot on the crown with the hem of his tunic before offering it over to Hatter. "Just keep that cane away from us."

He took the hat, tamping it down on top of his head with a fond little pat. "Ah, darling. How I've missed you!"

"Pardon me, Mr. Hatter, but—"

"Just 'Hatter,' if you please."

"As you wish. Hatter. Apologies, especially since you was kind enough to save us from that cursed cane, but we gots to take you in now. She'll have *our* heads if we don't. You understand, don't you?"

Hatter rolled his eyes and let out a long-suffering sigh. "That attached to your heads are you? Can't make do without them? Very well, then. Lead on." He waved the four Guards onward.

They jostled one another, forming a straight line, then began to march west, across the patio toward the open doors beyond it.

Hatter stamped his feet in time with theirs, marching in place until the Guards reached the doors. Then he took three long strides to the side to where a pair of bushes grew, and ducked down amid the greenery.

"Wait! Where'd he... Hatter!" The Red Guard called. "Olly, olly oxen free!"

Right. As if a little bit of children's fun like hide-and-seek could trick him into revealing himself. Did they think him such a fool? He rolled his eyes although there was no one to appreciate the gesture aside from the aphids marching along the plant stalks.

In the end, the thing he loved most was what gave him away. "There he is, in the hydrangea bushes! I can see his hat peeking through the leaves!"

Again, large, beefy hands grabbed him in an unbreakable grip, dragging him out of the bushes onto the patio. He fought them as much as his wounded ribs would allow, but to no avail.

Oh, why, he asked himself for the eleventy-thousandth time, *did I ever decide to become a hatter? If I'd listened to father and become a fishmonger instead, this never would've happened. A fish would never have given my position away. A cold fish might've made my attackers feel uncomfortable, and a slippery fish might've facilitated my escape. Indeed, a herring, particularly of the red variety, might've led my pursuers in a false direction, but no fish I can think of would've exposed me to the Guards.*

Damn me for having a flair for fashion and a deep and abiding love for all things chapeau!

He gave another half-hearted attempt to escape, but his wriggling only caused the Red Guard to tighten their grip on him. They dragged him across the patio and through the double doors on the far side, which led to a long interior hallway of the castle. To his dismay, more so perhaps than his capture, was the knowledge that his cane remained behind, lying in the dirt behind the bushes, and the Guards, convinced of its Curse, refused to return for it.

That would teach him to summon up Curses willy-nilly, whether they actually existed or not....

The hallway was familiar to him. Flocked red velvet wallpaper swathed the walls, and a thick crimson carpet striped the flagstone floor in a straight line, reminding Hatter of a long, red tongue. He wrinkled his nose, thinking—not for the first time—that walking down that particular hallway always made him feel like a waste product working its way through the castle's digestive tract. *Through the teeth and past the gums....*

Portraits of previous queens and kings, each one having a body shorter and rounder supporting a larger and more bulbous head than the previous, all wearing the royal red and identical sneering frowns, hung in gilded frames for the entire length of the wall. Each successive generation's crown was larger and more ostentatious than the last, until finally, in the only remaining portrait, the crown was nearly the same height as the King's body. The portraits continued in a long, curving line of pretentiousness for the length of the hallway.

Hatter knew where the hallway terminated. It was the path leading to the throne room. He also knew what was on an outside patio adjacent to the throne room, and that was what took the starch out of his knees.

The Executioner's Block—home to the Axe.

The bones seemed to flee his flesh, and he sagged in his captors' arms, head flopping forward as his toes dragged furrows into the red carpeting. He was doomed.

He'd thought it a blessing at first, when he, Dormouse, and the White Rabbit had managed to literally tick off Time, and were cursed to relive the same teatime hour over and over again, particularly when he found a way out of the tea party while still retaining the gift of youth. Now, he thought it simply a waste. After all those years spent in prison he still looked as young as he had when he took his first sip of tea, but what good would it do him? His head, young or not, would still roll. He only hoped the Curse of Immortality faded when his head left his shoulders. He would hate to be a disembodied head, perhaps stuck on a pike in the throne room, doomed to entertain party guests and serve as a hat rack.

Two additional Red Guards stood sentry at the throne room doors. Moving in unison, they wrenched the heavy doors open. Hatter's honor guard dragged him inside and down the long aisle to the Queen's dais. There they dropped him like an unwashed sock, to lie in a most undignified heap on the floor.

"Off with his head!"

Hatter knew that cringeworthy screech. It always made him want to clean out his ears with white-hot pokers. There was only one creature in Wonderland who could make that sound.

The Red Queen.

Without moving from his place on the floor, he touched his fingers to the brim of his hat, tipping it ever so slightly. "Majesty. You're looking as fetching as ever. Would it be too much to ask for the royal hounds to bring you back to wherever it was they fetched you out of?"

Her scream of outrage echoed, making it thrice as painful on the ears. "Summon the Axe!"

A new voice intervened—happily for Hatter's head—before the Axe answered the Queen's call. "Majesty, a word if I may?"

The Queen addressed the newcomer with the same consideration she offered everyone else, which, of course, was none. "What is it now, Cat? Speak now, or else be silent! We're losing the light and I want his head to roll before supper."

Hatter knew the second voice too, and liked its owner only a smidgen more than he did the Queen. Admittedly, the voice was definitely easier on the ears than hers—it purred and rumbled in pleasant tones—but it spoke in annoying riddles whenever possible. Damn Cat. What was he doing in Red Castle, and how had he won the ear of the Queen? Last Hatter heard, she'd hated the feline almost as much as she hated Hatter.

Against his better judgment, Hatter tilted his head up so he could see the dais. The Queen, as round, vertically-challenged, and big-headed as any of her forebears, sat on her throne, the heels of her tiny feet drumming an irritating tattoo against the legs of the chair. Her gown of red silk trimmed with fluffy, red-dyed ermine enveloped her in billows and folds, leaving only her head, hands, and feet exposed. She clutched a golden scepter in her hand, which was, Hatter thought snidely, not nearly as striking as his now-lost cane.

The Queen's face was not so much beautiful as it was striking, in the same way a venomous snake was attractive— interesting to look at, yes, but much better when seen from a distance. Her face was oval, her eyes a curious shade of yellow that deepened to orange when her temper flared, which was basically all the time. Piled high on her head were intricate coils of hair the color of blood, fastened in place with many carnelian pins. A diadem of ruby-studded gold encircled the base of her towering coif.

On a stool placed within reach of her right hand sat an enormous crown of gold and precious gems slightly surpassing her in height and girth. It was so large that had she actually tried to wear it, the weight would probably snap her neck like a chicken bone. When she did need to don it—for those rare, special occasions like royal familial beheadings and the like—wires suspended it from the ceiling, and positioned it to appear to be sitting on her head. In actuality, she merely sat beneath it.

Hatter noticed the Red King's throne set off to the side of the room, covered in dust and cobwebs. She'd driven her husband batty, they said. He'd simply stormed out of the castle one day and never returned. They never found his body, so there was a chance he still lived. Of course, there was the distinct possibility the Queen had the King's royal head secretly lopped off and the body buried deep.

Either way, unless proven otherwise, technically the King was alive and remained in power, and the Queen ruled in his stead, unopposed.

Personally, Hatter, who'd always found the Red King a likeable sort, hoped the King remained among the living and was never found. It was rather nice to think he escaped the Queen. Hatter took great pleasure in imagining the King living a life full of danger and excitement, perhaps as a pirate or brigand, even though it was far more likely his remains were moldering under the earth somewhere on the castle's grounds, his head tucked securely under his arm.

Nearer the throne, on the Queen's left, completely unsupported by anything other than air, sprawled the Cheshire Cat. Furry, plump, orange and white, he had the largest green eyes and the whitest, sharpest teeth Hatter could recall seeing on a feline. He spread his limbs in a long, lazy stretch, then rolled on his side and smiled a wide, toothy grin. "Mustn't be too hasty, Majesty. Without a head, where would Hatter's hat rest? It wouldn't do to have a stray hat rolling about the queendom willy-nilly, tripping people up. People might think us untidy."

She shot him a withering stare. "Can you never speak plainly? Perhaps it's your head I should order lopped off."

Cat's grin grew wider as his body disappeared, leaving only his head behind. It was a most disconcerting sight, which, of course, was why Hatter suspected Cat did it so often. "I fear that's already been tried, Majesty, and most unsuccessfully as I recall." The rest of him reappeared, just as fat and furry as ever. "Think for a moment, your Most High Redness. Without his head, no one would know he's the Hatter. I believe—and please, correct me if I'm wrong—the personage now in Wonderland seeks the Hatter, not merely the Hat. It simply wouldn't do to send a headless Hatter to… our guest."

The Queen's face grew as red as her castle walls. One hand tightened on the arm of her throne until her knuckle joints crackled. The other hand squeezed the golden scepter she carried so hard she left finger marks embedded in the metal. "Intruder! Interloper! Trespasser! It shan't be allowed! Off with his head!"

"Now, Your Highness, we agreed that his head must remain attached until we find out how he got here and what he wants, didn't we?"

Her lower lip jutted out in a magnificent pout, quite worthy of royalty, and she gave an almost imperceptible nod. Her eyes darted back to Hatter, her lips spread in a wicked little grin, and she pointed a pudgy finger. "Then off with his head."

"Majesty, we've just been over this. I'm afraid you can't behead him, either. Not yet, at any rate."

Hatter grimaced. Couldn't Cat just leave it at not beheading him at all? Was it truly necessary to add in the "not yet" part?

The Queen bounced on her throne. "Of course I can! I'm the Queen. I can do anything I wish. Off with his head! Off with her head! Off with all their heads!" Her eyes bulged so much Hatter feared they might pop out of her skull and fly across the room like a pair of peas tossed by misbehaving children at the dinner table.

Cat's voice remained velvet-like, unruffled, as if her crazed fury was no more than a toddler's temper tantrum. "Now, now, Majesty, if you put everyone to the Axe, who would you have left to rule?"

The Queen fretted for a moment, hemming and hawing and huffing, clearly wanting all the heads in the queendom to roll, and not wanting to admit Cat had a point. She blew a strand of hair from her eyes and pouted. "Well, someone's head has to come off."

"That is why we are sending the Hatter to our guest—to lure him here for questioning."

"And head-rolling! Don't forget that!"

Cat's grin grew a bit too predatory for Hatter's liking. "Of course, Majesty. They'll both kneel before the Axe… in good time. For now, we need their heads to remain where they are if we wish our questions answered. Remember?"

She hedged, trying to bargain, and pointed at Hatter. "But this one's just aching for a good lopping. Perhaps just a little scrape, then? A nick on his neck with the blade? Only a scratch. No one will even notice. No one will care. I'll settle for a close shave at this point."

Cat clucked his tongue at her. "No, Majesty, not now. You know the rules. Off or not, no in-betweens."

"Oh, well…. Fudge." That was the closest the Queen ever came to an expletive. She could order beheadings enough to flood Wonderland with an ocean of blood, but having a four-letter word pass through her lips was simply too gauche for her to stomach. Even the mild confectionary oath she managed caused those in the throne room to gasp in shock, including Cat and Hatter. "Then both their heads shall roll as soon as possible!"

"That's the spirit, Your Redness," Cat purred.

Hatter blinked, and forgetting for a moment it was his head so recently in jeopardy, lifted it from the carpet. "Whose head are we talking about now? Is it mine or someone else's? Is it coming off or staying on? And why? I'm really quite confused."

"Yes, we're speaking about your head. It's staying on, for now. The why of it is… is…." The Queen pursed her lips for a moment. "Cat, tell me again why I must keep his head on his shoulders?"

"Boy Alice asks for him, and in turn, we need him to bring our visitor to us for questioning."

The Queen shrieked and slammed her hands over her ears, knocking her diadem askew. Her feet kicked a rapid beat against the chair legs. She pointed at Cat. "You know it is against the law to say that name in my presence! Off with your head!"

Cat's body disappeared again, and he rolled his overly large, green eyes. "Majesty, try to stay focused, yes? We've just discussed that already."

Pouting, her cheeks mottled with red fury, the Queen lifted her chin in defiance. "Oh, well, then off with his head, instead!"

Hatter leaned up on one elbow and asked again, more confused than ever. "Off with whose head?"

"His! His!" The Queen jumped up, and stamped her tiny feet. Her gown swished around her like a garnet flood. She bared her teeth, her voice slipping between them in a venomous whisper. "Boy Alice!"

Now Hatter was intrigued enough to heave himself into a sitting position. He reached into his pocket, and pulled out a full cup of steaming hot tea, then noisily sipped it. It was, after all, nearly four and he never missed teatime if he could help it. Blame it on the long practice he had at the never-ending tea party with Dormouse and Rabbit. "Might I inquire as to who this 'Boy Alice' might be? That doesn't sound like a proper name to me."

Cat rolled to his back, scratching playfully at the air. "So says the one named after an insane haberdasher." He rolled back, and grinned at Hatter. "Isn't that the pot calling the kettle a skillet?"

Hatter frowned, drained his cup, and carefully replaced it in his pocket. He chose to ignore the remark rather than admit Cat had a point. "Who is this person called 'Boy Alice,' and why would he be asking for me?"

"Majesty, cover your ears." Cat waited until the Queen finished shooting him her blackest and fiercest scowl, and slapped her palms against her ears again. She began humming a ditty that might have been catchy had it not been so awfully off-key. Cat turned toward Hatter. "We don't know his true name yet. He is, as best our reconnaissance tells us, Alice's brother, which is why we've referred to him as 'Boy Alice.'"

Hatter's eyes opened wide, and his mouth popped open. "You mean… the Alice?"

Cat nodded. "Do you know of anyone else by that name in Wonderland?"

"I wasn't aware she had a brother."

"Well, it seems she does, and now he's here, and asking for you."

"Me? Why me?" Hatter frowned, his fingers worrying one of the large purple buttons on his slightly worn, slightly shiny brocade vest. "I don't know him. Never met the chap. Barely knew his sister when she was here. It all seems a bit forward, don't you think?"

"Ah, that's the question, isn't it? We don't know why he's here or why he's asking for you. He refuses to answer any questions. Not even from Caterpillar, and you know 'Pillar has ways to make people talk."

Hatter smirked and nodded. "Most potent whackweed north of the Rabbit Warren, and don't get me started on his mushrooms." He glanced at the Queen. Her singing had grown louder and more off-key than before. Her cheeks were as red as her gown, and her frown was so deep you could hide treasure in the folds on her forehead. She was clearly as frustrated that a relative of the much-hated Alice dared step foot in Wonderland, and that said relative, again like the loathed Alice, refused to be forthright about their business in the queendom or follow protocol by visiting the Red Palace first off, as she was at her own inability to have anyone's head chopped off.

He looked at Cat for answers. "So, we haven't the foggiest idea what his name is, why he's here, or what he wants with me?"

"No." Cat gestured toward the Queen. "Majesty thinks he wants the same thing she thought Alice wanted, mainly to overthrow her regime. If you recall, just before she left Wonderland, Alice was Queen… for a very short time."

He remembered. It was probably the best and happiest five minutes the queendom ever knew.

He glanced at the Queen again. If she grew any angrier, Hatter worried her head might explode. *Not that it would necessarily be a bad thing*, thought Hatter, *but she'd make a horrific mess, and I'm in the splash zone.* He knew better than to give voice to that particular thought, and wisely kept it inside his head where it belonged. "What does Her Majesty wish me to do?"

As if unable to contain her ire any longer, the Queen lashed out and cracked Hatter on the head with her scepter. It made an unsightly dent in his top hat. "Imbecile! We want you to find Boy Alice and chop off his head!"

Cat tsk-tsked her. "Now, now, Majesty. Think. What did we say earlier?"

The Queen rolled her eyes, then turned her head, refusing to make eye contact with Cat, and mumbled half under her breath. "People can't talk once their heads are removed."

"Correct. And what do we want Hatter to do?"

She sighed heavily. "Find Boy Alice and bring him here so we can ask him questions." She quirked an eyebrow, and curled her lips into a sly smile. "And then chop off his head!"

"And Hatter?" Cat prodded. "It occurs to me he should be given some sort of reward for bringing Boy Alice in, else he might not be very accommodating."

The Queen huffed and made a face, as if the words were bitter enough to choke her. "Oh, very well. If he brings Boy Alice to me, he can keep his own head."

"And...?" Cat nudged her.

She bared her teeth. "And I shall grant him a full pardon for his crimes."

"Excellent. You are quite magnanimous, Majesty." Cat turned his grin toward Hatter. "Understood?"

"I'm mad, not deaf."

The Queen rewarded him with another knock of her scepter. "Then why are you still here?"

Hatter swept his hat off and after punching out the dents, bowed low. His hat—not to mention his body—had taken enough of a beating for one day. "I'm off."

Cat laughed, rolling to his back. "You can say that again."

Seriously, sometimes he hated that damn Cat.

Hatter narrowed his eyes and straightened his hat, running his fingers smartly over the brim. He strode out of the throne room, back straight and head high. He tried not to worry overly much, but it was difficult. He had no idea what sort of trouble the Cat and Queen were sending him to meet this time. When he'd met Alice, although he'd known her a very short time, he'd very nearly lost his head as a result. What might he be in danger of losing with Alice's brother?

Chapter Two

Henry sat up, rubbing his head. It ached, not as if he'd bumped it, but as if he'd been sick, although to the best of his knowledge he hadn't been. He squinted at the bright sunlight beaming down at him, but quickly averted his eyes before the intensity seared his corneas. When had the sun risen, and where had he been while it was rising? Last thing he remembered, it'd been nighttime, and he'd been feeling fine.

Where had he been? He tried to think, fighting through the cobwebs in his mind that obscured his memories. Oh, yes. He was beginning to remember, although everything was still foggy. There'd been a party. It'd been a dinner party, hosted by his sister, Alice, hadn't it? He frowned, trying to remember more.

There'd been pizza, he remembered that much, but cheese and pepperoni wouldn't cause memory loss, would it? It never had before.

Wasn't there an argument? Well, of course there'd been. That might not be a memory as much as a good guess. He and Alice always fought. In fact, it was a rare occasion when they didn't trade words. Sometimes fists flew. And on one memorable occasion, they sent a half-dozen fine china plates whizzing at one another's heads.

This hadn't been just any old brother/sister argument, though, had it? No, it'd been *the* argument, the same one they'd carried on since they were kids in one form or another. She insisted she'd fallen down a rabbit hole, and then later, stepped through a looking glass into a fabulously topsy-turvy world called "Wonderland."

He'd insisted Mother must've repeatedly dropped her on her head as an infant, and if she continued to insist rabbits wore waistcoats and dormice held tea parties, he might just need to talk to Alice's husband, Phillip, about arranging a nice long vacation for her at the local insane asylum. Perhaps a few hundred volts of electricity between her ears would be sufficient to un-scatter her brains.

Honestly, he couldn't wait for June, when he would at long last reach twin milestones in his life within days of each other—his eighteenth birthday, and his high school graduation. The combination would free him, and he planned to leave his parents' home, his sister, and their shared past in his dust as he bolted toward a future free from lunatic tales of pocket-watch-wearing rabbits and head-shearing Red Queens.

A future where he would be free to be himself, where there would be no hiding, no ducking his head, no pretending he didn't hear the whispers and taunts about his crazy sister, and no remorse at leaving it all behind.

Then Alice apologized for making him upset, and handed him a glass of punch. He almost hadn't taken it. It was just so out of character for her to give up and concede the argument so quickly that he felt strongly something was wrong. He wouldn't put it past her to try to poison him. There was no love lost between him and Alice, not since she'd disappeared and returned with those wild stories of hers.

He was certain to the very core of his being that Alice's unbelievable tales were blatant cries for attention, tolerated from a seven year old, perhaps, but not from a grown girl in her teens, and certainly not now, from a married woman in her early twenties. She was his older sister by several years—she should be setting a good example. He was old enough to handle the truth of whatever horrible thing had happened to her when she'd disappeared.

Even if she truly believed her audacious lies, he felt wholeheartedly her disappearances and refusal to tell the truth of where she'd been had driven their father to the bottle, and their mother to an early grave.

Nowadays, their father rarely left his suite of rooms, staying in a mind-numbing state of inebriation. He didn't care if the house caught fire as long as long as his liquor was delivered. Henry doubted he'd seen his father more than a half dozen times in the past year. Heard him, yes. Father's drunken tirades were practically legendary. But *seen* him? No, hardly ever. It was just as well— Father was a mean drunk who often let his fists talk for him. Another reason Henry counted the minutes until he could leave home forever.

Henry placed the blame for his father's condition directly at Alice's dainty little feet. To Henry, their father was an unapproachable giant who'd always ruled their home with an unbending, unyielding iron will. Surely he would never have sunk so low had it not been for the weight of Alice's ridiculous lies pulling him down.

Then there was their Uncle Leonard, his mother's brother, who'd arrived several years ago, soon after their mother's death, and hadn't left since. Uncle Leonard was kind enough, Henry supposed, but even he believed Alice's tales. That was the extent of Henry's family, and no one, not a single soul in the house, sided with him against Alice.

Not only could Henry never bring himself to believe Alice's nonsense, he could never find it within himself to forgive Alice, either. There were many times when he could barely abide being in the same room with her. If only she'd apologize, tell the truth about Wonderland, admit it was a dream or a fabrication, and tell what had really happened to her, then maybe. However, as long as she insisted her lies were the truth, he wanted no part of her. In fact, he'd only agreed to attend the party because Alice 's husband, Phillip, asked. Phillip was a nice enough fellow,a nd Henry had always liked him. After all, it wasn't Phillip's fault Alice was bonkers.

Last night her smile seemed genuine though, and he'd taken the drink from her hand. Now it seemed he should've listened to his instincts. What had she put in it? It looked like punch and smelled like punch, but it definitely hadn't tasted like punch. He remembered a complicated taste filling his mouth, the flavor reminding him of butterscotch, fig pudding, liver and onions, and cabbage all rolled into one, singularly horrid combination. Before he could complain, though, the taste was swiftly followed by a feeling of the world shifting on its axis, and then… nothing.

Nothing, that is, until he'd awakened on a soft bed of moss, with spikes of pain in his head and the taste of dirty feet in his mouth. He spat on the ground, and wiped his lips with the back of his hand—for all the good it did him. The taste clung to his tongue like a frightened toddler to its mother's skirts.

One perfunctory glance around told him he was in a garden, but he didn't have the foggiest notion who the garden belonged to, or where it was located. Nothing looked even the slightest bit familiar to him. It wasn't the lovely, carefully tended rose garden at his parents' home where he still resided, nor the far more pedestrian patch of daisies and forget-me-nots in Alice's yard. Nor was it a garden in any park he frequented, nor did it belong to any one of a number of his friends and acquaintances. He'd never seen it on his school grounds, or anywhere in town. No one he knew would have a garden such as this attached to their homes. It was altogether too strange, too odd, too… too.

For one thing, the flora here was ridiculous. Each plant was outrageously oversized, sporting huge, heavy blooms of overly sweet-smelling, brilliantly colored flowers, and thick stalks of greenery that loomed well over his head. They formed a large, seemingly impenetrable rectangular area of foliage, and he had to crane his neck to see the tops of them. Thorns the size of bayonets precluded him from considering climbing over or pushing through the floral walls.

For another, there was a large caterpillar-like creature lounging nearby on an enormous mushroom. The bug was the size of a small pony, and covered with bright blue, spiky fur spotted with pale yellow. Worse, it was smoking from a huge purple hookah pipe. A lazy curl of bluish smoke coiled around its head, and a sweetly spicy smell hung heavy in the air, making Henry feel a bit lightheaded.

Wonderful. Just what he needed. A contact high from a hallucination.

"Boy Alice, we are bored. Perhaps you would amuse us. Tell us… why are you?"

Great. He was hearing things as well as seeing and smelling them. Could seventeen-year-olds have strokes? Perhaps he'd had one of those. He put a finger to his throat, feeling for his pulse. It was strong and steady, and gave no explanation as to why he was being delusional.

The caterpillar responded to his silence by blowing a series of smoke rings toward him.

Henry coughed, waved a hand in front of his face in a futile effort to bat away the smoky air, and tried not to inhale. "Why am I…?"

"Yes, dull boy. Why are you?"

"What?"

"As dense as your sister, we dare say. We ask why you are and you answer you are what." The Caterpillar took a deep drag on his pipe. After a moment or two, he let out another long stream of smoke that encircled Henry's head and neck like a hangman's noose. "Why should we care what you are? You are you and we are we. Our only interest is why you are."

Henry coughed again. "Why am I even having this conversation? You're not real. Caterpillars do not grow to the size of lawn furniture, and even if they did, they don't talk, and they definitely don't smoke. You're a hallucination." He gestured around him, batting at a daisy the size of a truck tire. "I've had some sort of psychotic break. All of this is part of a delusion, probably brought on by whatever foul little concoction Alice made me drink last night. She poisoned me, the little twit!"

"Who is Twit? A relative, perhaps, of Tweedledum and Tweedledee?"

"Who?" He shook his head. "Never mind. It doesn't matter. I need to get home."

"And where is that, Boy Alice?" The Caterpillar gestured in a circle with his pipe. "In which direction should you go?"

"Home is… it's…. Well, I don't know which way, exactly. I don't know where I am."

"It should be obvious. You are here, with us."

"But… but where are you?"

"Again, the answer is obvious. We are here, with you." The Caterpillar inhaled again, then blew out another thick stream of blue smoke. "Really, you must pay more attention to the conversation."

Henry's head was beginning to spin pleasantly. He resisted the urge to take a deep breath, or better yet, ask for a toke on the Caterpillar's pipe. "Look, all I know is Alice made me drink something that knocked me on my butt. The last thing I remember is her voice telling me to find the Mad Hatter. There was something else, too, but—"

That name widened the Caterpillar's eyes. He leaned up, gesturing toward Henry with his hookah pipe, cutting Henry off. "The Mad Hatter, you say? Why him?"

"I don't know why. I don't even know if such a person exists, or how he could help me."

"Ah." The Caterpillar lay back down, and smoked for a moment. "Hatter exists, or at least, he did. Do you?"

"Do I what?"

"Exist."

Henry shoved his fingers through his hair, pulling tight enough to bring tears to his eyes, nearly at his wits end with the irritating creature. Or hallucination. Or whatever the Hell this thing was. "Of course I exist! I'm standing right here."

"Perhaps you are a figment of our imagination." The Caterpillar blew an especially thick ribbon of smoke at Henry. "It would not be the first time we conversed with ourselves. We rather enjoy it, actually. We're quite witty, you know."

"You're crazy!"

The Caterpillar's laugh sounded wet, like pipes gurgling. "But of course. All the best people are. Just ask Hatter."

Henry gritted his teeth, trying to keep his voice level and his temper under control. He nearly succeeded. "Screw Hatter!"

"Please. We could care less about who Hatter chooses to sleep with or not. We might add, neither should anyone else."

He frowned, and shook his head, then turned his back on Caterpillar. After a moment or two, he brightened. "Maybe I'm still unconscious, and this is all a dream. Perhaps whatever Alice gave me knocked me out, and I'm still sleeping." His mood just as quickly deteriorated into a funk. "On the other hand, maybe I'm dead, and this is Hell. Can't be heaven, because I doubt giant, irritating caterpillars are allowed there, stoned or otherwise. I don't feel dead, though, not with this wicked headache." He began to massage his temples. "Although if I'm in Hell, it stands to reason I'd be damned to endure all manner of suffering. Both pains in the head"—he glanced back toward Caterpillar—"and pains in the ass."

He dropped his hands, determined to ignore the pain. Focusing his attention, he paced the rectangular area of the garden, looking for holes in the thick foliage large enough for him to squeeze through without being shish-ka-bobbed by the thorns, but found none. He couldn't climb over it for the same reason. Tunneling out was not an option, not without a shovel. Finally, in desperation, he turned back to the Caterpillar. "How do I get out of here?"

Caterpillar took a deep drag on his pipe, seeming to contemplate the question. "Well, we suppose you could fly out." He peered at Henry over the pipe. "Can you fly?"

"Do I look like I can fly?"

"You don't look like you can do much of anything. That was not our question. We are well aware that looks can be deceiving, so we asked whether or not you can fly."

Henry ground his molars, his jaw tightening. "No. I can't fly."

"Pity. It would be a very marketable talent."

Henry smirked. "I'd say you're flying enough for the two of us. Come on, there must be some way out of here!"

"Hmm." Caterpillar gestured toward the thick foliage walls. "Can you not just push through to the other side?"

"No. It'll hurt." Henry took a step away from the wall of greenery and thorns, just to be safe.

"Perhaps the pain will not be as terrible as you fear it will be."

"And perhaps it'll be worse. Have you seen the size of those thorns? There's got to be another way!"

The Caterpillar smoked a while, seemingly lost in thought. Then he suddenly sat forward, and jabbed his pipe at Henry, looking stern. "Beware the Jabberwock, my son! The jaws that bite, the claws that catch! Beware the Jubjub bird, and shun! The frumious Bandersnatch!"

Henry gaped at the Caterpillar. "The Jabberwho? I never heard of a Jubjub bird, and 'frumious' isn't even a word. Do you want to know what I think? I think that rank stinkweed you've been smoking has rotted your brain. Either that or this is still all a hallucination, one that's devolved into total nonsense."

The Caterpillar sat back, tapping his chin with his pipe. "Hmph. Interesting. Alice didn't understand it, either. We can only surmise the dullness in your family is genetic."

Henry had had enough. Finding a few nooks and crannies in the giant mushroom to serve as foot- and handholds, he clambered up to the broad, smooth head. Reaching over, he yanked the hookah pipe out of the Caterpillar's hand, and held it just out of reach of the Caterpillar's short, skinny arms.

The Caterpillar screeched a thin, fragile, desperate sound. "No! What are you doing? Oh, you bad boy. You terrible boy! Give it back to us! Give it back!"

"Absolutely. As soon as you tell me how to get out of this garden! There has to be a way. You got in. I got in. Logic says if there's a way in, there must be a way out." He jiggled the pipe, taunting the Caterpillar.

"All right, all right! Logic lies. The way out is illogical."

"That doesn't make any sense!"

"Now you're getting it. Perhaps there's hope for you after all. We told you the secret, boy! Give it back to us now!"

"You told me nothing but nonsense! How do I get out of here?"

The Caterpillar banged ineffectual fists against the slightly slimy surface of the mushroom head. "To go up, one must go down. To go back, one must go forward. To get out, one must go in!"

"Go in? If I go in, the thorns will slice me to ribbons!"

"This! This!" The Caterpillar banged the mushroom harder. "This will allow you to go in."

Henry's lip curled as he looked at the giant fungus on which they stood. "Do you mean I have to eat some of this slimy crap? I hate mushrooms."

"Fine. Then stay. It is your choice. Now, we answered your question. Give us our pipe!" The Caterpillar reached toward Henry, all sixteen hands making grabby motions toward the pipe, his face twisted in a snarl.

"Fine! But if eating it doesn't work or makes me sick, I'm going to come back up here and stuff that hookah up your ass!" He didn't know if the Caterpillar actually had an ass, or if it did, where it was located, but it sounded like a good threat to Henry anyway. He tossed the pipe to the Caterpillar.

Caterpillar grabbed the pipe and held it close to his chest, greedily guarding it against illicit snatches by terrible boys or otherwise unexpected mishaps.

Henry found an edge of the mushroom head that was soft, and was easily able to break off a small piece, about the size of a slice of bread. It felt a little bit slimy, and smelled like dirt, but he managed to take a tiny bite.

"As stupid as his sister!" The Caterpillar snarled from behind him. "Annoying, irritating, and frumious! Get off my mushroom and out of my Lair!"

Henry felt something hit his back, pushing him over the edge of the mushroom. He tilted wildly for a moment, his arms windmilling, but he lost the fight with gravity and tumbled off, falling helpless through space. His last thought was that it seemed much, much further going down than it had going up. It had to be Caterpillar. The damned bug must've done something to him. He hoped he wouldn't break a leg or his back in the fall, so as soon as he finished falling, he'd be able to climb back up and strangle the Caterpillar with its own damn hookah pipe hose.

Chapter Three

The trip from the Red Castle to the Caterpillar's Lair was uneventful, aside from a barrage of stones thrown at the royal coach by villagers, a close call with a rampaging Bandersnatch, and the overall bone-jarring, teeth-rattling, spine-shattering motion of the wooden carriage wheels clattering over stone-strewn, hole-infested dirt roads.

Still, Hatter mused, *I suppose it beats walking. As uncomfortable as the ride was, it shaved at least a day and a half off my travel time. Also probably shaved an entire quarter inch off my height by compressing my spine, but one can't have everything.*

The stone-throwing villagers were par for the course. He would've been more shocked had they not appeared and hurled rocks at his conveyance. After all, he was riding in the ridiculously red royal coach, an ostentatious and pretentious eyesore on wheels if ever there was one, a vehicle that practically screamed, "Here Comes the Red Queen, the Cause of All Your Woes." Hatter knew the villagers bore him no personal grievance—they fully expected the Sovereign to be inside, not the Hatter. The villagers simply thought they had a shot at beaning the Queen squarely on her crimson noggin with one of their rocky missiles. They'd be ever so disappointed to find out they never had a chance since the Queen was safely ensconced in her throne room back in the Castle. Hatter didn't want to be the one to disillusion them, and would emit a loud, ear-piercing scream every so often just to hear the swell of cheers that inevitably followed it.

The Bandersnatch was another story. Foul creatures they were, full of teeth and claws and sour attitudes, but surprisingly tasty if well-salted and cooked long and slow. Hatter sorely wished the one that nearly took a bite out of him was already seasoned and roasting over a low fire. The ugly thing may have succeeded in getting a mouthful of Hatter, had not one of its feet caught on a root that sent it tumbling into a nearby marsh. He fervently hoped a snaggle-toothed crocodile might make its home in that marsh, one that thought the Bandersnatch would make an excellent and tasty meal. Hatter's dislike of Bandersnatches really knew no bounds.

It was nearing teatime on the second day when the coach finally pulled up in a neck-wrenching stop in front of a rectangle of thick greenery. The foliage walls soared up so high that, had he been inclined, he would have had to crane his neck to see the tops of them. Having had his back and neck tortured by the rough roads and rougher ride for the past several hours, and having seen said hedge tops on previous occasions, Hatter kept his gaze glued to the ground as he clambered awkwardly out of the coach. His face wrinkled in a grimace of pain as his spine slowly, if noisily, returned to its original, uncorked, uncompressed state.

A sign posted on the nearest wall had the word "Lair" written on it in exquisitely rendered calligraphy, full of delicate swirls and curlicues. Next to the sign, a tasseled purple velvet rope-pull dangled.

The Caterpillar's Lair, known well to everyone who lived in Wonderland as a place to avoid entering at all costs, was also one of Hatter's least favorite locations. Not because it was as difficult to escape as a Chinese finger trap—he was, after all, one of the few people privy to the secret of escaping it—but because of its garrulous owner.

Caterpillar, with his absurd, drug-induced questions and habit of always referring to himself in third person, was enough to make anyone who wandered into his Lair consider impaling themselves on one of the gigantic hedge thorns as preferable to remaining in his company, Hatter included.

Still, he had no choice if he was to find Boy Alice, or whatever the fellow's real name was, and in doing so, hopefully eliminate his own date with the Axe. Not to mention feed his own curiosity, which was, at times, more of a ravenous beast than the most fermicious Bandersnatch, and probably even more likely to be the means of his demise. He sighed, and reached out to gently tug on the purple velvet rope-pull.

From somewhere deep within the green walls, a dainty, musical bell chimed. It sounded like crystal fairy laughter, so delicate, fragile, and sweet it nearly gave Hatter a toothache from hearing it.

"Who's come to our door?"

"It's Hatter, Caterpillar. Is someone called 'Boy Alice' in there with you?"

Caterpillar's wet laugh made Hatter grind his teeth. "Now, now. We have rules, as you are most well aware. We ask the questions."

"Come on, 'Pillar. Don't be a prat. Just answer the question so I can get on with my life, and you can get on with... er, whatever it is you get up to in there besides sucking on that damn hookah."

"Rules, Hatter! Without rules, the world is chaos. Without rules, civilization falls. Without rules, we get bored and will take a nap."

Hatter gritted his teeth hard enough to hurt his jaw. "Fine. What's your question?"

He could hear sixteen tiny hands clapping in joyous anticipation of an energetic round of riddling, and rolled his eyes.

The sound of Caterpillar clearing his throat floated through the leaves. It sounded like he was gargling glass. "What is cold at times and warm at others, and red for all, though some Red thinks theirs blue?"

Gods, how I hate these stupid games! He thought for a moment, then sighed. It was so obvious! Caterpillar must be losing his touch. He used to come up with riddles that actually tested the intellect.

"The answer is blood, of course. Mammals are warm-blooded, reptiles are cold-blooded, and the royals claim their blood is blue." He could practically smell Caterpillar's disappointment because he'd gotten the answer so quickly. "My turn, now. Is Boy Alice in there?"

"No, no! There are no turns. We ask the questions, not you. You know the rules, Hatter!"

"'Pillar—"

"We are going to go to sleep. It shouldn't be a long nap... only three or four days."

"No! No, don't go to sleep. Go ahead, ask me another!" Hatter's hands curled into fists as he fought to contain his temper. Naps for Caterpillar were more like drug-induced comas, and the last thing he wanted was to cool his heels outside the Lair, waiting for Caterpillar to go through days of self-induced detox.

Caterpillar's voice was thick with smugness. "Very well. Another riddle, then. We see far, we see close, we hold spirits, we count hours. What are we?"

Hatter touched the tip of one of the huge thorns. It pricked his finger, drawing a bright drop of blood. He swore and stuck in it his mouth. *Just as sharp as I remember them.* No pushing through the greenery then. While Hatter knew of a secret door through which a person might exit the Lair, he also knew it was one-way only. There were only two ways to enter that he was aware of—the first was by dropping in from the sky, and the second was waiting for Caterpillar's invitation. Since he had no wings, the former was out; he had no choice but to opt for the latter.

Damn Caterpillar and these stupid riddles! He sat on the grass, watching a flutterby's erratic pattern of flight. Think, Hatter! Far, close, spirits, hours... "Oh, of course!" He jumped up, and went to the wall. "The answer is glasses, of course. Spyglasses see far, magnifying glasses see close, shot glasses hold alcoholic spirits, and hourglasses tell time."

He took little pleasure in Caterpillar's frustrated moan. He simply didn't have time for any more foolishness. There was, he realized, one way to get answers without actually getting inside the Lair. It was dirty pool and a bit underhanded, but he was desperate. He dug in his pocket, his arm sinking in to the elbow, rummaging around for one particular object. A smile lit his face as his fingers closed around it and withdrew it. "Do you know what I'm holding right now, Caterpillar?"

"No questions! No questions! You know the rules."

"Oh, I daresay you'll want the answer to this one, 'Pillar. That's all right. I won't force you to play. I'll give you the answer.

It's a matchstick. A lovely, red-tipped, wooden matchstick. One strike against the sole of my shoe, and I will burn your precious Lair to the ground."

"What? No, you lie!"

"Do I? You should know me better than that. I may be mad, and on occasion may make the truth seem like a crooked street in a twisted town, but a liar I am not." Hatter lifted a foot and scraped the match across the sole of his shoe. A tiny flame burst into life, flickering at the end of the wooden stick. He held it toward the wall of greenery and gently blew on the smoke rising from the flame, watching the thin tendril snake between the leaves into the Lair. "Smell that? That's plain ol' smoke, my friend, but as they say, where smoke is, fire can't be far behind."

Hatter knew that, contrary to what most might think, the whackweed in which Caterpillar imbibed didn't dull his senses, but instead, made him hyperaware of the slightest changes in his Lair. Caterpillar would perceive the thin plume of smoke from the lit match as a billowing, noxious cloud. Hatter smiled to himself and waited for the inevitable explosion.

There was a sudden cry of "Smoke!" followed by a cacophony of crashes, screeches, bangings, and bumpings from within the Lair. Hatter could picture Caterpillar in a tizzy, unsure of what to do, all sixteen hands flailing in panic. Bring Hatter in? Answer Hatter's question? What to do? What to do?

Hatter seized the moment to press his advantage. "Where is Boy Alice, Caterpillar?"

"Gone! He's gone. Got little and left!"

Oh, no. No, no, no! "You didn't make him eat the damn mushroom, did you? 'Pillar, you know better. The Queen forbade you from feeding anyone a piece of that mushroom ever again!"

Caterpillar's voice thinned into a whine. "We had to, Hatter! He was upsetting us. He refused to play by the rules. He raised his voice at us, Hatter."

The flame ate the rest of the wooden stick, burning Hatter's fingers. He shook it out and dropped it, shoving his slightly burnt fingertips in his mouth. His voice sounded a bit distorted as he tried to enunciate around his thumb and forefinger. "You're a grown caterpillar, Caterpillar. I would think you could hold your own in an argument without resorting to feeding poor, unsuspecting people bits of your slimy fungus. Which way did he go?"

"Did you blow out the match?"

"Answer me, and I'll tell you."

"He went... down."

Well, of course, he did. The only other direction was up, and unless Boy Alice kept a cannon in his pocket with which to shoot himself into the upper stratosphere, down would've been his only option. "And then where?"

"We don't know. We didn't watch. We didn't care."

Hatter sensed Caterpillar was telling the truth. If Boy Alice was anything like his sister, he was probably annoying at best, disagreeable at worst, and positively frumious if the mood struck him. Chances were good Caterpillar couldn't wait to get rid of him, hence why he risked the Queen's ire by making Boy Alice eat the mushroom.

Eating the fungus was not the Caterpillar's only recourse. There was a much easier, safer way to leave the Lair—through a secret door in the foliage that only Caterpillar, Hatter, and a select few others knew about. Making Boy Alice eat the mushroom was an indication of just how much Caterpillar disliked him.

"Have you doused the flame, Hatter? Please, Hatter?"

Hatter sighed. For all Caterpillar was annoying, he was in essence a harmless, simple creature, who minded his own business unless you made the mistake of trespassing in his Lair, or letting him talk you into partaking of his pipe. His riddles were bothersome but benign. He'd done no real harm to Hatter this time, either, and he had answered Hatter's question. Just because Hatter wasn't happy with the answer didn't mean Caterpillar's Lair should burn. "Yes, it's out. You're safe."

The relief in Caterpillar's voice was quite audible. "We thank you." Purple smoke again began to drift out from between the leaves of the walls as the smell of whackweed again filled the air.

Hatter turned his mind back to the problem at hand, namely, finding Boy Alice. The best place to begin his search, in fact, Hatter supposed, the only place, since he now knew for certain Boy Alice had eaten Caterpillar's mushroom, was the ground under the towering mushroom. That meant the search was to begin with Hatter on his knees, since that was likely where Boy Alice would be— whether or not he survived the fall from the mushroom to the Lair's floor.

If he was dead, Boy Alice's battered and broken corpse would be lying somewhere in the grass in the shadow cast by the mushroom. If he'd lived through what was surely an extremely rough landing, he'd be wandering—most likely bruised, bleeding, and limping—among the jungle of grass stalks, no doubt trying to remain alive.

Sampling 'Pillar's mushroom made the eater shrink to the size of a largish bit of dandelion fuzz. That was how it was said the Red King met his fate—he ate 'Pillar's mushroom and a strong wind carried him away. They had yet to find the poor man's body.

Of course, the King could be playing dead, Hatter mused, not for the first time. Faking one's own death would be a bloody brilliant way to escape life with the Queen.

In any case, that was why the Queen forbade Caterpillar to feed his mushroom to anyone else. If she found out Boy Alice ate some, she'd have Caterpillar's head. Even though Hatter didn't harbor any particular fondness for Caterpillar, he disliked the Queen even more. No more heads for her, not if he could help it.

"Caterpillar? Let me in, please."

"We have rules—"

"Do not start with me again. I have an entire packet of matches. Shall I light another?"

"Do come in, Hatter."

Just like that—because, after all, that's how magic works— Hatter found himself able to pass through the thick green walls of the Lair to the inside without earning a single scratch from the bayonet-like thorns. He knew, though, that going back out the same way would be impossible without them skewering him. This magic was one-way only.

Hatter dropped to his knees and began searching through the grass at the base of the mushroom. It wasn't like looking for a needle in a haystack. Oh no, that would've been much easier because the needle rarely tried to be found, which he greatly suspected was indeed the case with Boy Alice.

Shrunk to the size of a largish dust mite, Boy Alice's best survival tactic would be hiding from everything, including Hatter, who would look like a giant from Boy Alice's point of view.

Hatter's keen gaze slowly swept the ground. He found acorns, feathers, a stone shaped like a peanut, a peanut shaped like a stone, and a key, which he pocketed because you never knew when you might stumble across a lock in desperate need of one. He also found a half crown, a whole crown, and a tiara missing only two or three diamonds, all of which also found their way into his pocket.

He saw centipedes trundling along on a hundred marching feet, and millipedes, having ten times as many legs, speeding past them, causing the centipedes to spew foul curses. There were ants aplenty—red ants, black ants, elif ants, gi ants, pique ants, ascend ants, descend ants, girl ants and boy ants, and he thought he may have seen a clairvoy ant, but it must've sensed him coming because it disappeared before he could be sure. He found bottlecaps, snowcaps, hubcaps, and nightcaps, as well as jewelweed, hawkweed, carpetweed, and fireweed, which burned his fingers when he accidentally touched it.

The one thing he didn't find was Boy Alice.

He sat up and stretched, feeling his spine pop like corn on the fire. It felt like he'd been searching for days, but a glance at his pocket watch showed less than an hour had passed. Why was it Time slowed down or sped up adversely to whatever he wished? If he wanted Time to pass quickly, the clock dragged its hands around its face with the speed of a dead snail. When he wanted Time to slow down, it sped up, zipping by him in a blur. Time, he decided, had a decidedly contrary nature, and still carried a grudge against Hatter from the whole Tea Party debacle.

Hatter blanched and immediately tried to erase the thought from his mind for fear he'd irritate Time again and end up searching the damned patch of grass forever, just as he'd nearly spent his life in eternal teatime when last Time cursed him. Time was much too sensitive and far too full of itself, as far as Hatter was concerned.

"Boy Alice! This would be so much easier if you'd just show yourself!" His keen gaze scanned the grassy area at the foot of the giant mushroom, then slowly panned out toward the towering green wall. The area within the Lair wasn't so large, perhaps a mere quarter the size of the Queen's ballroom, yet if he had to search it all on his hands and knees, he'd probably be a bearded old man by the time he finished. Or at least have extremely sore hands and knees.

He could claim Boy Alice was dead. March right up to the Queen and tell her Caterpillar ate him. Or smoked him, which might be more believable.

At which point, she would do one of two things: Call for Caterpillar's head, or spiral into a deep rage over losing her chance to kill Boy Alice herself, and lop off Hatter's head as an inferior substitute.

Perhaps lying wasn't the best of plans after all.

Sighing heavily, he resumed his search.

He bent down low so his nose practically touched the dirt, scanning the ground for any sign of Boy Alice. At last, after he'd searched as wide an area as he felt Boy Alice could've covered in the few short hours since eating the mushroom and shrinking, he spotted a pair of teeny-tiny footprints in a mound of soft dirt.

Many hundreds of slightly larger footprints surrounded them. Then the teeny-tiny footprints vanished, and all that remained, leading away from the soft mound of earth, were the slightly larger prints.

Hatter knew those other prints, and cursed aloud when he saw them.

The Ants, it seemed, had captured Boy Alice.

He looked around again, stepping gingerly so he wouldn't inadvertently smash the Ants' Hill and Boy Alice with it. There, a foot or so away, seemed the likely culprit. An Anthill rose like a pimple from the black dirt.

He bent down again and peered closely at the Anthill. A few remaining ants disappeared down the hole at its center.

Red Ants, to be precise, which drew another curse from Hatter's lips. Of course it would have to be Red Ants. They were by far more vicious and bloodthirsty than any other group of Ants, marching in well-trained, regimented armies, and ruled by a fierce and cruel Red Queen Ant.

Hatter faced yet another choice: Go back to the Non-Ant Red Queen and tell her the Ant Red Queen had Boy Alice in her Hill, and he was as good as dead, or get small and go into the Red Anthill and attempt to rescue him.

The first scenario would no doubt result in Hatter's head rolling from the Executioner's Block since the Queen would likely place the blame for the Ants eating Boy Alice fully at Hatter's feet. The second would probably see him eaten and shat out as a Red Ant turdball.

While neither option was particularly appealing, he admitted he might stand at least a miniscule chance of surviving if he chose the second.

Rolling his eyes heavenward and uttering a half-remembered prayer from his childhood, Hatter turned back toward Caterpillar's mushroom and prepared to get small.

Chapter Four

Henry instinctively drew in a deep, ragged breath when he realized there was nothing under his feet but air. Whether it was in anticipation of a hard landing or a scream, he didn't know. In either case, he'd expected to hit bottom soon after tumbling off the edge of Caterpillar's mushroom, but instead, continued to free fall, the air rushing past his ears in a roar.

Was Caterpillar's mushroom situated on the edge of a cliff? Henry didn't think so, but it seemed the only rational explanation. Perhaps Caterpillar had some sort of secret trapdoor installed at the base of the mushroom stalk through which Henry now fell. It was unlikely, but really, had anything been logical since he'd awakened?

As he fell, he realized something strange. Although he'd considered the flowers and leaves of Caterpillar's Lair huge before, now they seemed enormous, as if a giant grew them in a Titan's garden. Cabbage roses were bigger than the actual heads of cabbage. They seemed to grow even larger as he fell. Now they were bigger than armchairs, bigger than houses! How could that be? It was strange indeed, and he pondered the possibility as he continued to drop.

It took him quite a while to conclude that, contrary to what he originally thought, the leaves and flowers of the plants enclosing Caterpillar's large mushroom had not grown to impossible, gigantic sizes, but instead, he had shrunk to the size of a largish dust mite.

This was not a conclusion he came to easily. Indeed, an internalized argument on the subject warred within him for a while. No man, least of all Henry, would want to admit they were small, would they? Small intimated weak, puny, frail, and helpless... at least, that's what Henry's father would say. What would his father, who could barely abide Henry now, think of him if Henry had shrunk?

No, he wouldn't believe it. Not ever. He hadn't gotten smaller. As far as he was concerned, he was the same healthy, normal size he'd always been. It must be that everything else had swelled to unbelievable proportions.

As he fell, though, a curious thing happened. He began to question why size should matter so much to him. He had friends who were shorter than he was, and others who were taller. Some people he knew were thinner than he, some fatter. They were all good quality, solid people, generous, and dependable. Their physical size certainly had nothing to do with the size of their hearts.

Was it then, as his father believed? That size alone made one superior? Of course not. He had one friend, Marcus, who barely reached Henry's shoulder, yet held a black belt in Tae Kwon Do, and could easily knock Henry on his butt. Another friend, Mallory Ames, was petite and frail, yet possessed a mind so sharply brilliant that she'd graduated a full two years ahead of the rest of their circle of friends and was already well on her way to earning her university degree.

Henry's father believed big was better in all things. Of course, being drunk most of the time, his father said many things that were more lie than truth. Things Henry already suspected were rubbish, like his father's belief that the color of one's skin, or where one went to school, or how much money one's family had, or who one loved, made a person better or less than the next. Maybe it was time Henry reexamined more of his convictions instead of blindly believing whatever his father told him.

The truth in this case, he realized, was that the size of the body didn't matter much in the scheme of things. It was the size of the spirit, the depth of the heart, and the power of the mind that counted more than inches of bone and pounds of flesh. His friends were worth more than gold to him, regardless of their size, color, or background.

The argument was irrefutable and seemed to settle the matter of whom or what had grown or shrunk. For some strange reason, in some bizarre way, he'd grown much, much smaller. To him, this was a newly sized planet where there were bumblebees the size of helicopters and ants the size of Clydesdales, but he knew that, whatever his size, he would adapt. Heroically, largely, and seamlessly adapt, because within his chest beat the heart of a giant.

At least, that was what he hoped was true.

One problem posed by shrinking occurred to him. While he was grateful the clothes he was wearing had shrunk with him, he realized that if he remained tiny, he'd need an entirely new wardrobe when he finally got home again. Nothing hanging in his closet would fit him anymore. The proposition of replacing all his shirts, jackets, pants, jeans, and underwear was an expensive one—even if he could find largish dust mite-sized ready-to-wear, and didn't need to have it all custom made—but that still wasn't his most immediate problem.

The fall was, because it didn't seem to want to ever end. Could a person fall forever? How long before he died from thirst or starvation, and only his bones continued their downward plummet?

He screwed his eyes closed tight as he plunged toward the earth, worried that when he finally hit bottom he'd shatter into a million pieces like a fine crystal decanter dropped onto a tile floor. Therefore, the first bounce took him quite by surprise.

One moment he was falling; the next he'd bounced off a leaf as if it were a trampoline, and somersaulted through the air. He landed on another leaf and bounced off that one too. After a few more involuntary bounces, he began to enjoy himself, springing from one leaf to another with surprisingly good aim.

He bounced a few more times, aiming for a lower leaf each time, until he felt confident he was close enough to the ground to jump to it without hurting himself. His luck held out—a mulch of last year's fallen leaves covered the hard earth. It was surprisingly soft and cushioned his landing.

Henry paused for a moment, hands on his knees, breathing hard, his senses overwhelmed as he took in his new surroundings. Everything seemed overly brilliant and fragrant—the green of the grass, the brown of the dirt, the yellows, reds, and oranges of fallen leaves, and the elemental smells of earth and vegetation. It was incredibly lovely, sweet and unsophisticated, and made him smile despite his circumstances.

This was a brand new world for him, a place where everything was giant-sized. All too soon, he realized that meant giant-sized trouble as well. He had shrunk to roughly the same size as a period at the end of a sentence, and no matter how strong his heart, or indomitable his will, or sharp his mind, that meant his life could be in danger merely because his body was so very, very small.

Just a stone-throw away from where he stood, a spider the size of a small car dangled from a web as thick as bridge's cable. The arachnid's multiple red eyes watched him carefully, patiently, as if the creature was certain Henry would, sooner or later, invite himself into its web for lunch.

An anthill rose like a small mountain in the distance. He could see the worker ants trundling up and down the sides, carrying leaves and other bits of vegetable matter in their incredibly strong mandibles, and could almost picture them carting him inside it, presenting him to their queen as some sort of delicacy.

Far above his head, birds the size of bomber planes zoomed between the trees, no doubt searching the ground for choice little morsels like him to scoop up with their sharp talons.

Nearby, glimpsed through the towering blades of grass, slithered a golden brown, sinuous shape that looked to him as if it were nearly two stories tall. He could hear the rattle its tail made thrumming in his bones like thunder, and froze, hunkered against a root until he was sure it was gone.

Even otherwise innocuous creatures, those that ordinarily didn't sting or bite or peck, could be deadly to him in his current size. A butterfly settled on a nearby blade of grass and fluttered wings as big as circus tent flaps. The breeze they stirred nearly knocked him off his feet.

A frog the size of a tank nearly gave him a heart attack by jumping over him, landing with a thud that made the earth under Henry's feet tremble, and snatching a biplane-sized dragonfly out of the air with its incredibly long, red tongue.

Henry quickly realized this was a life-or-death situation, and he was at a distinct disadvantage over the local fauna. He had no weapons, no fangs, venom, claws, or pincers. He couldn't fly away, or burrow beneath the dirt to escape predators, or cleverly change his color to blend in with the background.

As he stood there in a forest of grass blades and oversized, monstrous insects, for the first time he seriously considered the possibility he wasn't engaged in some sort of drugged fantasy brought on by whatever was in the cup Alice gave him the night before, but rather wide awake and perfectly sane.

If he was, it could mean only one thing: he was in deep, deep shit.

A sound caught his ear, and he cocked his head, listening. Tramp. Tramp. Tramp. He realized it was the sound of many feet marching, like an army on the move. Tramp. Tramp. Tramp. And it was getting closer.

Twisting around, he felt panic clawing at his throat as he scanned the immediate area, looking for a potential hiding place. He was small—tiny, really. He should be able to hide just about anywhere, right?

Wrong.

The area around him, while thick with tall slender blades of grass and many hip-high pebbles, provided as much scant cover as a forest of palm trees might in the world he'd left behind, had palm trees actually grown in a forest, which he doubted.

In other words, little to none.

Finally, he spotted a huge, desiccated nut lying on the ground. The size of a large boulder, the nut's blackened, cracked shell might provide a place for him to hide. He hurried over and ducked behind it. His luck seemed to hold. It proved to be only half a shell, cracked open and the nutmeat eaten long ago by some creature, the empty half shell discarded. He curled up in the empty space left by the missing nutmeat, hoping the shell would provide enough cover to protect him from whatever was marching his way.

Tramp. Tramp. Tramp.

The sound was closer now. Tremors rippled in the ground under the shell. He could hear odd clicking sounds in addition to the tramping of many feet. It sounded like an entire army was on the march.

Curiosity reared its ugly head, and completely ignoring the old adage about it killing cats, forced him to set aside his fear for a moment and peek out from behind the nutshell.

Ants.

Humongous red ants, each as big as a city bus, had gathered near the nut, standing in a straight, regimented line that stretched as far as he could see. Their massive mandibles clicked while bullwhip-like antennae waved in the air.

His fear, so recently shunted aside by his curiosity, elbowed its way back to the forefront of his consciousness like a fourth-grade bully through a crowd of kindergarteners, freezing the breath in his lungs. Unfortunately, his breath didn't stay frozen. It thawed rapidly, flowing like a river past his lips in the form of a high-pitched, ragged scream.

Every pair of mandibles ceased clicking, and every pair of antennae swiveled in his direction. Henry ducked back into the shell's hollow, his hands clamped over his traitorous mouth, hoping the ants' antennae weren't sensitive enough to hear the thumping of his heart.

The next thing he knew, he felt the shell holding him rise into the air. Looking down over the edge of the shell, he saw that an ant had clamped its mandibles around it and was carrying it—and him—off.

Now what was he going to do? It was a long, long way down. He couldn't jump, not if he didn't want to risk breaking a leg or getting mashed under the ants' marching feet. Nor did he want to alert the ants to his presence inside the shell. They might decide he'd do nicely for a quick on-the-road snack. His only choice seemed to be to wait until, hopefully, the ant set the shell down and he could make his escape.

The ant carried him for what seemed to him to be a long time, and he was almost lulled to sleep by the even sway of the ant's gait. Then the world suddenly tipped at a sharp angle, and he slid a short way before his feet hit the opposite side of the shell. Peeking over the side again, he realized the ant was descending into a tunnel of some sort.

No, not a tunnel.

A hill. An anthill.

Oh, man. And he'd thought he'd been in trouble before.

Chapter Five

The steep path the ant traversed leveled out again after a while. Henry tried to keep track of the twists and turns the ant made so he possibly might find his way out again should an opportunity to escape present itself, but there were so many, he soon became confused. Deeper and deeper into the ground they went, all light fading, until the darkness became thick and suffocating. He could hear the ants all around him, clicking and clacking.

There finally came a small bump as the ant placed the shell on the ground. He froze, panic digging ice-cold talons into his gut as he waited for the ant to discover him inside his hollow hiding place, but after a few moments, he realized the ant had gone away.

Now was the time, perhaps his only chance for escape! But how? It was so dark, he couldn't see his hand in front of his face.

"Psst."

Henry cocked his head. What was that sound? It didn't sound like the ants. It sounded like a hoarse whisper.

"Psst. Boy Alice."

Now that definitely wasn't the ants. The ants might click and clack and chitter on occasion, but they never used words, in particular not his sister's name. "Who are you? Where are you?"

"I'm Hatter. Take two steps to your right, then another four steps forward."

"Do I know you?"

There was no mistaking the sarcasm in the whispery voice's tone. "Oh, I do apologize. Perhaps we should have a formal introduction while the ants eat us! Would that satisfy your need for social convention?"

Henry swallowed a sharp retort at the sarcastic reply, and took two steps to the right and four forward. He barely stifled a yelp when a hand clamped down on his shoulder.

Amazingly, a soft yellow glow illuminated the owner of the hand. The man who called himself "Hatter" was an inch or so taller than Henry, and had longish black hair hanging in silky tangles to his shoulders. His face was handsome in a craggy sort of way, his strong jaw shadowed by a day's growth of whiskers, his eyes as dark as his hair. Impossibly, he wore a top hat, a waistcoat, and fingerless gloves. In one cupped hand, a ball of light seemed to hover, the source of the pale light.

Henry reached out to touch a finger to the glowing orb. "How are you doing that?"

"Really? We're surrounded by giant man-eating Red ants, and you want to waste time with a science lesson? It's a basic, everyday emergency lightning bug lantern. Every schoolchild can operate one. Caterpillar was right. You really are as dull-witted as your sister."

Henry felt his last nerve stretch and snap. He gave Hatter a push. "I'm nothing like my sister!"

"Shh! Do you want to get us eaten? Look, I'm getting out of here. Are you coming, or do you want to stay behind and discover whether ants prefer dark meat or light?"

Henry sputtered, so angry he almost forgot how frightened he was. Almost, but not quite. "No, let's go." He put his hand on Hatter's shoulder. "But when we get out, you're going to tell me how you can do that with lightning bugs, and how you know my sister."

"Sure, sure. Come on, before they realize their lunch is running away."

Hatter led Henry down a long tunnel. They hugged the earthen side, staying low, ducking into one of the many alcoves whenever an ant came too close to them. Gradually, the darkness lightened until the glowing orb Hatter held was no longer necessary. He released it, and it fluttered away.

It seemed to take forever, but the path finally took a steep turn upward, leading to the surface. "Now what?" Henry peered up toward where the sun—and freedom—beckoned. "Do we try to climb out?"

"Not necessary." Hatter removed his top hat and thrust his hand in into it. Amazingly, it went in up to Hatter's elbow, and then to his shoulder. He rooted around for a while, but eventually pulled his arm out. In his hand, he held an umbrella.

Henry rolled his eyes. "In case you didn't notice, the sun is shining."

Hatter shot him a black look. "Would you care to get us out of here? No? Then let me work." He held the umbrella up and opened it. The umbrella sprung open, shading them both. Hatter grabbed Henry's hand just as the umbrella began spinning madly, whirling like a top. Unbelievably, it began to rise up the tunnel, carrying both Hatter and Henry with it. They floated up and out of the Red Anthill, and over a field thick with wildflowers.

Henry's eyes bulged as he scanned the ground far below them. "Holy crap! What kind of umbrella is this?"

It seemed to be Hatter's turn to roll his eyes. "Um-brella? No, no, don't be silly. This is an up-brella. You really are quite stupid, aren't you?"

"I'm not stupid!"

"Stupid is as stupid does. Might do you well to remember that."

Henry had enough. He yanked his hand out of Hatter's, and immediately began falling... again. This time, there were no trampoline-like leaves to break his fall. He fell like a rock, and landed just as hard as one, knocking all the air out of him.

Hatter touched down lightly next to him. "See? Just as I said. Stupid."

"Stop calling me stupid."

"Then stop trying to kill yourself. Eating unknown mushrooms, allowing Red ants to carry you off, not to mention falling into Caterpillar's Lair from the sky.... Really, you're making my job exceedingly difficult."

"Who are you?"

"I told you. I'm Hatter. Now, you can tell me why you're here, and why you were asking the Caterpillar about me."

Henry sat up, feeling his arms and legs for the broken bones he was sure he'd find. He felt solid and unbroken, if badly bruised. "Alice told me to find the Mad Hatter. Are you saying you're him? That's ridiculous—he doesn't exist. Where are we, anyway? I asked the Caterpillar, but he wouldn't tell me. Seriously, I think there's something wrong with him. You know, in the head."

"Well of course there's something wrong with his head. He smokes whackweed continuously. That stuff doesn't exactly make you a scholar, you know." Hatter tapped the side of his head. "Kills the gray matter. But don't tell 'Pillar I said that." He folded his up-brella and stored it away inside his hat before replacing his hat on his head, setting it at a jaunty angle. "I would think it obvious that you're in Wonderland. And of course I exist. I'm here, aren't I? Now, I've answered your questions. It's only fair for you to answer mine."

"Wonderland? You mean the place Alice always talks about? That's ridiculous. There's no such place!"

"Yet, curiouser and curiouser, here you stand squarely in the center of it. And that was another question, by the way. Really, do I need to explain the rules again?"

Frustration made Henry want to scream. Did everyone talk in riddles around here? "What rules? What are you talking about?"

"Tsk, tsk. Those are two more questions! Really, you're as thick as mud. I'm beginning to think Alice is the bright one in your family."

This time a frustrated sound broke free of Henry's control. It began as a rumble deep in his chest, rolled up through his throat and exploded through his lips in a fierce snarl.

Hatter's dark eyes widened, although there was no fear in them, only interest. His lips quirked in a half smile. "My, my. Alice certainly never growled. I'll give you points for originality. Very ferocious." He crooked a finger at Henry to follow, and began walking. "All right, since you obviously have a sad lack of understanding regarding the rules, let me explain." His hands, encased in tatty, gray fingerless gloves, had long, elegant fingers, and they traced patterns in the air as he spoke. "Here in Wonderland, there are rules we must follow. These rules keep the universe in motion, the planets aligned, and the cosmos free from chaos. Rules must be followed at all times, without deviation… unless, I suppose, the rule is to break the rules, in which case, following the rules may actually be regarded as breaking them. So sayeth the Queen. Do you understand now?"

Henry shook his head. "No."

The Hatter grinned. "I should have expected nothing less." He beckoned Henry to quicken his step. "Come, come. It should be around here somewhere. Oh, wait… there it is! That's what I've been looking for. Thank goodness those mimsy creatures, the borogroves, didn't carry it off. We'd have a devil of a time getting it back from those gloomy birds."

"Mimsy? Borogroves?" Henry shook his head. "You're making that up. Just like Alice did."

"Me? I beg your pardon. I never speak anything but the truth. It might be bendy at times, perhaps a bit swirly, but still, in the end, always the truth." Hatter led Henry to a large bottle, easily the size of a Buick. The bottle was dark blue, and lying on its side in the grass. "Mimsy, for your information, means something that is both miserable and flimsy. The borogroves certainly fit that description, I can tell you. Floppy, glum birds, they are, and prone to snatch away anything they find so that whoever lost it is bound to be as depressed as they are." Hatter looked at Henry. "Give me a hand with this. We need to roll it over."

They placed their hands on the bottle's cool, slick side, and pushed until their teeth ground and their spines popped. Just as Henry was sure the bottle would never budge, it began to roll, inch by inch. They kept pushing until a golden label was revealed. It was grimy from its time spent lying in the dirt, but the words printed on it were perfectly legible.

It read, "Drink Me."

Hatter laughed and slapped the bottle with the flat of his hand. "This is the very same bottle your sister drank from, if I'm not mistaken, and it looks like there's plenty left over. Now, you have repeatedly said you are nothing like your sister. In other words, you are her opposite. If that's the case, then the potion in this bottle should have the opposite effect on you than it had on her, and make you grow." He gave Henry a push toward the bottle's neck. "Go on. In you go."

The round opening at the tip of the bottle's neck was wide enough and tall enough for Henry to walk through as easily as if it were the Arc de Triomphe considering his current vertically challenged state. He hurried down the long neck to the bottle's barrel, which turned out to be a much longer walk for him than he anticipated. By the time he reached the very bottom of the bottle, where there was a small puddle of purple liquid, he was exhausted.

He took a sniff, and nearly gagged. It smelled like a combination of the locker room at school after an especially rough football game, and the dumpster behind the Mickey D's on a hot summer day. He glanced back toward the mouth of the bottle. Did Hatter really expect him to drink this nasty crap?

Hatter's voice called to him from the bottle's mouth, as if Hatter had heard his thoughts. "Go on! Take a sip!"

"What about you?"

Laughter floated down the long bottleneck, the sound growing louder and louder until it rumbled like thunder. Suddenly a pair of huge, dark eyes were looking in at him through the green bottle glass. A mouth stretched into a smirk as wide as train car. "I'm the Hatter. I don't need potions. Magic is in my blood. Go on now. Take a sip. We haven't got all day."

It felt like Hatter had somehow tricked him, which made him angry all over again, but there was nothing he could do about it while he was still so very small, and Hatter was now so very big. He felt he had no choice but to drink from the small pool of liquid ugliness floating at the bottom of the bottle, but he made himself a promise. As soon as he got big again, he was going to punch Hatter right in the mouth. Let's see how that smirk works for him with a few teeth gone.

The thought somehow made him feel a bit better.

Holding his nose closed with two fingers, he dipped his hand into the purple liquid, gathering a bit up in his palm. He put it to his lips and drank it down as quick as he could, trying very hard not to taste it as it slid over his tongue and down his throat.

Tried, but failed.

It tasted every bit as ugly as it looked, viscous and slimy at the same time, but happily, he didn't have long to explore the horrid flavor because at that moment, things started happening that took his mind off his mouth.

No sooner had he swallowed the muck but he began to grow. His body expanded in all directions—upways, downways, sideways, and slantways—quickly filling the bottle. For a heartbeat he was stuck there, unable to move, unable to breathe, his face smooshed flat against the glass. He could feel the pressure building as his body insisted it continue to expand, and the non-giving glass refused to bend. Then… smash! The bottle splintered into millions of tiny glass bits, exploding away from him in a shower of fragments glinting in the sun.

Freed from the glass, he grew even more quickly, as if someone was using a tornado to blow up a balloon-shaped man. Within seconds, he'd grown to his former height and weight, or as close to it as he could tell, anyway.

And found himself facing a pair of mischievous, sparkling dark eyes.

He barely felt his fingers curling into a fist, or his arm pulling back to throw a punch squarely at Hatter's handsome, smirking face.

Chapter Six

Hatter scarcely had time to blink as Henry's hard fist caught him just under his jaw, the force of the punch lifting him off his feet, and planting him on his ass in the dirt. He rubbed his jaw, feeling—for the first time in a good, long while, if ever—completely stunned. "You... you struck me!"

Henry, busy dancing around with the hand he used to strike Hatter tucked under his armpit, muttering all manner of foul epithets, shot him a black look, as if the entire incident was Hatter's fault.

It was more than a little irritating. After all, who was down on the ground on his rear end, with a sore jaw and what felt like a loose tooth, and who was still standing upright? He struggled to his feet, still cupping his jaw. "What are you so angry about? I'm the one who got hit!"

That stopped Henry in his tracks. Without warning, he bellowed out a half-strangulated scream, and launched himself at Hatter. The combination of his weight and gravity flattened Hatter to the ground again.

Hatter struggled to free himself, but Henry kept him firmly pinned to the ground. Fear made his blood pound in his ears as he watched Henry raise a fist he knew from experience was rock-hard. "Um, would you kindly consider not hitting me again? Teeth, sad to say, do not grow on trees. At least, not anymore they don't, not since the Molar Wars, and I would have a dickens of a time trying to replace these." He beamed a high wattage smile at Henry.

"You made me go into the bottle. You made me drink that purple goop, when all the time you had the power to get big! Why? Why would you do that? What did I ever do to you?"

Hatter shook his head. "You misunderstand. Yes, I can work a little magic, but only on myself. Even I had to eat Caterpillar's mushroom to get small. I don't have the power to make you big. If I did, I would've done so back in the Red Anthill instead of risking your neck—and my own, might I add—escaping the way we did."

"Well, then, why didn't you get big and carry me out?"

Hatter blinked. "Because... because...." The question took him aback, mostly because he didn't have an answer. He honestly just hadn't thought of it, not that he would admit to it. It took him all of a half minute to regain his poise. "Because then you would've missed out on a Grand Adventure and an Important Lesson! Yes, that's why! Of course, that's why!" He finally succeeded in pushing Henry off and regaining his feet. He watched Henry out of the corner of his eyes while he brushed the dirt from his pants and coat, straightened his lapel, and tugged on his cuffs. "What sort of person would I be if I denied you such an experience?"

Henry snorted. "The kind that wouldn't get slugged for making me drink that purple crap. Grand Adventure and Important Lesson? I can practically hear the capitalization. What a load of horse crap." He looked away for a few moments then turned back to Hatter. "I guess I owe you an apology. It's just this place. It's getting to me! First the Caterpillar, then shrinking and falling, then the ants, then having to drink the purple slop...." He thrust his fingers into his hair, twisting the blond strands. "I'm still not even sure where I am or how I got here, never mind how to get back home!"

"Speaking of which, Caterpillar said you were asking for me."

That made Henry blink again. "Um, yeah. Yes. The last thing I remember before blacking out was my sister telling me to look for the Mad Hatter. That's you, right?"

"So it seems. Though there are many other creatures here that either claim to be mad or were proven so, I'm the only Hatter in Wonderland."

All the air seemed to escape from Henry, leaving him looking as deflated as an old balloon. "So it's true, then? This is Wonderland? Alice hasn't been lying all these years?"

Hatter gave Henry's shoulder a reassuring pat. "Lying? Why would you think that of your sister? For all that I disliked her and thought her dull, she was not one for spinning untruths. This is Wonderland, in all its topsy-turvy, insie-outsie, backward-frontsie glory."

The expression on Henry's face was blatantly defeated. "Great. So… what do I do now? How do I get home?"

Hatter smiled again and then winced at the pain in his jaw. "I'm so glad you asked. It just so happens that I was sent to fetch you back to the Red Queen for the express purpose of getting rid of you."

It wasn't a lie, after all. Not exactly. He just left out the fact that when she did rid Wonderland of Henry, he would be in two distinct pieces.

Henry frowned. "Alice used to talk about the Red Queen. She didn't seem to care much for her."

"No one did. I'm afraid your sister was a bit of a nuisance."

"I meant my sister didn't care for the Red Queen. Alice said she was crazy."

Hatter gasped and his eyes grew wide. He slapped his hand over Henry's mouth. He lowered his voice into a hoarse hiss. "Shh! Her spies are everywhere. Never speak ill of the Queen aloud while out in the open where you can be easily overheard!"

Henry peeled Hatter's hand off. "She's not my Queen."

"While you're in Wonderland, she is. She's the ultimate authority here, her only rival being her sister, the White Queen. She can lock you away until you're so old you trip over your own beard, or starve you until you're nothing but bone and sinew, or cover you in honey and feed you to a Bandersnatch." Not to mention lop off his head, but since that's what actually lay in store for Henry, Hatter thought it would be gauche to mention it. Why ruin the surprise?

"The White Queen? What about her, then? Would she send me home? Perhaps we can go to her instead."

"Can't."

"Why not?"

"The Red Queen had her head chopped off soon after Alice left the last time. The White King's head rolled as well."

Henry gulped and grabbed his neck as if to keep his own head from rolling. "Her own sister and brother-in-law? As much as I detest mine sometimes, I'd never try to decapitate Alice. That's awful!"

Hatter shrugged a shoulder. "No, that's politics. It caused quite the scandal, as I recall. The two queens met on the same chessboard your sister won her crown on, both accusing the other of aiding and abetting Alice on her quest to become a Queen of Wonderland. The gauntlet was thrown down." Hatter sighed. "One would think after spending a lifetime as a blood relation of the Red Queen, the White Queen would've known how badly she cheats and been prepared for it. But no, the White Queen rather stupidly tried to play according to the rules." Hatter made a slicing motion with one finger across his throat. "And well, in the end, off came her and her husband's heads."

"You make it sound like she was wrong to want to play by the rules. Rules bring order. You said so yourself."

Hatter raised the volume of his voice, as if wanting anyone eavesdropping on their conversation to better hear him. "Yes, I did, of course. The Red Queen has ordered everyone to obey the rules. Very wise of her." Hatter looked about, and lowered his voice to a whisper again. "But what fun is there in being orderly? None. Rules are merely a fistful of conundrums, obstacles, and barriers knotted and twisted together for the sole purpose of sucking the last bit of fun out of every experience. I should think they'd be riddled with cracks given how many times they're broken, and if I ever found out which fool keeps pasting them back together, I'd give him a good clobber with my walking stick."

Henry gave his head a shake. "Without rules, there'd be chaos!"

"No, no. Without rules, there'd be freedom."

"Not a half hour ago, when I was small, you stood there and told me rules were meant to be followed at all costs!"

"I believe my exact words were, 'so sayeth the Queen.' That doesn't mean I believe it."

"You know what? You're nuts, and I think I'll be better off on my own." Henry lifted his chin and began walking off in a different direction, as if he knew where he was going. "I'll find my own way home, no thanks to you."

Hatter knew very well that Henry wouldn't last half a day in Wonderland without him. Nor would he last half a day if he returned to the Red Palace without Henry in tow. "I wouldn't go that way if I were you."

Henry glanced back over his shoulder and made a rude noise, but continued walking.

Stubborn man. No, modify that. Thickheaded lout is a more apt description, Hatter thought. He ignored the tiny voice in his head that wondered if Hatter might just not find that quality a bit attractive. Aloud he reiterated, "I really wouldn't go that way."

"Stop talking to me." Henry continued walking, and did not turn around again.

"Fine. But when you find yourself sunk up to your chin in the Great Sinking Sands of Wonderland, don't cry to me for help."

Henry's step faltered, slowed, then stopped. Still, he didn't turn around. "Sinking Sands? You mean quicksand?"

"Ha! There's nothing quick about it. It sucks you under slowly, inch by terrifying inch, until it eventually pulls you under the surface and fills your lungs with thick, wet sand. It's a horrible, painfully slow way to die, and quite frankly, not one I'd choose were the choice mine to make."

Henry took a small backward step toward Hatter. "Perhaps I was a bit hasty."

Hatter's lips lifted in a bemused, half smile. "So he can be taught! Perhaps your stupidity is not a permanent condition. Excellent."

Finally, Henry's head swiveled in Hatter's direction. "But you want to take me to the Red Queen. She's a villain, according to Alice. Hell, according to you, she's practically evil incarnate! She killed her own sister."

"She also has the power to send you home. Alice didn't magically find her way home not once but twice, you know. That was the Queen's magic." Hatter had no idea if it was within the Red Queen's power or not. For all he knew, Alice's return home was nothing more than a pair of happy accidents.

Even if the Queen had possessed such magic, he rather doubted she would've lifted her pinkie finger to help Alice. Indeed, now that Hatter thought about it, if the Red Queen could send Alice home, she would have straightaway at the beginning, but he also knew admitting so would only serve to push Henry to take his chances in the Great Sinking Sands or with another of Wonderland's equally deadly environs alone. Going to see the Red Queen really was the safest choice for the unarmed, uninitiated foreigner. In addition, there was still Hatter's own head and its tenuous attachment to the rest of him to consider. She had, after all, promised him immunity should he deliver Henry to her.

Henry seemed to be mulling it over as well. He shifted his weight from foot to foot, chewed on his lower lip, and cast long glances in the direction of the Sinking Sands. Finally, he turned back to Hatter. "Okay. I guess I don't have a choice. I'll go with you… for now."

Hatter grinned, whipped his hat off, gave Henry a rather sardonic half bow, and gestured toward the west with his free hand. "Your guide—for now—at your service. This way, please."

He straightened when Henry took a few tentative steps in that direction, then replaced his hat and gave it a thump to settle it on his crown. "All right, then. On we go."

Hatter led Henry around the west side of the Caterpillar's Lair. He scanned the area, but there was no trace of the Queen's coach. He swore an oath so foul it startled a nearby dragonfly into spewing a tiny stream of flame. *Stupid driver. I suppose it never occurred to him that I might need a ride back to the Castle!* He turned to Henry. "While I'd hoped we would have a conveyance to speed our journey, it looks as though we're out of luck. We'll have to walk."

Henry looked both surprised and irritated, as if distance hadn't occurred to him before, and he was annoyed now that it had. "How far is it to the Red Queen's castle?"

Hatter considered his answer. "I'm not sure. Longer than a knick-knack, but certainly shorter than a paddywhack."

"Why is it that everything you say either makes no sense, or is jumbled into a giant, convoluted knot?"

Hatter shrugged. "Gifted, I suppose. Well, on we go." He stepped forward and began to lead the way toward the west, across a wildflower-strewn meadow reaching toward the horizon, beyond which the Red Queen's castle lay.

He hoped.

Direction was never really his strong suit. Hatter once got lost in his own closet, and might've starved if it hadn't been for the biscuits he kept in his coat pockets.

Wisely, he refrained from sharing that tidbit of information with Henry.

Speaking of biscuits, he remembered it'd been a long while since last he ate. He reached into his pocket and fished around for a bit before pulling out a couple of lovely scones. He graciously offered one to Henry, who, after a few moments of hesitation, took it. Munching, they walked on.

Darkness was falling when they arrived at a low, split rail fence running in both directions as far as they could see. Hatter called a halt and peered over the fence. Those trees, those flowers.... He felt the wind blowing against his face when only a moment ago it had been at his back, and knew where they were, though he hadn't realized they'd need to pass through the area to get to the Queen's castle. He certainly didn't remember passing it on the way to the Lair.

Still, there it was. Better to deal with it in the morning.

"We'll camp here for the night. Get a fresh start in the morning."

"Why? It's not dark yet."

Hatter resisted pulling something with heft out of his pocket—he had a hardcover edition of *Tea Time Etiquette* in there somewhere—and smacking Henry with it. How could someone so handsome be so very stupid? "Darkness comes swiftly in Wonderland, and all manner of uglies ride its coattails. Goblins. Trolls. Fidgits. You don't want to run into a Fidgit in the dark of night, believe you me! Now, let's settle down as best we can, and get a few winks, eh? Besides, this fence marks the beginning of the Drawrof. It isn't an easy land to cross, and only a fool would attempt it without a good night's sleep."

He knelt on the ground, and began digging in his pocket again. Before long, he'd brought out dinnerware for two, a pot filled with a hearty stew, a stone jug of iced tea, and a small, crackling campfire that spat green and purple sparks. He set the pot to warm on the fire, and poured tea for them both.

"How did you do that?" Henry gaped at the collection Hatter pulled out of his pocket.

"Do what?"

"Carry all that stuff in your pocket? Are you a magician? That's it, isn't it? You're like Copperfield, or Criss Angel."

"Never heard of them. Do they live in Wonderland?"

"No. They're magicians. They do tricks… sleight of hand."

"I can't imagine what the size of one's hands has to do with anything."

"No, not slight… sleight." Henry huffed a stand of hair out of his eyes and looked frustrated. "They do magic."

"How does one do magic? Magic just is."

"Not where I come from it's not. Back home, magic is just misdirection and sleight of hand. Tricks."

Hatter cocked his head. "Hmm. How very dull. It does explain much about you and your sister, though. In Wonderland, magic is as much a part of us as our skin. It's possible to live without it, but it would be oh, so very uncomfortable. Oh, look. The stew's ready."

He ladled some into bowls for the two of them. For the moment, Henry seemed more inclined to feed his face than exercise his tongue, and since Hatter was hungry as well, silence descended on their little campsite.

Afterward, they each stretched out on the grass, making themselves as comfortable as possible. Hatter fished around in his pocket until he found a pair of clean, if threadbare, blankets, and gave one to Henry. Rolling himself up in the second, he feigned slumber until he heard Henry's soft snores.

Peeping out from under his eyelids, he watched Henry doze, thoughts spinning through his own mind too fast to allow for slumber.

Hatter noticed Henry's face was quite attractive when sleep softened its almost constant surly expression. His hair was as blond as his sister Alice's was, with a slight curl to the silky strands that made Hatter's hands inexplicably itch to touch them. Long, light brown lashes edged eyes he already knew were the color of a summer sky. The lines of his high cheekbones and sharp, square jaw were indisputably masculine, yet still quite beautiful. Hatter could see Henry's stubborn streak in the set of his jaw, even while asleep.

Henry's lips were full for a man, soft-looking, although Hatter already knew from experience the sharp tongue that lay behind them. Day-old whiskers dusted Henry's jaw, so pale they were practically unnoticeable except when viewed up close. *A few more days,* Hatter mused, *perhaps as long as a week, and he'll sport the beginnings of a strawberry blond beard.*

All in all, Henry was more than easy on the eyes, a fact Hatter knew would make traveling with him both interesting and extraordinarily dangerous, because if there was one thing Hatter loved most in the world, it was beauty. He was drawn to it, whether he wanted to be or not. Beautiful women, beautiful men, both stirred a fire within him that, as often as not, got him in trouble sooner or later.

A thought bubbled up from the back of him mind. What might Henry do if Hatter tried to kiss those soft, plump lips?

Probably punch Hatter squarely in the face.

Again.

Hatter ground his teeth and turned his back on Henry.

Don't be stupid, Hatter. Don't even think about such things. One kiss inevitably leads to a second, then before you know it, your emotions get involved, and things get intolerably complicated. You need to turn him over to the Queen, remember? Such an involvement, however pleasant, would only serve to leave you broken in the end, and quite possibly without a head.

He was still trying to talk some sense into himself when he finally fell asleep.

That night, rolled up in a threadbare blanket on a bed of grass, Hatter dreamt of sky-blue eyes and strawberry blond whiskers, and almost too-full lips.

Chapter Seven

They broke their fast over a quick meal of tea and biscuits pulled from Hatter's pocket, during which Hatter barely spoke more than a handful of words.

Henry wondered why that was, what had changed, since the day before he feared the only way to get Hatter to shut up would be by nailing Hatter's lips together. He'd prayed for silence yesterday, but today, now that it was here, he found it a bit disconcerting, although he didn't want to admit it. The silence made him uneasy, and he found himself wondering whether he'd said or done something wrong, only to question why it should matter to him even if he had. Therefore, it came as a sort of relief when Hatter finally deigned to speak, if only to quiet the bewildering voices in his head.

Until, that is, he tried to make sense of what Hatter was saying.

Hatter had packed everything up by depositing each item, one at a time, into his pocket—a feat Henry still couldn't figure out—and hopped over the split rail fence. He was facing Henry, and motioned for Henry to join him before taking a few steps backward. "Ti fo kcank eht teg uoy litnu tluciffid si ereh gniklaw, Yrneh, tnaligiv eb."

Henry cocked his head. "Why are you talking like that? You're speaking gibberish, Hatter."

Hatter glared at him. "Yob diputs." He turned away and walked backward toward the fence again, then climbed back over. "Weren't you listening last night? I told you this marked the boundary of Drawrof."

Henry merely shook his head and hunched his shoulders. "Never heard of it."

Hatter rolled his eyes. "I should have known. Tell me, Henry, what did they teach you in school? You did go to school at some point, didn't you?"

"Of course I did! I was getting ready to graduate this June, hopefully with honors."

"Well, what sort of school was it? A school of fish? Because it certainly couldn't have been a school of learning if you never heard of Drawrof before!"

Henry ground his molars, trying hard not to give in to temptation and punch Hatter. "It was high school, and I'm willing to bet no one else in my class has heard of this place before either. Just tell me what's going on."

"Fine. Everything in Drawrof is backward. Once you clear the fence, you need to speak backward, walk backward, think backward, eat backward, pee backward, and practically bend over backward or else Snilmerg, the guardians of Drawrof, will send you back over the fence to the beginning, forcing you to do it all over again."

"Backward. Everything? How do you think backward?" He really didn't want to think about how one might pee backward He promised himself he'd hold it until his eyes turned yellow before finding out, too.

Hatter seemed to consider this for a moment. "It's best not to think at all. Now, are you ready?"

Henry sighed. He really didn't see where he had a choice. He nodded. "I suppose so."

"Then, let's be off! Daylight, as they say, is wasting." Hatter hopped over the fence again, and began walking backward. After a moment or two, Henry joined him.

It was disconcerting to walk backward through unknown territory, to say the least. Surprisingly, he didn't bump or trip at all, though. Perhaps it had to do with the magic of Wonderland. Surely if he tried this at home he would've broken an ankle or been run over by a car long before now. Then again, he'd seen nothing larger than a squirrel about, so being trampled really wasn't much of a threat.

He still thought it was unnerving not to be able to see where you were going. It dawned on him that he'd never really appreciated the gift of sight before. He'd always just taken it for granted, but now that he couldn't see the road before him, he missed it, and was very grateful for his 20/20 vision.

Hatter chose that moment to get over his self-imposed silent treatment and spoke. What he said, and what Henry heard was "Emithcnul erofeb edis rehto eht hcaer dluohs ew .Ssorca ediw yrev ton si Forward yllufknaht" but what Henry understood was "Thankfully Drawrof is not very wide across. We should reach the other side before lunchtime."

Well, what do you know? It seemed that while in Drawrof, one's brain ran backward as well, allowing one to easily understand backward speech. That made things much easier, and encouraged Henry to continue the conversation. It still felt strange to have his lips forming the words backward, although he was confident Hatter would understand him when he said, "Is the Red Queen's castle on the other side of Drawrof?" but it came out "Forward fo edis rehto eht no eltsac S'neeuq Der eht si?"

Hatter nodded, and of course, Henry understood the gesture to mean "no." "Wonderland is usually a very large place. I doubt our journey will be so short."

"Usually? How can a place usually be large?"

"How could it not? Ask yourself this: Are there always the same number of blades of grass in a field year after year? The same number of birds in the sky, or deer in the forest, or Bandersnatch chicks in a clutch?"

"Um, no?"

"Of course not! So therefore, the area in which they live must at times be larger, and at other times, smaller. It's only logical."

"I… but that…."

"It's best not to think about it overly much. Logic can be toxic if taken in large doses. Suffice it to say, it will take us some time to reach the Queen's castle."

They walked on for a while in silence as Henry tried hard not to think about Hatter's convoluted and thoroughly flawed logic, and marveled at how Wonderland, riddled with such rules, managed not to collapse in on itself like a dying star, leaving a gaping black hole behind.

He found distraction easily enough by watching the native fauna going about their backward business around him. Bees flew backward and deposited nectar from the hive to the flower. Frogs hopped into ponds and changed into tadpoles. Birds flew backward, taking worms from their offspring and delivering them to the ground. He found out quickly enough that sand here felt wet, but water felt dry, and roses stunk like dirty feet, while dandelions smelled a bit like heaven.

It was all very confusing. And oddly beautiful at the same time. The colors were all so luminous, although they were also backward. The sky was a perfectly unmarred stretch of rich emerald green, while the grass, trees, and shrubs came in every shade of blue from navy to periwinkle. Flowers painted in shades of gray paled next to vibrantly colored weeds, while butterflies wore somber cloaks of gray and black, but moths, beetles, and spiders dazzled the eye with a rainbow of hues.

It was then that he noticed something so very strange that once realized, it stood out among all the other peculiarities of the place. "Hatter? This place is very beautiful. I would think people would like to live here. Where are they? I haven't seen anyone since we came over the fence. In fact, so far, you're the only person I've met since arriving here."

Hatter looked shocked. "Of course there are no people! And people say I'm mad."

"What do you mean? Why are you looking at me like I'm crazy?"

"Just when I was ready to concede you might not be as dull and witless as your sister.... Most people here, evidently myself excluded, know to steer clear of Caterpillar's Lair lest they want to spend their days in a hallucinogenic fog. And here? Think about it, Henry. Everything in Drawrof is backwards! People would be born old here, and progressively grow younger as they grew. What sort of parents would children make, I wonder? What sort of infants would full-grown adults make, toddling about in diapers, sucking on pacifiers? How difficult would it be for an adult-child to burp a child-adult? And toddlers in the throes of the terrible twos! Why, the first temper tantrum might end in bloodshed!"

Henry's mouth formed a perfect letter O. "Oh. I didn't think about that. I suppose that wouldn't work well for anyone, would it?"

"No, indeed. In fact, by the time we reach the fence at the far side of Drawrof, we'll be younger than we were when we first entered it. Unfortunately, once you cross back over the fence, the effects begin to fade and you begin to age normally again. There are those in Wonderland who visit here regularly just for the purpose of shaving a few years off their age."

"Do you come here often? How old are you?"

"Bah. As a wise man once said, I'm as old as my tongue and a little bit older than my teeth, and that's good enough for me. I don't need to be any younger, thank you. Age is just a number, anyway, and only a good one for a very short time, so why bother keeping track? Besides, I'm a special case. I was once cursed by Time, and there's no reversing its effects, even if I wanted to."

"You didn't answer my question."

"I'm older than you, but younger than the dirt under your feet. Satisfied?"

Henry threw his hands up in the air. "Gah! You make everything complicated, even the simplest questions."

"Why, thank you!" Hatter shot him a wide, delighted smile.

"That wasn't a compliment!"

"Of course it was. Why would anyone purposely seek to be dull and succinct? That would make for a horribly boring person, I should think. No, it's much better, in my opinion, to be large and delightfully intricate as much as possible."

They both suddenly came in contact with a hard, unmovable object, bringing their walk—and their conversation—to a grinding halt.

"Ah! Good. We're across." Hatter began crab-crawling backward over the wall.

Henry rolled his eye and began to turn around to climb the fence, but Hatter stopped him.

"No! You're still in Drawrof! You must move backwards or the Snilmerg will force you all the way back to where we first crossed over!"

Henry froze, his body halfway turned. From the corner of his eye, he thought he saw horned and vaguely threatening figures moving through the tall blue grass. He quickly turned back and carefully scaled the fence backward, holding his breath until he dropped over the other side.

"You can turn around now. We're clear of Drawrof." Hatter patted his shoulder. "You did well. We didn't get sent back once. That's rare for a first-timer."

"Thank you." Henry slowly turned around; he half expected little clawed hands to grab him and drag him back over the fence. Before him spread a swampy, overgrown area that seemed much less inviting than Drawrof had. "Where are we now?"

"A place I'd never planned to revisit." Hatter removed his hat and swept his arm over his forehead, which looked damp with sweat. "Welcome, my friend, if one can ever truly be welcomed into a place as nasty as this, to the Neverglades."

Chapter Eight

The smell was nauseating and overpowering.

It was the odor of the sewer, of wet, slime, mold, and mustiness, of swollen and bloated dead things. Hatter fished in his pocket and retrieved a scented handkerchief, using it to cover his nose. Happily, it was one of the chocolate-scented ones. The last hankie he'd pulled out had been trout-scented, although even the stink of old fish would be preferable to the stench of the Neverglades. He found a spare and handed it to Henry. He caught a faint whiff of strawberry as he passed it over.

Henry's voiced sounded slightly muffled through the hankie. "What's that horrible smell? It smells like gone-over deli meat."

"It's the Neverglades. Thusly named because some things get in, but never get out."

"Never? What about us? Maybe we should go back."

"There is no way back. Look." Hatter pointed behind them. There was nothing there but a semi-solid screen of tangled trees and limbs, lianas, roots, and vines. The fence they'd just climbed was gone.

"Shit!"

"Oh, yes, undoubtedly, and of all sizes, shapes, and densities. I'd watch my step carefully if I was you."

Henry grabbed Hatter's arm, his fingers digging uncomfortably into Hatter's flesh. "Why would you bring us here?"

"You said you wanted to go to the Red Queen's castle."

"So? I never said take us by way of the bowels of Hell."

Hatter sniffed loudly, although more to cover the Neverglades stench than for any dramatic effect. "The way to the Queen's castle changes. It's a security measure she put in after Alice's last visit. You never get there the same way twice unless you're riding in her personal coach."

"Nice of you to mention that!"

"Would it have made a difference? No? I rest my case."

"But you said things never get out of here!"

"Open your ears. I said some things get in but never get out. Not all things. There's a chance we'll make it through."

"A chance?" Henry grabbed Hatter's other arm, no doubt making a matching bruise on that arm with his claw-like fingers.

"A good chance. Although if we stand here much longer, that will swiftly decline into no chance. Creatures that live in the Neverglades tend to claim any objects slow enough to catch as dinner." He nodded toward a long, scaly beast lying nearly submerged in a brackish pond. Only the nostrils and red eyes peeked above the waterline. Hatter knew that just below the surface was a wide mouth full of very sharp teeth.

It was slowly drifting toward them. Hatter could almost feel its reptilian smile. "That crocodile, for example. It's looking at us like we're a pair of Grade A prime chops."

He grabbed Henry's hands and pried them off. Keeping tight hold of one—he didn't trust Henry not to fall behind, and didn't fancy the young man's odds if left with the crocodile—he pulled Henry along as he slogged through the swamp.

Black muck sucked at his shoes and the cuffs of his pants. Slithery, scaly things, some finned, some fanged, swam through the brackish water, slipping between their legs and brushing against their calves.

Small, furry bats flitted above their heads, feeding on the enormous mosquitoes that called the swamp home. He could hear the leathery whir of wings, and felt them beating close enough to his head to cause a breeze. Every so often, a bat would settle on top of his hat, as if claiming it for its personal roost, and he would wave an arm at it to shoo it away.

"Hatter…." Henry's voice sounded thick with fear.

He gave Henry's hand a reassuring squeeze, although he admitted he didn't feel very assured himself.

The light was always gray in the Neverglades, murky, as if it were perpetual twilight, impairing vision and impeding movement except for those denizens who made the swamp their home. Hatter knew of many besides the crocodiles and bats, and all of them were equally dangerous and hungry.

Indistinct shapes moved through the twisted and tangled tree limbs and roots all around them, some seeming muscular and cunning, others sinuous and clever, but all potentially deadly. He began to speak, keeping his voice even and steady, as if the sound of it was an audible amulet to keep evil at bay. "The creatures in the water aren't the only hungry beasties in the Neverglades. Keep watch for a triangular fin cutting through the leaves above us, Henry. Tree sharks make their home here. Curious creatures, they can swim through the thickets of leaves, darting out to take a bite of whatever creature pauses too long below them.

"Crocodiles lurk at the edge of deeper water, waiting for some poor unsuspecting soul to wander too close to the rim. Piranha monkeys, swamp bears, and pygmy tigers live here as well; all of them much too happy to drag you home to their lairs to snack on at their leisure. The key to survival in the Neverglades is to keep your eyes open, and always keep moving."

"That's fine with me. I have no wish to spend any more time here than necessary. We could run, couldn't we? The faster the better."

"No, that's not a good idea at all! The faster you move, the harder the mud and muck sucks at your feet trying to slow you down. Move too quickly, and you'll find yourself stuck standing still, a perfect target for any of the hungry creatures that live here."

"You know, I'm beginning to really, really hate Wonderland."

Hatter clucked his tongue. "Don't judge the whole of Wonderland by the few places you've seen so far. Most of it is quite beautiful. For example, the Diamond Fields are particularly brilliant at harvest time, when the diamond fruit sparkle like a million fairies in the moonlight.

"There's the Frozen Lake, forever frosty even in the highest heat of summer. It's a favorite vacation spot, as is the Caramel River, with its smoothly flowing, utterly creamy waters. There are many pleasant towns, as well, filled with interesting people and creatures. Wonderland lives up to its name, by and large."

"Well, based on what I've seen so far, it sucks."

"Exactly my point. You've seen us only at our worst. You should give us a chance before passing judgment." He spotted a gray, triangular fin in the leaves above his head and ducked, pulling Henry down with him, and just in time. A pointed maw full of sharp, crazily angled teeth dropped down toward them from the trees, snapping closed with the sound of a hundred scissors slicing, missing their heads by inches. It returned to the thicket of greenery just as quickly as it appeared. Hatter watched in relief as the fin moved swiftly through the leaves, heading south.

Hatter gave Henry's hand another squeeze. "Perhaps we should discuss this later and just concentrate on walking at a steady pace. The sooner we're out of here the better, and I'd very much like to leave without any chunks of me missing."

They trudged through the thick sludge for hours, or at least it felt that way. Hatter couldn't really be sure. The light never darkened or lightened in the Neverglades, but remained a steady, murky gray, and he certainly couldn't see the sun or moon through the thick canopy of vegetation above his head. It might be dawn, noon, or midnight, or sometime in between. He had no way of telling how much time had passed since they entered the swamp, and therefore, had no idea of how long it would be before they cleared it again.

He still held Henry's hand. It was warm, the grip strong. It was a good hand, a sturdy one, created for hard work and perfect for hand-holding in general. He wondered how many other hands it had held, and if any of their owners were special to Henry.

To his surprise, he found himself hoping there was no particular set of hands waiting at home for Henry. He liked the feel of Henry's hand in his, and more, found himself beginning to like the rest of Henry as well. Perhaps he had misjudged Henry when they first met in the anthill. Perhaps Henry wasn't as much like Alice as Hatter had surmised.

He tried to sound casual. "So, Henry, do you see much of Alice? Do you get along well?"

Henry snorted. "Alice and I are like onions and ice cream. We don't mix often, and in the rare circumstances we do, it's usually a disaster."

Aha! He was right. Henry wasn't close to Alice, and seemed to dislike her almost as much as Hatter did. That came as a bit of a relief, although Hatter wasn't exactly sure why he should care.

"I know why I don't like my sister—I have a lifetime of reasons, actually—but what did she ever do to you, Hatter?"

Hatter decided to be honest, something he usually strove to avoid whenever possible. *How very unlike me,* he thought, *perhaps I've caught an illness of some sort. I'll need to see the Physician, I suppose.* He plunged ahead anyway. "Many, many years ago, I was cursed by Time to spend eternity living and reliving a Tea Party with a Dormouse and the White Rabbit. Over and over again, drinking the same damnable cup of tea, eating the same stale cakes... It was awful, but I suppose I got used to it."

"What's that got to do with my sister?"

"Oh, well, she stumbled upon our Tea Party, you see, and rudely invited herself to join us. Then, she nitpicked and picked nits terribly, going on and on about the simplest mistakes, asking question after question, so much so that she even managed to upset the Dormouse, a difficult feat for certain, since, as I'm sure you already know, dormice are practically comas with legs. Then she stormed off, leaving the rest of us to sort it out. And why? Because I asked her a simple riddle. Time was so upset by her behavior, he forgot about the curse and let us all go."

"But wouldn't that be a good thing? Ridding yourself of the curse?"

Hatter shook his head sadly. "You would think so, and perhaps once upon a time I would've felt the same, but I'd been in that damned Tea Party for so long, most of the people I knew and cared about were long dead! My family, my friends… I would've been happier if I'd been left to drink tea for eternity."

Something shadowed Henry's eyes, something that looking suspiciously like sympathy to Hatter. "Sorry, Hatter. She's a true twit sometimes. At least, she was when she was little. She's changed some since she got married." Henry blushed, as if he were somehow to blame for his sister's shortcomings.

"No worries. I've adjusted rather well, I think." *Except for the part where I nearly lost my head, of course, but I needn't burden Henry with all that.* Hatter summoned up a smile.

"So, what was the riddle?"

Hatter blinked. "What riddle?"

"The one you asked Alice. What was it?"

"Oh, that. Why is a raven like a writing desk?"

"Huh. That's easy. I'm surprised Alice didn't know the answer."

"We've already established that you're much smarter than your sister." Hatter glanced at Henry out of the corner of his eye to see his reaction to the small compliment, and was pleased to see a smile curve Henry's lips. "So, what is the answer?"

"Ah. Because they both produce notes."

Hatter blinked again. "Huh. Yes, I guess that works, doesn't it. Good show."

Henry tugged at their joined hands, but Hatter refused to let go. "So what is the real answer?"

"The real answer?"

"To the riddle. What was the original answer?"

"Um, you guessed it." Hatter cleared his throat and refused to meet Henry's eyes.

Henry's eyes narrowed, and Hatter knew he'd been found out. "You didn't know the answer when you posed the riddle, did you? That's what made Alice so mad."

"Who side are you on, anyway?" Hatter grumbled, but he brightened a few moments later. "Look! We're nearly out of the Neverglades!"

Sure enough, the light ahead was slowly becoming brighter, cutting through the dense dimness of the Neverglades swamp, and chasing away the shadows. Hatter picked up the pace, anxious to leave the swamp and all its deadly, toothy residents behind.

Only after they'd cleared the last of the dismal swamp and stood under the bright Wonderland sun once again, did Hatter realize he was still holding fast to Henry's hand. Henry seemed to realize it at the same time, because they dropped each other's hands and took a step away, neither meeting the other's eyes.

Hatter took advantage of the moment to scan the area, trying to figure out where they were. He knew in an instant. The sweet, syrupy, yeasty smell on the breeze gave it away even more than the gently sloping foothills in the distance. They were on the Sugar Plains, which eventually led to the Confection Mountains.

"We have a few hours left before sunset. Best to keep walking." He hoped they'd have enough light to get up into the gently rolling hills before needing to make camp. The area adjacent to the swamp was relatively flat, and dotted with sweet-smelling wildflowers. It would come as a relief after the all the turmoil they'd suffered since leaving the Caterpillar's Lair, but Hatter knew it still held its own unique dangers.

One glance at the gray smoke gently puffing from the mountaintops told him the ovens were warmed up and ready to bake in the Confection Mountains. If that were the case, then it wouldn't matter whether it was midnight or high noon. Trouble would come for them either way, and there'd be no talking their way out of it, either. The Bakers were not a rational lot when it came to plying their trade.

Chapter Nine

"What's that smell?" Henry lifted his nose in the air and sniffed. "I can't quite put my finger on it, but it reminds me of my grandmother's kitchen."

"It's nothing. Your imagination. Keep walking."

"No, it isn't. I can smell it. It smells warm, and spicy, and sugary… and familiar." Henry took another couple of deep breaths. "I know! Cookies! That's what it is. I smell cookies baking."

"You're daft. We're out in the middle of nowhere. Do you see a bakeshop anywhere nearby? Keep walking."

Henry glanced at Hatter, then took a longer look. Hatter was chewing the inside of his cheek, and worry lines creased his forehead. He looked frightened, although about what, Henry couldn't guess. After escaping the monstrous ants in the Red Anthill, and managing the backward nature of Drawrof, and navigating the treacherous Neverglades, their walk across the flower-strewn meadow in the bakery-scented breeze was almost a vacation. What terror could the smell of a fresh, oven-baked treat possibly hold? "Hatter? What is it? You need to tell me. You look practically scared out of your pants."

Hatter's eyes bulged and he swallowed hard. "You don't know where we are, do you? Those are the Confection Mountains we're approaching!"

"So? What's so frightening about that? They don't look difficult to climb."

"The mountains aren't the problem. It's the Bakers we need to worry about. Their ovens are built into those foothills."

"So? I like cookies and cake. I particularly like gingerbread, although I also enjoy chocolate chip cookies, but—"

Hatter gasped, and stopped, clamping his hand over Henry's mouth. "Shh! You can't take sides! That's a sure way to get dead!"

Henry pulled Hatter's hand away from his mouth. "Will you please stop doing that?" He scowled, and folded his arms across his chest. "I'm sick and tired of your double-talk and riddles and nonsensical blathering. Tell me what's going on, or I'm not taking another single, solitary step."

Hatter wrung his hands, and shifted his weight from foot to foot. "We've no cover out here. I'd hoped to get past the foothills and up onto the mountain before the ovens were fired up, but I was wrong. We need to find someplace to hide. Maybe we could pick some of those flowers and use them as camouflage." He reached down and plucked a daisy, holding it up to his face. "Can you see me?"

"Seriously?" Henry raised one eyebrow. "Of course I can. It's a freaking daisy."

"Damn." Hatter tossed it away, and scanned the ground. "Then maybe we could dig a hole. I might have a shovel somewhere." He pushed a hand into his pocket and began to feel around.

Henry grabbed both of Hatter's arms, and gave him a little shake. "No! No camouflage, no hole digging, no hiding. Not until you tell me what's going on!" He gestured toward the empty meadow and the hills beyond. "There's nothing out here but us!"

Hatter's eyes were huge and practically glowing with fear. "The Bakers must be at war again. That's the only reason why the ovens would be lit at this time of day."

"The Bakers?"

Hatter nodded. "They're a race of giants who live up in the mountains and supply all of Wonderland with baked goods. Cookies, cakes, tarts…. Every baked treat comes from here. Their huge ovens are built into the foothills."

"So?"

"Don't you understand? The ovens are never fired this late in the day. They're only operated in the wee hours of early morning! The Bakers go to work in the middle of the night."

Henry lifted a shoulder. "So they decided to sleep in and bake later in the day. So what?"

Hatter swore softly, as if Henry were an idiot who failed to grasp the most rudimentary of explanations. "The Bakers are dedicated to their craft. Each clan has their own recipes, and each of them insists theirs is the best. Usually the Court of Confection settles disputes, but sometimes war breaks out between them. Then the hill ovens steam day and night baking their armies. It's the only reason the ovens would be hot in the middle of the day!"

Poor Hatter looks terrified, but really... a cookie army? What sort of damage could that do? All you'd need is a glass of milk to defeat them! A chuckle bubbled up and out from between Henry's lips before he could stop it.

"It's not funny!"

"Well, yeah, it sort of is. Hatter, we just came out of a swamp filled with tree sharks and crocodiles and other toothy, hungry nasties I don't even have a name for, and yet here you are, knock-kneed over a bunch of cookies!" The chuckle deepened into a true laugh that shook Henry's shoulders and brought a tear to his eye.

Hatter sputtered with indignation. "Don't laugh! There's nothing funny about war, cookie or otherwise." He looked off into the distance, but his gaze seemed to turn inward. When he spoke again, it was in a whisper. "I was only a small child during the last Confection War, but you never forget something like that, never. The noise. The smoke. The icing." A visible shiver raced across his shoulders.

Henry bit down hard on his tongue to stop laughing. Hatter was truly terrified. "I'm, um... sorry, Hatter."

Hatter looked away, and lifted his chin. "As if I believe you."

"No, really. I'm sorry." He really did feel badly, and placed a hand on Hatter's arm. Henry knew from experience that being mocked wasn't pleasant. People had laughed at him his entire life because of Alice's tales. "Please forgive me. I was out of line. It must have been awful for you."

"It was. The Bakers are not known for compassion."

Henry took Hatter's hand and patted it. He nodded toward the hills. "That's not such a huge mountain range. Perhaps we can find a way around them."

"No. There's no other way to go." Hatter shook his head. "The Neverglades are behind us, and going backward won't do us any good anyway. To the east lies the Endless Sugar Sand Desert. People rarely go there, and only someone with a death wish would attempt to cross it on foot."

"If no one goes there, how do you know it's endless?"

Hatter gave him a dark look and pulled his hand away. "First, it's right there in the name. It's not the Practically Endless Sugar Sand Desert, you know. Second, no one who tried to cross it ever came back. They're either dead or still walking. In any case, it doesn't sound particularly pleasant to me."

Henry smirked. "Maybe they reached the other side and liked it better there, and that's why they never came back. Didn't you ever think of that?"

"And maybe they're lying out somewhere on the scorching hot sugar sand, with nothing left to them but a jumble of bleached bones. Prove me wrong, and I'll happily lead the way in."

"Point taken."

"Really, I do live here, you know. Why must you question every word that comes out of my mouth?"

Henry thought about it. Why did he? He had the sneaking suspicion it was because Hatter—and Wonderland in general—was tied so closely to Alice. Since he'd spent nearly his entire life disbelieving her, doubting Hatter seemed a natural progression. "Sorry. You're right. I guess I have issues with anything Wonderland-related. I never believed Alice's stories, you know. I always thought she made it all up to get attention. I guess I owe her an apology when I get back."

"Hmph." Hatter nodded. "She was utterly annoying, a pain in virtually everyone's posterior, and no one was sorry to see her leave here, but the one thing she wasn't was a liar."

Henry nodded, and sought to change the subject. He found talking about Alice's virtues to be an unfamiliar and uncomfortable pastime. He pointed to the west. "What's that way?"

"Venom River. It's a waterway that begins at Headless Falls, just west of Caterpillar's Lair. It cuts through the Confection Mountains, and empties into the Undead Lake. The water is poisonous and acidic. It's a river of rocks, rough, roiling whitewater, and swirling vortexes that'll melt your raft out from under you and the flesh from your bones within five minutes of setting sail on it. And that's only if you can manage to navigate the shore to get to the water in the first place. The banks are the feeding and breeding grounds for venomous snakes, basilisks, spiders, and an especially ferocious species of firedrake."

Henry suppressed a shudder. "And you really call this place 'Wonderland,' huh?"

"Yes, of course. It's named that because many parts of it are wondrous, but also because it's a wonder anyone ever survives some of it." Hatter grabbed Henry's hand and began to pull him along toward the hills. "Our only choice is to go over the hills. Once we're in the mountains, there will be plenty of cover to keep us hidden from the Baker armies as we cross. Let's go. Keep your head down, and if you hear someone yell 'fire'… duck."

The meadow gradually grew steeper, wildflowers and grasses thinning, thickets of thorny bushes growing more abundant and closer together as they approached the base of the first hill. It was the largest one in a collection of six. The gently rolling mounds were the gateway to the Confection Mountains, which rose up sharply behind them. Hatter said people called them the Six Mother Hounds.

"They are aptly named," Hatter said as they stared up at them. "Because each one is a bitch in her own right."

Ice covered the first and smallest hill in a glittering, slippery-smooth glaze. Hatter said it never melted, not even when the huge oven buried within it grew hot. The ice made it nearly impossible to scale.

The second hill was a volcano, continually spewing lava in snaking, steaming streams, and belching gray clouds of ash and gas high into the air. Hatter said the air near that one stank of brimstone, and killed birds that made the mistake of flying too close to its poisonous clouds. Several fell out of the sky as Henry watched, horrified.

A lush tropical garden covered the third hill. Even from a distance, Henry could see trees heavy with colorful fruit, and ribbons of sparkling water threading through the foliage and unusual rock formations. He smiled. "Let's climb that one. I'm hungry."

"Are you daft? That's Forgetful Hill. Eat anything, drink anything on that hill and you'll instantly forget everything you ever knew. Not only difficult subjects like arithgebra and quadrometry, but simple stuff, like who you are, how to walk, how to talk, how to eat, and how to breathe."

"So, we won't eat or drink anything. It still looks safer than any of the other hills."

Hatter shook his head. "You really don't think it would be that simple, do you? The flowers on Forgetful Hill produce a narcotic pollen. It's thick in the air over there, and unavoidable. The pollen is toxic, and is so powerful, you won't be able to resist eating or drinking everything in sight." He pointed toward the hill. "See those lumpy pale things scattered around the hill?"

Henry nodded. "You mean those rock formations? Yeah, I see them."

"Those aren't rocks. Those are the calcified bodies of people who stupidly believed the pretty little hill was safe."

"Oh." Henry bit his lip and considered the remaining four hills.

Hatter pointed to the one furthest away. The hill seemed to float within a huge ball of water. "That's Shark Hill. Care to venture a guess why it was given that name?"

Henry didn't have to guess. He could see sharks of all different sizes swimming through the water, including several species he knew and many others he didn't. Hammerheads, tiger sharks, bull sharks, and at least three tremendous great white sharks continuously circled the hill, along with purple sharks, striped sharks, and one that looked almost as big as a whale and ate several smaller sharks as it swam.

Hatter drew Henry's attention to the fifth hill. It seemed to bulge and shrink randomly, as if something were encapsulated within it and struggling to break free. Considering everything he'd seen thus far, Henry was inclined to believe that was happening.

"That's Egg Hill. Nobody's sure what's incubating inside, but whatever it is, we're all fairly confident it'll be ugly and hungry when it hatches. Which, from the look of the cracks crisscrossing the surface, might be any time now."

That left the final and largest hill. Thorny brush covered it, but Henry couldn't make out anything living, pulsing, bulging, swimming, spurting, biting, or glowing on it. "What's that one?"

"Stinging Hill. It's covered in brambles that sting like wasps." He looked at Henry. "Are you allergic to bee stings?"

"No. Not that it means I like getting stung, though."

"Ha! I expect not. I ask because the brambles contain minute amounts of venom, much like bee stings. In any case, it's Stinging Hill or one of the others. Take your pick."

Henry looked over the six hills again. While climbing Stinging Hill might be a possibly painful experience, it seemed the least likely to kill them. "Maybe if we run fast enough we won't get stung."

"I suppose stranger things have happened. So, Stinging Hill it is. Remember; keep your head down, and your eyes peeled for the Bakers' Armies."

Chapter Ten

It was much tougher going than Hatter remembered. Then again, he hadn't been in the area since he was a child, and children were notoriously limber. No matter how carefully they stepped, the thorny brush snagged on their trousers, biting through the fabric to scratch the skin beneath. This wasn't like taking a few bee stings. This felt as if they were wading through a pool filled to the brim with pissed-off hornets.

"Ouch! Ouch, ouch, ouch, ouch." He lifted his knees up high as he stepped, hoping to give at least one leg at a time a respite from the biting thorns, however temporary.

Henry took a different approach. He took long, awkward hops through the thorns, looking like a whackweed-smoking rabbit. His method didn't seem any more successful than Hatter's, but Hatter admitted it was far more amusing to watch.

Or would be, had Hatter been in any frame of mind to be amused. As it was, his legs were beginning to feel flayed of skin, leaving his muscle, sinew, and nerve endings raw and screaming, putting him in a slightly less than jovial mood.

"We should've taken our chances with Egg Hill." Henry sounded a little out of breath, no doubt from all the intense hopping he was doing. "Whatever comes out of that hill—ouch—can't possibly be any worse than these thorns."

"Never say never. Ouch. I've learned the one thing all creatures great and small, be they human or animal, have in common upon being born is hunger. I would rather be stung than serve as some newborn nightmare's first meal."

"You can't possibly know it would want to eat us. Ouch. Maybe whatever is in that egg is a vegetarian."

Hatter looked at him askance. "After seeing all you have of Wonderland thus far, do you really think things would work out that way? Ouch."

Henry snorted. "Maybe, ouch, but then I would probably automatically turn into a giant zucchini and be eaten anyway, wouldn't I?"

"Ouch. Now, you're getting it."

"You'll pardon my saying, ouch, but so far Wonderland sucks big, fat, hairy monkey balls."

Somehow, despite the stinging pain, Hatter laughed. "That it does, my friend. At times, that it does."

They crested the hill and paused at the top to gain both their breath and a brief respite from tramping through the stinging brambles. Before them, at the bottom of the hill, was a narrow valley.

Within the confines of the valley stood row upon row of brown, man-like figures. One look told Henry they weren't human. Their heads, hands, and feet were too large and too round, and their bodies, when viewed sideways, were too flat.

He nudged Hatter. "Who—or what—are they?"

Hatter swept off his hat and swiped an arm across his forehead, wiping away the perspiration beading it. "That's the Gingerbread Army. They're the first line of defense for the Molasses Baker Tribe. In battle, they're fearless and deadly. Practically unstoppable, really."

Movement from far down the valley caught the corner of his eye. A dust cloud was swirling in the distance. Henry turned, squinting to see. "What's that down there?"

Hatter stuck his hand in his pocket and withdrew a telescoping spyglass. He pulled it out to its full length and put it to his eyes, studying the churning dust. He swore and removed the spyglass, handing it to Henry. "Take a look. It's the Chocolatier Baker's Sugar Militia. Looks like the Gummy Cavalry is in the lead."

Henry peered through the spyglass, swinging it in the direction of the dust cloud. Indistinct shapes began to emerge; jewel-toned candy riders mounted on puffy marshmallow horses rode slowly toward the waiting Gingerbread Army, with rows of chocolate soldiers marching behind them. They stopped about halfway down the valley, and all grew deathly quiet.

Suddenly, a thunderous boom split the silence, and echoed down the valley. Henry watched in horror as a brown ball flew through the air and punched a hole in the middle of one of the Gingerbread Soldiers' chests. The Soldier fell forward and lay still.

Hatter grabbed his arm and tugged him to the ground. "Keep your head down unless you want a chocolate malt cannonball to take it off. The battle has started!"

A long figure stepped out from the front line of Gingerbread Soldiers. He wore yellow licorice epaulettes, and carried a rock candy sword. He raised it and pointed at the Sugar Militia. His voice was surprisingly deep and rumbly for a cookie. "Charge!"

A roar rose up from the valley as the Gingerbread Army surged forward. Advancing in a stiff-legged, shambling run, they fired their icing guns at the Sugar Militia. Streams of sticky white frosting hit the cavalry, sending marshmallow horses and their gummy riders sprawling.

Additional booms sounded in response, followed by more Gingerbread Soldiers blown into cookie crumbs by deadly chocolate malt cannonballs. The Chocolate Soldiers marched double-time, pressing onward up the valley, spearing Gingerbread Soldiers with sharp, candy cane lances. Every so often, a Gingerbread Soldier would throw a Red Hots hand grenade in an arc over the heads of the Sugar Militia, where it would explode in a spray of melted chocolate.

As they watched, a marshmallow horse caught fire, galloping away from the fray until it blackened and fell to the ground in an oozing, bubbly marshmallow puddle.

Hatter pulled on Henry's arm. "Come on! This is our chance, while the armies are busy trying to kill one another."

"What? We can't go down there! We'll get ourselves killed."

"It's our only chance. They're too busy trying to destroy one another to see us. If we wait, we're likely to be captured by whichever side wins this skirmish. Now, let's go!" He began running down the side of the hill into the valley, dragging Henry along with him.

The smell of smoke and cinnamon lay heavy in the air on the valley floor. Henry had to swallow hard at the sight of fallen Gingerbread men strewn across the ground, most missing limbs, and all sporting terrible wounds. Chocolate malt cannonballs lay here and there, covered in gingerbread crumbs.

War, even of the confectionary variety, was Hell.

Hatter tugged him along, sidestepping puddles of icing, melted chocolate, Gingerbread, and Gummy bodies. The smoky air made it difficult to see where they going, though. More than once the soles of Henry's shoes stuck in something sticky, pulling up taffy-like strands of goo when he finally broke free. He didn't want to look at the puddles too closely. They smelled strongly of marshmallow.

A whistling sound caught his attention. Before Henry could react, Hatter pushed him to the ground and fell on top of him. Over Hatter's shoulder, Henry saw a chocolate ball the size of a bowling ball arc, crashing to the ground next to them.

"Oh my God! That could've killed us!" Fear froze Henry's chest, making it difficult to breathe. It had been a really close call. If Hatter hadn't pushed him down, the ball might've taken off Henry's head. He turned his gaze to meet Hatter's. "You saved my life."

The corner of Hatter's mouth quirked into a halfhearted smirk, but since he remained lying atop Henry, he couldn't really hide his fear. Henry could feel Hatter's heart racing. "Nothing to it."

Hatter made no move to get up. The longer Henry lay there, the press of Hatter's body pinning him to the ground, the more the sounds of battle seemed to fade away. He began to notice how the dark hair dusting Hatter's jaw accentuated its sharp edge. How Hatter's eyes were a warm, dark brown, not fully black as Henry had first thought. And mostly, how full Hatter's lips looked, and how soft. He wondered if they would feel warm, and what they'd taste like.

How is it, with war raging so close by, with chocolate malt cannonballs flying, and icing guns firing, that I can be thinking of kissing him? This freaking place has finally pushed me over the edge. I must be nuts. Crazy. Certifiable. Why are we just lying here? We need to get out of here before we get killed!

In his head, he fiercely berated himself, but he spoke not a single word aloud. Instead, he lifted his head and touched his lips to Hatter's.

As it turned out, they were every bit as soft and twice as warm as Henry had supposed, and tasted like peppermint tea.

Nothing surprised him more, though, than when Hatter kissed him back, his tongue teasing at Henry's lower lip. Except maybe for the fact that for a long, happy moment, Henry was perfectly content to lie there on the battlefield in Wonderland, bits of Gingerbread Soldiers and Sugar Militia all around him, chocolate malt cannonballs flying, being kissed by Hatter.

It was Hatter who finally broke the spell.

He cleared his throat, and rolled off Henry, clambering to his feet. "Um, sorry. Well, I think we should, um, go. There. Away."

Henry smiled and pushed himself to his feet. "Definitely. We should go." Hatter looked positively dazed, and somehow, that made Henry feel as if he'd won a skirmish.

Another chocolate malt cannonball whizzed by them, striking the ground nearby. They both jumped and let out half-strangled screams. It was all the impetus they needed to get them moving.

They began running, bent nearly in half, keeping their heads down, and quickly crossed the valley floor to the other side.

In front of them, the first of the Confectionary Mountains rose steeply from the valley floor. He and Hatter took a moment to stare up at its intimidating presence. A narrow, well-trod path of firmly packed graham cracker crumbs began at its foot, winding its way up the face of the mountain.

Hatter broke off a small piece of rock from the foot of the mountain, and popped it into his mouth. "They're made out of rock candy, you know. The mountains, I mean. I've heard that Confectioner's sugar dusts the peaks in six and eight-foot drifts. Legend has it the Bakers built the mountains to keep enemies from stealing their recipes, but they're so paranoid about their secrets that they often suspect one or more of their own brothers of trying to steal them. That's when these wars break out. He clapped his hands together, rock candy dust flying. "Well, we'd best get climbing. I'd like to get to the other side of the mountains before dark."

They climbed for what seemed to be an eternity to Henry. The path was steep, and before long his knees and back were aching. He looked back once, and saw the valley and its war-sundered baked goods spread out far below. They'd come farther up than he'd thought.

A thunderous pounding startled him, so deep he could feel the reverberations in his bones. He grabbed Hatter's arm. "What was that?"

Hatter looked around wildly, then pulled Henry into a tight crevice in the mountain wall. They barely fit inside, chest to chest. Hatter's dark eyes were wide, and fear sparkled in them. "Shh. Don't make a sound."

Henry held his breath and waited as the crashing sounds came closer, getting louder by the minute. A huge shadow, seemingly almost as large as the mountain itself, fell over them. It was as if night had suddenly fallen. Henry could no longer see Hatter's face, even though it was mere inches from his own.

The booming sounds continued, growing farther away, and within a few moments the shadow passed, and the sun returned. Hatter made them wait another full five minutes before slowly creeping out from their hidey-hole.

Henry was still almost afraid to speak. He could see a gigantic figure blotting out the sun at the far end of the valley. He lowered his voice into a feathery whisper. "What was that?"

"One of the Baker Giants. They're not especially neighborly folk. Everyone is a potential spy to them. Had he found us, he would've likely ground us up and added us as flavoring to the next batch bound for the oven."

Henry kept casting glances over his shoulder as they continued to climb but eventually, in the absence of any more Baker

Giants, his mind began to wander. Once freed from fear, it made a beeline directly back to their kiss.

Neither of them mentioned it aloud, but for Henry, at least, their kiss never quite left his mind, not even when the Giant passed so close Henry could smell the Giant's aftershave—a bit spicy and nutmeg-y, like his grandma's pumpkin pie. He found the memory of it almost as nice as the kiss itself was, but he couldn't help but wonder what Hatter thought about it.

Hatter seemed content to pretend nothing had happened. Henry could understand that, to a point. He wasn't so stupid as to believe everyone was out and comfortable in their own skin. Some people denied the attraction they felt.

It wasn't the first time Henry had kissed a boy. He'd had a boyfriend once. He and James had dated for almost six months as sophomores, and done more together than simple kissing. A lascivious grin creased his cheek as he remembered. He'd dated Sarah before James, and Rachel afterward, and neither one of the girls had worn purity rings, either.

Still, none of them had been what Henry would consider "serious" relationships. They'd been fun, but he hadn't been too heartbroken when they'd ended. All his life he'd felt as if he were looking for something, that something missing in it that he couldn't even name, but he did know neither James nor either of the girls had been it.

Could it be he'd been seeking Wonderland all along? Even when he berated Alice for telling lies and believed it couldn't possibly exist? For the first time, he began to question his own motives for disbelieving Alice. Had it been because he truly thought she'd been lying, or had some small, ugly part of him been jealous of her tales?

He didn't know. It was all too confusing. What he did know was that no one he dated before had kissed him blind in the dust of a battlefield, while chocolate malt cannonballs whistled overhead, and the smell of gingerbread hung heavy in the air. None of their kisses had so burned themselves into his memory that not even the thundering footsteps of a giant could dislodge them.

None of them had kissed him like Hatter.

He was smiling as he followed Hatter along up the mountain path.

Chapter Eleven

Surprisingly, it never got any colder no matter how much higher they climbed. The temperature stayed warm because of the enormous ovens inside the foothills. Heat traveled up, and they produced enough to warm even the uppermost mountain peaks.

The steep path wound around the western face of the mountain, evening out for a while before beginning its descent on the other side. The snow—which was actually confectioner's sugar, powdery and dry—while not as deep as it was on the higher reaches of the mountain, was still enough to slow their travels. It was knee-deep in places, and the breeze lifted it into the air, blowing it into their faces, making breathing difficult. Hatter dug into his pocket for his handkerchiefs again, which they tied around their faces to keep the fine particles out of their noses and mouths. Heads bent into the wind, they pushed on.

The going got much easier as they crested the mountain peak, and the path dipped downward again. As they left the heavy drifts of confectioner's sugar behind, the trail led them into pretty forests of slim lollipop trees and fat gumball bushes, interspersed with a few marzipan shrubs.

Wildlife, conspicuously absent on the Baker Giants' side of the mountains, reappeared. Colorful birds darted between the trees in rainbow streaks. Hatter caught sight of a few shy deer hidden deep in the foliage, a family of raccoons cautiously watching their progress, and a white rabbit wearing a pocket watch and a shamelessly dated brocade waistcoat—

Wait. What?

"Rabbit!" Hatter swore and gave his head a violent shake. "No. Absolutely not."

Rabbit gasped and hopped up to Hatter, shoving a large, gold pocket watch in his face. "Have you any idea what day it is? What time? Where have you been? You're late, Hatter. Very, very late. You've put the Queen in a most disturbing temper." He glanced at his watch again, his small pink nose twitching, and began to whimper. His overly large feet nervously thumped the ground. "Oh, look at the time! I'm to accompany you straightaway to the Red

Castle, Hatter. Your sentencing is set for this very afternoon, and you mustn't be late for that. Heavens, no. It would be most unpleasant."

"Sentencing? Rabbit, what are you talking about?"

"Her Majesty has accused you of the crime of killing Time. Again."

"What? Oh, not again! Why, I haven't even seen Time in—"

"It matters not. The Queen believes you've done it. Oh, your trial was quite spectacular, I dare say. Arguments raged on for so long, the Queen actually yawned. I've never seen such an exhibition. Of course, in the end, you were found guilty."

Hatter folded his arms across his chest and glowered at Rabbit. "Of course I was."

"Very sensible of you to agree. Now, if you don't mind, what's say we hurry, yes? We're late." Rabbit showed Hatter the face of his pocket watch again, as if to prove to him how late they really were.

Hatter gently pushed Rabbit's watch away. "I am not late. I did not kill Time. I've barely even poked it a little. I've been very busy securing the presence of Henry, also known as Boy Alice, and going to great and quite exhausting lengths keeping him out of harm's way while escorting him to the Red Castle. Quite a grueling and vexing project, for which I may not expect recompense, might I add."

Henry frowned at him, but Hatter pretended not to notice, keeping his attention on Rabbit. He'd deal with Henry's dented feelings later.

Rabbit's eyes opened wide. "Heavens, is this really Boy Alice?" He stepped up and peered closely into Henry's face, whiskers twitching. "Why, yes, I can see the family resemblance now. Well, if he's anything like his sister, that explains why you're late, Hatter."

"I am nothing like Alice!" Henry glared at Rabbit, his lip curling over his teeth.

Hatter took a step to the left, effectively stepping between Henry and Rabbit. "You see? There are extenuating circumstances. He is most disagreeable. Tiresomely so. I didn't kill time. If anything, I saved it by making him hurry despite his argumentative nature."

"Hey! Whose side are you on? I am not argumentative!" Henry put in.

Hatter smirked at Henry from over his shoulder. "Thank you for proving my point."

The Rabbit waved a dismissive hand at both of them. "Doesn't matter. You know how it is with the Queen. She never changes her verdicts."

Hatter scowled. "Rubbish. This is just her way of getting out of her promise to me, that's all."

Henry pulled on his shoulder. "What promise? You didn't say anything about a promise from the Queen, Hatter."

Hatter cursed himself silently for slipping up. "Er, it's nothing. Never mind. You heard Rabbit! We're late! Let's go. Come on, double time."

"You just said we're not late!" Henry shouted, his cheeks growing very red.

"I lied." Hatter turned away, not wishing to see the hurt and anger in Henry's eyes. Lying about lying about lying. It was a new low, even for him. He tried not to slouch from the weight of the guilt pressing down on his shoulders as he followed Rabbit through the woods toward the Red Queen's castle.

Henry grabbed his arm and pulled him to a stop. They watched the Rabbit hop into the distance, never slowing, obviously convinced the two of them would hurry behind him now that he'd proven how very late they were. "What did you mean when you said you lied? What did you lie about?"

"It's really nothing. Look, plans have changed. We can't go to the Queen's Castle."

Gaping at Hatter, Henry's jaw dropped. "What are you talking about? Of course we do. You said she was the only one who might be able to send me home!"

"Yeah, about that... that would be the part I lied about."

Henry folded his arms across his chest. The look on his face was positively murderous. It was obvious to Hatter that Henry wasn't taking a step until he got an explanation.

Gods, how Hatter hated the truth. It was almost never pleasant, and usually quite painful, which is why he usually liked to bend and twist it into more palatable shapes. He sighed. "The Queen believes you're here to execute a coup against her regime. When Alice became Queen, even though it was only for a few short hours, the Red Queen nearly lost her mind if not her head. She won't let that happen again. She aims to question you, then lop off your head as a warning to other interlopers."

"Lop off... you mean...." Henry's hand went to his neck as if to protect his tender throat. "I intend nothing of the sort! I'm here by accident. I'll just explain things to her, and—"

"Explain? To the Red Queen?" Hatter couldn't help a sardonic laugh from escaping his lips. "No one explains anything to the Queen. She's built of nothing but maliciousness and stubbornness held together by a few threads of narcissism and a nice big helping of conceit. She'd cut off your head if you tried to talk her out of cutting off your head."

Pale as milk, Henry began to pace, his hands clamped to the sides of his head as if to keep his brains from leaking out of his ears. "Why? Why did you lie to me?"

"I didn't. Not really. If you remember, I said the Queen wanted me to bring you to the castle, and that was the truth. I merely omitted the part about losing your head." Hatter felt hollow inside. He sounded like a jerk even to himself. Then again, he never expected to have feelings for Henry, other than gratitude for providing a way to keep his own head attached to his shoulders. The new charges against him for killing Time were false; the Queen was trying to make sure Hatter—and in turn, Henry—would be delivered to her by Rabbit. He wasn't worried about them, but he was worried about Henry. "Listen to me. The Queen is not a good sport, but we don't need to see her to get you home."

"Oh? Why should I ever believe a word you say again?"

"There is no reason. You're right to doubt me. I behaved abominably, and for that I'm truly sorry." Hatter swallowed his guilt like a bitter pill, and stood tall. "But I'm not lying now. If you go to the Red Palace, you will lose your head."

Henry stopped pacing and faced Hatter. "Then what am I supposed to do? Stay here forever? I have a life back home! Friends. Family." He picked at his shirt and pants, which were filthy from their slog through the Neverglades and Confection Mountain climb. "Clean clothes!"

"Family? I thought you hated Alice."

"I do not! She's my sister, and besides, I owe her an apology. I was wrong. She was telling the truth all those years. I have other family besides Alice, you know. There's my father.... He drinks, but he's still my dad. Plus, there's my mother's brother, Leonard, who showed up a few years ago. People depend on me. I have to go back!"

"Well, as I said—if you were listening, which you obviously have not been—there is another way. I know where the magic looking glass is, the one Alice used the last time she came to Wonderland." Hatter allowed himself a small triumphant smile. "It stands to reason that if she used it to get here, then you can use it to get home." His smile slipped, and he whispered, almost under his breath. "Unless it's one-way magic, like the door to Caterpillar's Lair."

"What's that? I didn't hear you."

"Nothing, nothing. The mirror is located in the White Queen's castle."

Henry cocked his head, and narrowed his eyes. "Didn't you tell me the White Queen was dead?"

"Oh, quite dead, yes." Hatter nodded. "Lost her head on the chessboard, and it is very rare that anyone survives that! However, her castle remains. Empty, of course, and some say haunted, but there nonetheless. And somewhere within it is the mirror."

Clasping his hands behind his back and tucking his chin down, Henry resumed pacing. It was obvious to Hatter he was thinking things over. "I suppose if the mirror isn't there then I'm no worse off than I am now. I can always come back to the Red Castle, right?"

"Well, yes, although the result will be the same, I assure you. Beheadings are the Red Queen's favorite pastime."

Hatter watched Henry's Adam's apple bob as he swallowed hard. "Okay. Lead on to the White Castle, but I warn you, Hatter... don't lie to me again."

"You have my word." Hatter solemnly crossed his heart, wondering how much his word was actually worth on the open market these days. Not enough to buy the holes in Swiss cheese, he figured, but again, Henry didn't need to know that. He had heard that the glass was in the White Castle; he hadn't lied. Whether it would work or not was up for debate. For the moment, though, making sure Henry's handsome head remained where it belonged was quite enough for Hatter. That and keeping his own firmly attached as well.

He looked off into the distance, where Rabbit was no more than a spot on the horizon, then turned to the northwest. His voice sounded far more chipper than he felt. "This way! Come on, let's step lively. We've got miles to go before nightfall. Miles to go." He set off at a brisk pace, with Henry at his side.

They walked in silence for several miles, each lost in their own thoughts. Then Henry finally broke the silence with a question.

"Did you say Alice was Queen of Wonderland? How could that be? For that matter, if Wonderland is all one country, how could there be a Red Queen and a White Queen?"

"Alice was Queen, once. Didn't she tell you?" Hatter sighed, and began walking. As he suspected, Henry kept pace with him. "It was years ago, at the end of Alice's last visit here. Of course, there are those who believe it true, others who insist it was nothing more than a dream of the Red King, and others who believe Alice was the one dreaming, but since they've both been gone for years, there's no way to verify it either which way. I'm not even entirely sure how it happened, since it's singularly unusual for anyone not born to the crown to wear it. All I know is that it supposedly involved a chess game, a White Knight, and some sort of cake."

"Cake? What flavor?"

"Do you know, I'm not sure." Hatter tapped his chin with a finger. "Certainly nothing as ordinary as plain vanilla cake. Perhaps it was something of the upside down variety, since it certainly turned the monarchy on its ear for a time. Of course, then Alice disappeared again, and things went back to normal, or for what passes as normal here on most days, so I suppose it really doesn't matter."

"Wait a minute." Henry put his hand on Hatter's arm. He could feel the heat soaking in right through his coat sleeve. "If my sister was Queen, what does that make me? Am I a Prince?"

Hatter frowned, thinking. He hadn't thought of that before. "I don't rightly know. Alice wasn't born to royalty—she was a commoner who won the crown. Still, she held it for a time, even if it was only a matter of hours, and disappeared having never formally renounced it. You're of her blood, but quite frankly, I don't know what that makes you."

Silence descended for another few minutes before Henry spoke again. "Alice and her dodgy queen-hood aside, what about my other question? How can there be two Queens in one land?"

"That's another story."

"Well, we've got time, right? I don't see the White Castle anywhere around here."

Hatter blew a stray hair out of his eyes. "Years and years ago, twin sisters were born to the ruling Queen. One was pure and sweet, and kind to everyone. Never a sharp word passed her lips. She was beloved by all who met her. The other twin was as crude and cruel as her sister was good. She had a crooked smile and a twisted soul."

"Let me guess. The good one was the White Queen, and the bad one was the Red Queen."

"Hmph." Hatter stopped and folded his arms across his chest, annoyed. "Have you heard this story before?"

"Um, no."

"Then kindly allow me to tell it."

"By all means, please do," Henry said, with only the slightest hint of sarcasm.

Hatter, somewhat appeased, continued both the story and their walk. "The current King and Queen decided the sweet twin would inherit the crown. This, of course, did not sit well with the other twin. She threw a tantrum so foul that it dropped birds from the sky and withered every flower for miles around.

"When her parents refused to change their minds, she stormed off and had her own castle built on the other side of Wonderland. She took a husband, a nice fellow who really ought to have known better, and proclaimed them King and Queen. She had everything painted red because it was the color of rage, and the color of blood. Eventually, even her servants, serfs, and soldiers took on a red hue. Her symbol was the Heart because she claimed her family broke hers. She swore vengeance on her sister, the White Queen, and finally got it when they met on the chessboard."

"So that's why she wants my head? Because Alice became Queen?"

"That's it in a nutshell." Hatter removed his hat and fanned himself with it.

"Why does she hate you so much?"

"Me? Because Time cursed me." Hatter replaced his hat on his head and tamped it down. "Time, you know, is the Red Queen's only real enemy. Nothing escapes the ravages of Time. Except me. Because Time cursed me, I haven't aged, and she's consumed by jealousy. My very existence reminds her that she grows old while I remain the same. As I said before, it isn't a blessing—it's horrible having everyone you knew and loved die while you go on—but she doesn't see it that way. She couldn't care less if everyone she knows turned toes up, as long as she went on just as she was."

"Wow. She's a total bitch."

"Really, calling her that insults female dogs everywhere."

Silence descended once more as they continued their trek to the White Castle. The sun breached the sky and was far along its path to the horizon again when they finally spied four gleaming towers in the distance.

Henry shouted and pointed. "Is that it? Is that the White Castle?"

Hatter nodded, not feeling the same jubilation. "That's it. We'll be there before dark."

Before night fell he'd find out if he could send Henry home through the looking glass, or if Henry was stuck here in Wonderland. Neither option made Hatter very happy. If Henry went home, Hatter felt he'd miss something wonderful before he even got a chance to appreciate it. If Henry stayed, they'd both live on the run from the Red Queen, or worse, lose their lives to her spiteful wrath. His was, as the old Wonderland saying went, a lose-lose situation.

Sighing deeply, he hurried his step to keep up with Henry.

Chapter Twelve

Lush meadows spread out before them. They were home to uncountable species of flowers, all of which produced blooms of white, from the giant, blindingly white Sunblockers, whose shade rivaled that of the largest oak trees, to the tiny Miniaturia, whose delicate ivory petals were no bigger than an exclamation point, and every size and shape of flower in between. Seen from afar, the meadows looked like softly rippling mounds of snow stretching out in all directions.

From the center of the meadow rose the four towers of the White Queen's castle, gleaming white under the sun, but as Hatter and Henry drew closer, they began to see decay had fallen upon the castle following its mistress's demise.

All the castle's beautiful stained-glass windows, which Hatter remembered told the history of Wonderland in bright splashes of color against the all-white background of the castle walls, were gone, leaving the frames looking like black, lifeless eyes. Gray mold grew in wide, furry patches on the castle walls, discoloring the rich whiteness of the massive stone blocks used in its construction.

There was no moat—Hatter recalled the White Queen being most welcoming to all who sought an audience with her—but even from a distance they could see the tall double entry doors hanging askew from their hinges. The entirety of the castle gave a distressing appearance, sad and somehow unbearably lonely, as if its purpose was to house life, but was now home only to ghosts.

Hatter paused, looking up at the four towers. The remnants of the White Queen's flag still rippled from a pole high up on the northeast tower. Although it was shredded and grayed from exposure, he could still make out the white rose at its center.

"The place looks like it was deserted a long time ago," Henry said. "Are you sure the mirror is still here?"

Hatter shrugged. "I hope so. It was here the last time I passed through this area, but the White Queen was very much alive then."

"Great. Just great. What do I do if it isn't here?" Henry began to huff and grumble, his hands balled into fists at his sides. "Hatter, answer me. What am I going to do?"

Hatter rolled his eyes. "First, you can stop worrying about things over which we have no control. Either it's here, or it isn't. If it is, then fine. If not, we'll worry about it then. I swear, you are the most worrisome worrywart I ever…."

His voice trailed off as he spotted something in the distance, approaching from the eastern edge of the meadow. His eyes grew wide, and his stomach lurched. "Henry?"

"Yes? What is it?" Henry's reply was short, his temper still flavoring his voice.

"Run."

"What?" Henry turned and looked east, where a dark shape was spreading through the white flowers like blood spilled in water. "What is that?"

"The Red Queen's Guard. Run!" Hatter grabbed Henry's hand and began running toward the White Castle, pulling Henry along after him. "Either the Rabbit overheard us talking and told the Queen where we were going, or she simply figured it out after we disappeared. I swear, if I find out it was Rabbit, I'm going to make stew out of him when I get my hands on him again!"

They ran past the askew double doors and into the castle, finding themselves in an immense entry hall. The high, arched ceiling was laced with long, gleaming planks of wood polished to a gloss. White marble blocks, veined with the palest rose, made up the walls. Under their feet, a thick carpet covered the flagstone floor. The carpet was gray with mold—the open doors had allowed the worst of the weather inside—but they could tell that at one time it had been creamy white.

Before them, twin curving staircases rose majestically to the second floor. Hatter hurried up them, taking two at a time. Henry followed him as closely as a shadow as they raced to the next floor.

Relying on his memory, Hatter led Henry down a long hallway to yet another set of stairs. This stairway was plain in comparison to the grandness of the former. As Hatter remembered it, it was a servant's staircase and led up to a hallway at the end of which was the Queen's boudoir, where he'd last seen the magic mirror.

As they fled, he noticed barely any decorations were left in the castle. No statues, few paintings, and only a stick or two of furniture. It had been well and duly ransacked. He began to doubt the mirror would still be there, although he didn't give voice to his fear. They'd find out soon enough if it was gone.

He could hear faint voices now. The Red Queen's Guard must have entered the castle. Putting on a fresh burst of speed, he grabbed Henry's hand again and raced down the long hallway. Finally reaching the end, he tried the handle of the door to the Queen's bedroom.

It was locked.

He jiggled it, and twisted it, pulled on it, and cursed at it, but the knob wouldn't budge. "Damn it! It's locked up tight."

"Use your magic!"

"What?"

"Your magic. Surely you can open a door with it, right? I mean, you could make yourself big, and you had the lightning bug light, and you have a pocket that probably has an elephant stuffed down in it somewhere. Tell me you can't open a simple door!" Henry's voice was shrill, and teetering on the edge of hysteria.

"I… I don't know how to…." Hatter paused. Magic. Could it be the door was guarded by a simple spell? He shrugged. It was worth a try. After all it couldn't hurt, and looking foolish if it didn't work was the least of his worries right now. Looking directly at the doorknob, he said, "Open."

Nothing.

"Um, unlock? Release. Disengage." He began jiggling the knob again. "Open, damn you!"

Henry growled and shouldered Hatter aside. Placing his hand on the knob, he said in a voice that sounded much calmer than he looked, "Open, please."

There was a brief glimmer of golden light around the doorknob before there was a soft click of the lock unlatching, and the door swung inward.

Hatter gaped at Henry. "How did you do that?"

"Please. Even I know that's the magic word, Hatter." Henry's lips curved in a small, satisfied smile, despite the direness of their situation.

Hatter felt inexplicably pleased that Henry seemed to have finally accepted the existence of magic, but he covered it in a sarcastic reply. "Well, Master Magician, if you're quite done with your phenomenal feats of prestidigitation, let's move, shall we? The Red Guard will be up here any moment now!"

They slipped into the White Queen's bedroom, and closed the door behind them. "Lock, please," Hatter said to the doorknob. He didn't know if it would work, but he felt it couldn't hurt, and was pleased to hear another soft click as the lock engaged.

Not that a mere magical lock would keep the Red Guard out of the room for long—they'd simply break it down to get inside, but it would buy Hatter and Henry a few more precious moments.

The White Queen's bedroom didn't look as though it belonged in the castle. Unlike the rest of the palace, there was little white to be seen. Instead, a rainbow of bright colors splashed the walls, floor, and furniture. Rich jewel tones abounded in all hues… except red. Red was the only color not represented in the Queen's boudoir. It didn't take a genius to figure out why, either.

Red was her twin's color, and no doubt the White Queen detested it.

Perhaps the lock-spell had done its job, because unlike the rest of the castle, this room seemed untouched. Under their feet, a thick, woven rug of brilliant colors cushioned their steps. A large swan bed dominated one wall, covered in fluffy pillows and a thick comforter the color of emeralds. Other large, ornate pieces of furniture, an armoire, a chest of drawers, and a dressing table were scattered about, their wood and hardware gleaming as if polished that very day. Not a speck of dust marred their surfaces.

Whatever cleaning spell the White Queen had cast must still be in effect, Hatter thought, looking around the room. Then he froze, pointing. "Look, Henry, over there! In the corner. That's it!"

Hatter and Henry dashed across the crazy-quilt rug toward a towering, ornately carved, freestanding mirror. It was easily seven feet tall and at least three feet wide, but the mirrored surface was not reflective. It was cloudy, as if in a steamy bath.

"Wow. It's huge. Why can't I see myself in it? It's all foggy." Henry reached out to wipe the surface, but Hatter caught his hand.

"It's not that sort of looking glass," Hatter said. "It's a traveling mirror."

"Wait a minute." Henry arched an eyebrow at Hatter. "You mean you have a magic mirror that links my world and this one? Why don't people travel back and forth all the time, then?"

Hatter huffed and looked at him as if he was an idiot. "Because every time someone steps through the mirror, they take a little magic with them. If too many people make the journey too many times, all of Wonderland's magic will be gone. Then where will we be? That's why the White Queen kept it here, guarded at all times."

It made sense, in a weird, twisted sort of way—like almost everything else in Wonderland, Henry realized.

There was a sudden banging at the bedroom door. The Red Guard had arrived. The doors shuddered as if something heavy was being slammed against it from the other side.

Hatter gripped Henry's shoulders and turned him toward the mirror. "Quickly, Henry. Step through the mirror!"

Henry nodded and squeezed his eyes shut. He took several deep breaths, and made a few false starts.

Behind them, the sound of splintering wood caught their attention. They turned and saw a broken panel of wood at the center of the door with an axe lodged in it. As they watched, an unseen hand worked the axe head free. Another brutal blow widened the crack in the door.

They gasped, and turned back to the mirror.

Hatter grabbed Henry's arm. "What are you waiting for? They'll break through any minute!"

"Okay, okay! Don't rush me."

"Stop procrastinating, and go!"

A crash thundered in the room as the rest of the door gave way. They risked a look back. The Red Guards, all armed with axes and swords, were spilling into the room through the broken door, and advancing on him and Hatter. From their grim expressions, it looked as though heads were going to roll right there in the White Queen's boudoir.

Taking a deep breath, Hatter pushed Henry into the mirror.

Chapter Thirteen

It was like walking through a pool of corn syrup. That was the only way Henry could describe the feeling of stepping into and through the looking glass. The not-quite-fluid was clear but gelatinous, and it filled every crevice of his body—his ears, his nose, and he suspected, his eyes and mouth had he not had instinctively squeezed them shut. It only took a moment to pass through the viscous fluid, but that was quite long enough as far as Henry was concerned.

Surprisingly, when he stepped through to the other side, he was as dry as he'd been before entering the mirror. Whatever substance comprised the membrane between the worlds, it dried instantaneously when it hit air.

Henry was thankful for small favors. He would've hated being bogged down by the syrupy glop, dripping long streamers of mirror-snot all over the place.

There was a wall of white before him, which he quickly realized was a sheet. Pushing it aside, he stepped out from in front of the mirror. He was in an attic, filled with boxes of junk and trunks, and castoff toys. He only hoped the attic was in Alice's house. He would've hated to have to explain his presence in someone else's.

"What is this place?"

Henry started at the sound of the familiar voice. Spinning around he came nose to nose with Hatter.

"What are you doing here, Hatter?" Henry gave him a shove. "Why did you follow me here?"

"Why not? My only other option was to stay behind and allow the Queen to chop off my head for letting you escape. I simply chose the less painful and, by all accounts, permanent option." He touched the tip of a rocking chair, and tsked at the dust left on his white glove. "I ask again... where are we?"

"I think we're at Alice's house," Henry answered absently, his mind running amok with questions. What was he going to do with Hatter here in the real world? What would Alice say when she saw Hatter? Or worse, vice versa? Most of all, why did he feel an overwhelming sense of relief that he hadn't left Hatter behind?

He motioned for Hatter to follow him. The only way out of the attic was by a staircase that folded up into the ceiling. The only problem was, it wasn't built to be opened from inside the attic—only from the hallway beneath. He guessed the builders hadn't counted on anyone magically appearing into the attic by way of an enchanted mirror.

He led Hatter to one of the only two windows in the attic. It was small and round, but big enough for each of them to fit through. Henry unlocked it and pushed it open. There was a large oak tree growing close to Alice's house, and its spreading limbs were in easy reach of the window. He climbed out of the window onto a small ledge, and jumped onto a broad limb. "Come on, Hatter. It's easy."

Hatter peered at the tangle of branches and leaves. "Are you quite certain there are no tree sharks in there?"

"Cross my heart. No sharks. Only a few sparrows, and they won't hurt you."

It didn't take them long to climb down using the oak's sturdy branches. It was only a short jump from the lowest one to the ground. Henry took Hatter by the hand and walked across a cleanly swept walkway, past a row of neatly trimmed hedges, and up the front porch stairs to Alice's door. There was a small, round buzzer next to the door handle, and he pressed it. From within the house, delicate chimes sounded.

They didn't have long to wait. The door opened to reveal Alice, dressed in a pale blue T-shirt and jeans. Her two-year-old twins, Carol and Louis, clung to her knees. Her smile was sardonic at best when she saw them. "Henry! I didn't expect you back so soon. And look who the cat dragged in! Or rather, look whom Cat spat out. I'd have a hard time picturing Cat wanting to take you anywhere, Hatter."

Hatter squinted, then dug in his pocket and removed a pair of glasses. He perched them on the bridge of his nose, and squinted again. "Alice? Can it be? Is that truly you? By all the Gullywhomps in Git, you're positively ancient. What happened to you? Were you cursed?"

To Henry's surprise, Alice laughed, and pushed the door open. "Nice to see you too, Hatter. Please, come in."

Henry followed Hatter inside, wondering at the relationship between his sister and Hatter. He'd thought they hated one another from the way they spoke about each other, yet Alice was laughing, and Hatter didn't seem too put out, either.

"What are these? Gremlins?" Hatter pointed to Alice's children.

"These are my twins, Carol and Louis." Alice patted their blond curls. They looked just like their mother. "They're two years old."

Hatter gaped at them. "Do you mean to tell me you spawned? I should think one of you is quite enough for both worlds, thank you very much."

Alice laughed again, and led the two of them into her living room. "Make yourselves comfortable. I'm going to get us some refreshments, and then you can tell me what you thought of Wonderland, Henry, and why on earth you brought Hatter here." She headed through an arched doorway leading to the kitchen.

For some reason, Henry felt as if he had to defend himself. He yelled after Alice. "I didn't bring him! He just... followed me home. Like a puppy."

He heard Hatter's haughty sniff, and offered him an apologetic smile. With just a single sentence, Alice made him feel like he was nine years old again and trying to explain how he came to break their grandmother's vase. Was that a talent all big sisters had, or was he just the lucky one? "Sorry. She makes me crazy sometimes. Listen, what is it with you two? From the way you talked back in Wonderland, I got the impression you hated Alice."

"Hate Alice? Me?" Hatter looked affronted, as if someone had accused him of shaving kittens. "How utterly ridiculous."

"But you talked badly about her all the time—"

"Of course I did. I had to. The Queen's spies are everywhere. I told you that. How do you think the Guard knew where we were going? Rabbit must've squealed on us. The Caterpillar reports back to her as well. One must be extremely careful what one says, particularly when it's about Wonderland's Most Wanted Criminal."

"Alice is a Most Wanted Criminal? My sister? Why?"

"She defied the Red Queen, and later seized the crown, even if it was only for a short while. The Red Queen would *love* to see her head roll. It's why she wanted *you* so badly. If she couldn't lop off Alice's head, her brother's would be a satisfying substitute." Hatter took of his hat and smoothed down his hair. "Alice and I agreed to speak ill of each other at all costs, so no one would suspect we were friends. I was thrown in prison to rot because the Queen suspected I didn't hate Alice as much as I said I did, but without any definitive proof, she couldn't order my head to roll—at least not while I might still prove useful to her, anyway."

Somehow, knowing Hatter and Alice actually liked one another made Henry feel strangely relieved... and a little bit jealous. Exactly how much did Hatter like Alice? Not that it mattered—Alice was a married woman with children, after all—but it still niggled at him, like a persistent itch he couldn't reach to scratch.

"Here we go!" Alice placed a platter on the coffee table in front of the sofa, and poured them all tall glasses of iced tea. "Lemon?"

"Please," Hatter said. His hat sat on his knee, and his back was ramrod straight. When he picked up his glass to take a sip, his pinkie finger extended gracefully. "Excellent tea. Dormouse would be most pleased."

Alice settled in an armchair. The twins took up sentry on either side of her, watching Henry and Hatter with somber, wide blue eyes. "How is Dormouse?"

Hatter shrugged. "Well, I suppose. Still serving tea and wishing himself a very happy unbirthday."

A sad look stole Alice's smile. "He's still cursed? He didn't escape when you did?"

"No, unfortunately. Time still has him."

Alice's expression turned steely. "That's awful. Poor Dormouse! It's all the Red Queen's fault. She's the one who accused you and Dormouse of killing Time. You were both innocent, too."

"I know. She's only gotten worse since you left. You wouldn't believe the chaos she's caused. She's quite off her rocker, you know. Without the Red King to temper her tantrums, heads have been rolling all over Wonderland." Hatter sipped his tea again. "Is there mint in this? It's most delightful."

For a moment Alice's eyes widened, then she sat back in her chair with a look of defeat on her face. "It's no use. I thought I could help, but I see now it was wrong of me." She stood up, and placed her glass on the table. "Watch the babies for a moment, Henry. I'll be right back."

Without another word, she hurried to the stairway and climbed it to the second floor. She disappeared down a hallway.

Henry turned to Hatter. "What the hell is going on here? Is she acting strangely? I mean, more strangely than usual? Do you have any idea what's happening?"

"Well, that one's mouth seems to be emitting some sort of glutinous liquid all over your pants."

Henry looked down, and blotted Louis's drool from his knee with a napkin. "Not with the twins. With you and Alice. What's going on?"

"Oh, that. I haven't the foggiest idea. I suppose we'll find out soon enough...." Hatter's voice trailed off and his eyes suddenly grew large and round. His glass slipped from his fingers and fell to the carpet, spilling tea onto the thick rug, as he sprang to his feet, his gaze glued to the staircase. His face paled, and his jaw hung open.

Henry looked up. A tall gentleman wearing a bright scarlet smoking jacket stood on the stair. Alice hovered just behind him. "Oh, hello Uncle Leonard. I didn't know you were staying with Alice. Hatter, this is my mother's brother, Leonard."

Hatter's mouth had dropped open until his jaw nearly touched his chest. He snapped it closed and jumped to his feet, then bowed low at the waist, his forehead nearly knocking against the coffee table. As he stood straight again, the oddest expression of wonder lit his eyes. "No, Henry. This is the Red King."

Chapter Fourteen

"Hatter! So very good to see you again, and with your head still attached! How did you ever manage it? I'd have thought the Queen would've lopped it off years ago." Leonard's voice was strong and vibrant, although his hair and neatly trimmed beard were silver. He descended the staircase with a light step, and sat in an overstuffed chair in the living room. "Please, sit. We don't stand on ceremony in this world."

Alice perched on a spindly-looking rocking chair, and Hatter slowly lowered himself to his previous seat on the sofa, but Henry remained upright. His mind was whirling with confusion. The Red King? How was that possible?

"Henry, my boy, do sit before you fall over." Leonard arched a bushy white eyebrow. He cocked his head. "Are you quite all right, Henry?" He turned to Alice. "Is he all right? Perhaps we should summon a physician. I knew we should have told him earlier."

"He wouldn't have believed us then, Your Majesty," Alice replied. She got up and went to Henry, urging him to sit down on the sofa. "I know my brother. He wouldn't have believed until he saw everything with his own eyes." She smiled at Henry. "My brother is all together too mulish to do otherwise."

He did believe, of course, and grudgingly agreed Alice was right about his stubbornness, but couldn't seem to lose the expression of shock and disbelief on his face. "He.... He...."

"Yes, Henry. Uncle Leonard is really the Red King. Well, actually, he isn't our uncle at all, of course. We only said that to explain his presence in our home to Father. Luckily, Father never met most of Mother's relatives, so the fib held." Alice patted Henry's shoulder. "You understand now why we kept the secret from you, don't you?"

"No, Alice. I don't understand. I don't understand any of it!" Henry shook off Alice's hand. He turned to Hatter. "Were you in on this? Did you know he was here? Is that why you followed me through the mirror?"

Hatter shook his head. "No, of course not, Henry. I swear upon my honor I didn't know." He glanced at the Red King. "Everyone in Wonderland thinks you're dead, Sire. I personally always hoped you'd simply run away, but never suspected you might've gone with Alice through the looking glass."

Leonard sighed. "Run away. I never quite thought of it that way. I always thought of it as my great escape, but now I wonder. Perhaps I *was* a coward. You say the Queen has gone—how do they say it here, Alice? Parcel post?"

"Postal, Your Majesty," Alice answered. "She's gone postal."

"Ah, yes." Leonard nodded. "Maybe leaving was taking the coward's way out."

"Nonsense." Alice shook her finger at Leonard. "She would've found a way to make your head roll. I'm sure of it."

Henry jumped to his feet again. Balling his hands into fists, he was visibly shaking. "Will someone please explain to me what's going on?" His voice was shrill, nearly hysterical. He felt as if he were losing his mind. It was almost funny, in a way. He'd never felt this close to losing it when he was in Wonderland, not even with talking caterpillars and baking giants and tree sharks, but here in his sister's living room, among plain and ordinary things like pitchers of iced tea and rocking chairs, he felt as if he were going insane.

"Sit down, Henry. I'll explain everything." The authority in Leonard's voice did more to convince Henry that Leonard was who Alice and Hatter claimed he was, than anything else. Henry sat.

"The second time Alice came to Wonderland, I'd already decided to leave the Red Palace. I couldn't bear what my wife was becoming, or what she was doing to the world I loved. I also couldn't seem to stop her. Perhaps I was just too weak, or…. Well, I did love her once upon a time, you know. In any case, I thought taking a short sabbatical would help me with the difficult decisions I needed to make." He turned and smiled at Alice. "Then dear Alice won the crown, and became Queen herself. She offered to take me home with her, so that I might get a respite from my problems, and I agreed. We came through the mirror at the White Queen's castle. I intended to return. I really did. I even brought a rare, bottled return spell with me in case something happened to the White Castle mirror in my absence." The Red King sighed, and within it was all the heartbreak he'd suffered. "I didn't count on it being so nice here. No one screaming day and night, no heads rolling across the carpet... I wanted to stay forever."

"And you would be most welcome to stay, Your Majesty," Alice said. She smiled at him. The fondness between them was apparent to everyone.

"Thank you, my dear." He looked at Henry. "You were a quite rude young man, as I remember. Always doubting your sister's stories, belittling her, threatening to have her locked away.... You should be ashamed."

Henry was, and it showed on his face. "I know that now." He turned to Alice. "It's one of the reasons I couldn't wait to get home. To apologize. Sis, I'm so, so sorry for everything I said and did. I wasted so many years we could've enjoyed together by being a pigheaded, stupid idiot." His face burned with his confession, but he forced himself to look Alice in the eye. "You were right all along. About everything. Can you forgive me?"

Alice smiled at him and jumped up, throwing her arms around his neck. She hugged him tight, and for the first time in as long as Henry could remember, he hugged her back. "Of course I forgive you. If you'll forgive me for sending you to Wonderland unprepared."

Henry grinned. "Well, there is that. Why did you do it? I'm glad you did, because I was too thickheaded to believe you otherwise, but what made you do it now?"

"It was my idea, Henry." Leonard touched his chest and gave a short bow. "Mea culpa. My fault entirely. I felt the animosity between you two needed to end, and the only way to do that was for you to see Wonderland with your own two eyes, so I used the bottled return spell on you."

Hatter cleared his throat. "Might I ask, Your Majesty, why my name was brought into this plot?"

The Red King grinned at Hatter. "Because I knew out of all my subjects, you would be the one most likely to bring Henry through Wonderland unscathed."

Hatter preened under the Red King's compliment. "And right you were, Sire. Got him back without a single scratch on him."

Henry elbowed Hatter. "Not for lack of trying, though. Confection Mountains, Neverglades… I'm surprised we survived to get to the mirror in the White Queen's ruins."

Leonard looked up sharply, the smile fading from his lips. "Ruins? What ruins?"

Hatter bit his lip, and looked at Henry. "He doesn't know. He left with Alice, remember?"

Henry felt terrible. Obviously Leonard cared for the White Queen as his sister-in-law. He'd blurted out news, however indirectly, that should've been broken to Leonard gently, with respect and kindness. "I'm so sorry, Leonard. The White Queen…." He trailed off, unable to finish.

Hatter took Henry's hand, patting it, and left his covering it. "The White Queen is gone, Your Majesty. She was met on the chessboard by your wife and defeated."

Leonard paled. "Tell me my wife didn't… not even *she* could be so horrible as to put her own sister to the Axe."

"She did. I'm sorry, Sire." Hatter's eyes looked wet, and Henry felt teary himself.

Alice moved to put her arms around Leonard. "Oh, Sire, this is all my fault. I should never have suggested you come with me!"

"No, Alice. You had no way of knowing how insane my wife would become. If anyone is to blame, it's me, for shirking my duty and leaving Wonderland unprotected." Leonard swallowed hard and wiped his eyes, then looked at Hatter and Henry. "You say she's out of control now?"

"Completely, my liege. There are frequent beheadings, and for the slightest transgressions—or no transgressions at all. It seems the Red Queen really doesn't need much of a reason. I believe she finds the executions entertaining, much as she used to enjoy croquet."

"That sick witch! Enough is enough. She's gone too far." Leonard stood up, seething. For all his age, the crimson smoking jacket didn't hide the way his muscles bunched under the fabric. He was still a strong man, despite his years. "I must go back. I will take back the kingdom, and see to it the Red Queen hurts no one else. Hatter, you've always been loyal to my throne. Will you help me?"

To his credit, Hatter hesitated only for half a moment. "Of course, Your Majesty."

"I'll come, Sire." Alice put her hand on the Red King's shoulder. Her smile was tremulous, but she held her head high.

"No, Alice. You have children now. Your responsibility lies with them and your husband." Leonard patted her hand, and looked at Henry. "How about you, Henry? You've seen Wonderland. Will you help me save it?"

Go back? He'd just made a journey he wasn't sure he'd survive to get home, and Leonard wanted him to go back?

Then again, there were parts of Wonderland that were beautiful, and even the scary parts held a certain uniqueness that should be preserved.

In addition, if he didn't go back he'd probably never see Hatter again. That thought made him feel a bit sick to his stomach, although he wasn't sure why it should. He didn't much like Hatter, did he?

The memory of their kiss filled his mind, along with the taste of Hatter on his tongue. Oh, that kiss, that miserable, awful, wonderfully astonishing kiss! Would it haunt him forever?

There was only one way to find out.

"Yes," Henry said. He felt Hatter squeeze his hand. "I'll come and help." He turned toward Hatter and saw a smile on Hatter's face that seared Henry to his toes. He returned it with one of his own.

He didn't see Alice and Leonard exchange a knowing glance, but heard Leonard say, "Excellent. We'll leave in the morning."

"In the morning," Hatter said. "Back to Wonderland we go."

In the morning, Henry thought. *Which means we have all night here.* He didn't question why the thought of spending time with Hatter in his own world made him happy, but it did.

Henry brought Hatter downtown, where Hatter continually marveled at everything he saw—once he'd conquered his fear, that is.

When they first left Alice's house, the street was quiet, but when they reached the main thoroughfare, traffic was much heavier. Hatter clutched Henry's arm, his dark eyes wide and round. "What manner of beasts are those? My God, look!" He pointed to a bright yellow school bus. That one's eaten dozens of children!" His expression was still fearful, and he kept eyeing the vehicles in the street as if one might jump the curb and swallow him up. "Oh, the horror!"

"Relax, Hatter. That's just a bus. These are cars, trucks, and taxis. They're machines, not animals. Sort of like carriages. People drive them and ride in them to get around faster. They run on a combustion engine, and are fueled by gasoline, although some are hybrids, and use a combination of electricity and gas."

Hatter blinked at him, obviously completely lost. "Gasoline? Is that anything like a trampoline? Tweedledee and Tweedledum had one of those. I remember the sound it made. Boingy, boingy, boingy."

"No, it isn't the same at all. Gasoline is made from oil, which is a fossil fuel."

"Where do the fossils go when they're fueled?"

"No, no. You don't understand. The fossils don't go anywhere."

"Then why fuel them? Isn't that a waste?"

Henry blew out a breath, exasperated. "Never mind. Just understand that they won't hurt you as long as you don't jump out in front of them. If one hits you, it could kill you."

"Ah. Is that how they ate all those people? They run their prey down, and then devour it? How ghastly."

Henry slapped a hand on top of his head as if to keep the headache he was developing from escaping the confines of his skull, and decided to leave the explanations for later. It was too frustrating. He wondered if he'd appeared half as dense when he showed up in Wonderland, and smiled a sheepish grin when he admitted to himself that he'd probably been even worse. "If you trust me, I promise nothing here will hurt you."

Hatter looked long and hard at Henry, then smiled and nodded, and seemed to relax. His curiosity was endless, though, as were his questions. At least, it seemed that way to Henry.

He insisted the skyscrapers, soaring forty or more stories above the street, had to be the work of giants. Henry tried patiently to explain about architects, construction crews, and the gigantic cranes used to construct the buildings, but he could tell Hatter didn't quite believe him.

"Do you seriously wish me to believe that men the size of you and me made that?" Hatter asked, pointing to one of the tallest buildings in town.

"Yes."

"Pshaw. You're pulling my elbow."

"The expression is 'pulling my leg,' and I'm not."

Hatter folded his arms and looked at Henry askance. "How could you pull my leg? I'm standing on it."

Henry laughed, and tugged on Hatter's jacket, leading him toward another building. "Come on. You'll enjoy this."

He bought two tickets at the kiosk, and led Hatter into the theater. Although it was warm outside, the cool air inside hit them both in the face when they entered the movie house. "Air conditioning," Henry explained.

"Conditioned air? Incredible." Hatter moved his fingers through the air, as if to feel it. "It feels the same as Wonderland air, but it's as cold as the peaks of the Confection Mountains even though it's quite warm outside! Amazing."

Henry bought them a bag of popcorn—which, after tasting, Hatter immediately dubbed the most perfect food in the world—and led him to the screening room listed on their tickets. They chose two center seats in a row halfway up the aisle. In front of them, the gigantic white screen was blank.

"This is an odd eating establishment," Hatter remarked. He removed his hat and placed it on his knee before stuffing another handful of popcorn into his mouth. "It would be much better if we were facing one another, wouldn't it?"

"This isn't a restaurant, Hatter. Just watch the screen."

The lights dimmed, and the coming attractions began. The instant the images appeared on the screen, Hatter let out a screech and jumped up. "Giants!" He pointed to the screen. "Run, Henry!"

Around them, people shushed him, and told him to sit down.

Henry chuckled and pulled Hatter back to his seat. "Shh! They're not giants. It's only moving pictures of people projected on a screen."

Hatter looked doubtful. "P-pictures? You mean they aren't real?"

"Nope. It's all a show. Like a play. They have those in Wonderland, don't they?"

"We have troupes of traveling players, yes. They go from town to town performing great works, like *Ode to a Jubjub Bird,* and *Oh, Jabberwock, I Hardly Knew Ye.*"

"This is like them. Think of them as paintings that can move and speak. I promise they can't hurt you."

Squirming a little in his seat, Hatter fiddled with the brim of his top hat, and refused to make eye contact with Henry. "I-I knew that."

"Of course you did." Henry grinned at him, and offered him more popcorn.

Crunching loudly, Hatter seemed to relax, and was soon caught up in what he later proclaimed "a marvelous history of magic and mechanical mayhem fought in the skies far beyond the sight of mere mortals."

"You do know it's just a movie, right?" Henry tossed the empty popcorn container into the trash on the way out of the theater. "*Star Wars* has been around since before I was born. It's a classic."

"You mean it's a fable, such as those told by traveling storytellers in Wonderland?"

"Yup. Exactly."

"It all looked so real! It seems your world is also a place of wonders, Henry."

"I suppose so. I never thought of it that way before. I grew up with things like skyscrapers, cars, and movies. I never thought of them as anything but ordinary before."

"Just as I never thought of tree sharks or giants as being anything but normal parts of my world, until you came along."

"You've got a point." Henry laughed, and led Hatter out of the theater. As they strolled down the block, Hatter suddenly froze and pointed across the street toward a small, white fast food restaurant.

It was a White Castle.

"Is that... no, it can't be. It's much too small!"

Henry patted Hatter's shoulder. "Wrong White Castle. This one just serves burgers."

"Oh? What does it serve to the burgers? And what, exactly *are* burgers? Why does this Castle serve only them? Are these burgers some sort of royalty?"

"No, burgers are food, and White Castle serves them to people."

Hatter shook his head. "I don't believe I'll ever understand your world, Henry."

"I live here and I don't always understand it." Henry smiled. "Speaking of food, want to experience something that's amazing?"

Hatter grinned and nodded.

"Okay. It's in here." He led Hatter into *The Leaning Tower of Pizza,* and ordered a large pie with extra cheese and pepperoni. "If you thought popcorn was good, wait until you taste this!"

Once the pizza was served, not another word was spoken other than happy little grunts and smacks as they devoured the entire thing. Hatter's mouth was rimmed with tomato sauce, and there was a bit of cheese hanging in a skinny thread from his chin. "Your world is amazing, Henry! First popped corn and moving pictures of giants, then this Pete's Ah. It's wonderful!"

"Pizza. One word. And I agree, it's pretty good. But so was the food you made in Wonderland. And I can't pull a campfire and pot full of stew out of my pocket here."

Hatter gave a solemn nod. "True. I can understand how that would be a hardship. When I get back to Wonderland, I'm going to need to learn how to make pizza, and find room in my pocket for the necessary equipment and ingredients."

Someone must've fed coins into the jukebox at the far end of the pizza parlor, because the first poignant strains of Queen's *Bohemian Rhapsody* began playing. Hatter's ears immediately perked, his head twisting to scan the room.

"You have troubadours in this world? Where are they? I can't see them." He stood up, trying to get a better view. "We had traveling musicians in Wonderland, too. They would sing of Wonderland's history, going from town to town. At least, they did before the Red Queen lopped off their heads. She was never overly fond of history. Still, I used to love to listen to the troubadours and bards."

"Um, if by that you mean music, then yeah, we have bands and singers. Rock and Roll, baby."

Hatter's head cocked and his eyebrows furrowed. "Do you mean to say you stone singers who are not well versed at their craft? That seems a bit harsh."

"No. Rock and Roll is the style of music. This is Queen you hear playing."

"Which Queen? Not the Red one. I've heard her sing, and she sounds like a Bandersnatch caught in a bear trap."

Henry grinned. "Not that kind of queen. It's the name of a band, the group of people you hear singing."

"Ah. An odd name, but fine music. Rather catchy. I like it. Now, where are these regal tune masters? I still don't see them."

"They aren't really here. What you're hearing is just a recording in a box, sort of like the movie we went to see."

"Oh! I understand. How wonderful to have music at your fingertips! The owner of this establishment must be very wealthy indeed to have such magic in his pizza emporium."

Henry shook his head again, and laughed. "Pizzeria, and you don't need to be rich to own music. When we get back to Alice's, remind me to introduce you to an MP3 player."

"Is that an instrument? This MP3? How does one play it?"

Henry laughed again. "You'll see." He glanced at his wristwatch and sighed. "Sorry, Hatter. It's getting late. We'd better get back to Alice's house. I think Uncle Leonard… er, the Red King wants to get an early start in the morning."

They left the pizzeria and headed back toward Alice's neighborhood. They'd just turned the corner onto Alice's block, when Hatter grabbed Henry's hand and pulled him to a stop.

"I just realized we probably won't be alone again after this. Henry, I wanted to say… I mean…." Hatter's tongue seemed to be tripping over words the way a drunk might stumble over curbs. "You and I, we… oh, bother. Sometimes words aren't enough anyway."

Henry's eyes flew open when Hatter pulled him into a deep kiss, but soon fluttered closed again. Unusual feelings shot through him like cloud-to-cloud lightning bolts, electrifying him from the inside out. Hatter's arms, strong and hard with muscle, wrapped around Henry's body and held him close. Henry's skin grew hot as his body responded to the intensity of Hatter's kiss.

The kiss seemed to go on forever, and not nearly long enough at the same time. Hatter pulled away long before Henry would've wanted. His breath was warm and smelled slightly of garlic from the pizza, but it made Henry feel slightly dizzy, like he'd been spinning in circles for too long.

"I don't know when I'll get the chance to kiss you again. I've been thinking of little else since that moment on the battlefield in the Confectionary Mountains." Hatter sighed and pulled Henry in a bit closer, until their bodies were flush against one another. Henry could feel every inch of Hatter's body pressed against him, and realized Hatter was enjoying the moment just as much as Henry was.

"Can I tell you a secret?" Henry's arms were around Hatter's slim waist, and he locked his fingers together, unwilling to let go. "I'm glad I'm going back with you. Every time I thought of you going to Wonderland without me, I got a sick sort of feeling in my stomach."

"I feel the same way. I suppose we'll have to think about separating sometime, though. But not tonight."

"No, not tonight." Henry tipped his face up toward Hatter, and was delighted when Hatter sought his lips again.

For the briefest moment, Henry wondered when he'd stopped actively disliking Hatter.... Perhaps on the battlefield in the Confection Mountains, or while slogging through the Neverglades. Or maybe Henry never really disliked Hatter at all, just the idea of liking him *too much*. Then the thought was gone, and Henry was again lost in the electricity of their kiss.

Their kiss this time had a gentler, longing feel to it. It made Henry hunger for more, but both knew it was past time to get home.

"We'd better get back before Alice calls out the police to look for us." Henry reluctantly pulled away. They began walking back toward Alice's house.

Henry was keenly aware they were holding hands, and from the look on Hatter's face, he was too. Henry wondered why the thought of leaving Hatter behind bothered him so much.

I can think about it later, like Hatter said, Henry thought, tightening his grip on Hatter's hand. "For now, all we should be concerned about is the Red Queen, and how we're going to overthrow her without losing our heads."

But thinking about their kiss was so much more fun than pondering war strategies, and soon all thoughts of the Red Queen were pushed out of Henry's head, replaced with the memory of warm lips, garlic breath, and bolts of lightning zinging through his body.

Chapter Fifteen

The following morning, the rising sun found them already gathered in Alice's kitchen for breakfast and a strategy meeting. Alice's husband, Phillip, and the children were the only ones absent, most likely still asleep at the ungodly hour.

Leonard had dressed in his full Red King regalia, presumably the same wardrobe he'd been wearing when he'd gone through the mirror with Alice into Henry's world. A small golden crown studded with rubies encircled the crown of his head. He wore a longish tunic of deep crimson, with matching leggings and knee-high boots. A heavy cape of bright red velvet trimmed with white, black-tipped ermine tails, thrown over his shoulders, made him look twice as broad as he actually was, and swept the floor behind him in a short train. He would've looked quite regal if it hadn't been for Alice's cats, Romeo and Juliet, who chased after the robe's fur-trimmed train, jumping and clawing at it. Perhaps they thought it was a rival cat, or more likely, just fun. Either way, Leonard found it necessary to flick the edges of his robe continually, trying to shake them loose. He finally solved the problem by taking a seat at the table and piling his robe on the chair next to him. The cats jumped up on the windowsill and stared at him, obviously irritated.

Alice placed carafes of piping hot coffee and tea on the table, along with a platter of scrambled eggs and another of crispy bacon. She added yet another plate piled high with toast, and set a few small jars of jams and jellies on the table before taking a seat herself. "Well, we're all here. What are your plans, Your Majesty?"

Leonard helped himself to the fluffy yellow eggs and a few strips of bacon, before passing the platters on to Hatter. "Well, providing the mirror allows us to return to the White Castle, and doesn't dump us off in the middle of the Great Sinking Sands, or Endless Sugar Sand Desert, our first priority will be to find our way to the Red Castle."

"What do you mean? The mirror sent Alice to the White Castle, and you and us here from there. Why shouldn't it send us back again?" Henry asked around a mouthful of toast and orange marmalade jelly.

"Depends on whether the Red Queen had the mirror moved." Hatter poured himself another cup of tea, and added a dollop of cream. "It sent Alice to the White Castle and us to here from the same place because that's where the twin mirrors are located. If the Red Queen had the Wonderland mirror image removed from the White Castle and dumped, say, into the middle of the Neverglades, then when we step through we'll find ourselves up to our rear ends in tree sharks and swamp trolls."

Leonard nodded. He buttered a piece of toast, stuck several slices of bacon and a wad of scrambled eggs onto it, folded it half, and took a huge bite. He waited to speak until after he'd swallowed, and although he dabbed his lips with a napkin, breadcrumbs and bacon bits still dotted his beard. "All too true, Hatter. Let's hope it remains in the White Castle, or better yet, that my wife had it moved to the Red Castle, which would save us quite a bit of time and effort."

"My guess is she's left it where it is, and perhaps has it guarded," Alice put in. "You'll excuse me, Your Majesty, but the Red Queen was never known for being very bright or having much initiative."

"That's quite all right, Alice. I agree." Leonard's eyes took on a somewhat dreamy, faraway look, as though he were seeing images Alice, Henry, and Hatter couldn't, something from his past. "When she was young, she was quite beautiful, you know, and could be extremely charming when it suited her. Her laugh was contagious, and her kisses were sweeter than anything the Confection Mountain Bakers could whip up. I did marry her, after all. However, the years weren't kind to her. We never had children, although we wanted heirs, of course. She hated the idea that her crown might go to someone other than a direct descendant of her bloodline, and grew bitter and jealous, and more ruthless and despicable with each passing day. I discovered there was something twisted in her soul, something wicked that once unleashed, grew unchecked, while at the same time every shred of decency and humor she once held shriveled and died away." He blinked, and looked at Alice, Henry, and Hatter in turn. "She's no longer the woman I married. She's become a monster, and she must be stopped before she finally destroys Wonderland."

"How?" Henry asked. "How do we stop her?" He hadn't thought about the Red King and Queen as a married couple, as his own parents must have been once upon a time, before his mother died and his father began to drink. It put a new spin on his opinion of the Red Queen. It didn't exactly change what he thought of her—he still agreed she was a monster and needed to be stopped before she cut the heads off everyone in Wonderland—but he realized she was, after all, only human. Or what passed for human in Wonderland, anyway.

"That would be the question, Sire." Hatter set his cup down in the saucer with a gentle ting. "She, herself, poses no physical threat, but she does still command the Red Guard. While most of them are getting a bit old, there're still plenty of good stomping years left in them. The three of us couldn't possibly overcome them all."

"We won't have to." Leonard reached up and tapped the golden crown on his head. "I am still the Red King, am I not? The Red Guards are mine to command."

Hatter gave a little shrug and averted his eyes. "Well, Sire, you did sort of disappear into thin air. Most of Wonderland believes you dead, and the rest think you abdicated and ran off with one of the chambermaids."

Leonard's eyes grew wide, and his cheeks reddened. "Nonsense! I am obviously quite alive, and I never ran away. I was on… er, sabbatical. I certainly never renounced my throne."

"Oh, I believe you, Sire," Hatter was quick to say. "The problem is how to convince the Red Guard of it."

Henry contemplated the problem. He wasn't so sure Leonard hadn't run away. In fact, he was quite sure that was exactly what Leonard had done. So, how did one go about convincing an army to follow a leader they believed abandoned them? The answer came to him like a poke from a sharp stick. He actually jumped. "Of course! By explaining that Leonard's leaving was necessary to overthrow the Queen."

The other's looked at him with blank, confused expressions. Finally Hatter gestured for Henry to continue. "Explain, please. I'm afraid we're all a bit confuzzled at your strategy. How, exactly, was it necessary for the Red King to leave Wonderland to the Red Queen's fits of temper?"

Henry tried to explain. "Suppose there was something in this world that the Red King needed, something that would assure him of victory over the Red Queen. He needed to leave to get it, but always intended to return."

"So, you think the best way to gain the Red Guard's trust is to lie to them? Henry, I'm ashamed of you." Alice scowled at him, as only a big sister was able.

Ordinarily that look would make Henry squirm, but not this time. He knew he was right. "No, you don't understand! He did come here to find something he needed to face the Queen—his courage, his pride, and his resolve." Henry smiled and patted Leonard on the arm. "After living with the Red Queen's madness for all those years, you simply lost your way, Your Majesty. You needed to come here to find it again."

Hatter laughed and slapped the table with his hand, making his cup rattle in its saucer. "That's brilliant, Henry! You wouldn't be lying at all, Sire, and knowing the Red Queen, I doubt anyone would fault you for it."

"You don't think it would be admitting failure?" Leonard chewed his lower lip, making his beard bob. "A king can't appear to be weak."

"Admitting a truth, even when it's painful, is never a failure, Your Majesty." Alice's smile was gentle. "It's a strength, one that not many people have."

"So is learning from your mistakes and overcoming them," Henry added.

Hatter nodded. "I agree most wholeheartedly, Your Majesty. I believe the Red Guard would understand and respect such an admission."

Leonard seemed to think it over, then sighed and placed his napkin over his plate. "I suppose then that we'll have to... " He looked at Alice. "How do they say it here, Alice? Fly it?"

Alice chuckled and shook her head. "I think the phrase you're looking for is 'wing it,' Sire."

"Oh, yes. Wing it. Indeed. We shall have to wing it when we get there." Leonard smiled gratefully at Alice. "I want to thank you, my dear, for allowing me to tag along with you to your world, and for finding me a place and protecting my identity for all these years. Time certainly flew by us, hmm?"

"Well sure, when Time likes you." Hatter said. He glanced at Henry, who snickered when Hatter rolled his eyes. "But get on Time's bad side just once, and it'll stick you in a never-ending tea party with a psychotic dormouse."

"Hatter!" Alice admonished, shaking her finger in mock anger at him. "Shame on you. Dormouse was not psychotic. He was just a bit... er, shy and retiring."

"Shy and retiring?" Hatter threw his head back and laughed. "You should have heard him after you left the party, Alice. His language was so blistering, it set the centerpiece on fire."

"Well," Alice said. "Maybe he was a bit peculiar. But then again, I was a petulant, obnoxious child, wasn't I?"

Hatter stood up, and tamped his hat on his head, his lips tilted in a wry smile. "I have learned it is never prudent to argue with a Queen, former or otherwise."

Everyone laughed, although the joke wasn't all that funny. Henry supposed it felt good because it provided a release of the tension that had been slowly building. He was acutely aware, as he was sure everyone else was, of the danger of their plan.

They didn't know for sure where the mirror would lead them, or if the Red Guard would be waiting, and if so, if the Guard would accept Leonard's claim to the throne. Indeed, they didn't know if Leonard would be able to make the claim before the Guard shot them all full of arrows.

Even if they did land in the White Castle, and the Red Guard accepted Leonard as King, they would still have trials to face on the march back to the Red Castle, and the final confrontation with the Queen promised to be anything but pleasant.

Henry put down his cup and did something he hadn't done in years. He took Alice in his arms and hugged her tight. "I love you, Sis. I'm sorry I didn't believe you before, and for being such a jackass about it."

To his surprise, there were tears in Alice's eyes when she finally pulled away from his embrace. "I know, and I'm sorry for being so stubborn about everything, and for sending you to Wonderland unprepared."

"It's okay," Henry said. "It's been an adventure, for sure. When I get back, I plan to make it up to you. I promise."

"Sure." The threatening tears escaped, rolling slowly down Alice's cheek, although a tremulous smile played at her lips. "When you get back."

Henry frowned. Why did he get the feeling Alice didn't think he'd be coming back? He shook himself. *Don't be stupid. Of course she believes you'll return. It's the stress, that's all. Everyone's on edge.* He returned her shaky smile, and stepped back as the others said their good-byes.

Alice led them up the stairs to the second floor of the house, cautioning them to keep quiet so they didn't wake her husband and children. She reached for a pull chain in a panel of the hallway ceiling, pulling down a drop-ladder to the attic.

They climbed it, one after another, and Henry and Hatter found themselves back in the spacious, pitch-roofed loft where they'd first arrived. Boxes, bags, and a few trunks were stored on the far side of the wall. A dressmaking model stood bare, a fine layer of dust its only covering. An ancient sewing machine cabinet, the rocking chair missing a few spindles with Hatter's fingerprint on it, and several dusty toys took up the rest of the floor space. In one corner a tall, flat object stood alone and apart from the other clutter.

Alice gestured toward the mirror, twin to the one he and Hatter had gone through in the White Castle. She stepped to the side, and smiled a smile she clearly didn't feel. "Here it is. Good luck, and Godspeed. Promise to find a way to tell me how it works out."

"What are you talking about? I'll tell you all about it when I get back." Henry frowned, and felt a shiver dance up his spine. Didn't Alice believe he'd return?

That same shaky smile returned to lift Alice's lips again. "Of course. How silly of me. I love you, little brother."

"Love you, too." Henry replied, still puzzled.

"Well, we'd better get going." Hatter swept off his hat and bowed deeply. "Many thanks, Alice, for everything."

"And thank you, Hatter, for seeing my brother through Wonderland. Give my best to Caterpillar and the Cheshire Cat." Alice kissed Hatter on the cheek.

"Bah, the Cat? He deserves a swift boot up his furry rear, not a thank you," Hatter huffed. "Never met a more contrary, frustrating beast in my life."

Alice waved off his concerns. "Oh, give him a chance. Something tells me you'll change your mind."

Hatter sniffed and raised his chin. "Not likely. He's all claws and teeth, held together with spite and an evil sense of humor." He stepped aside for Leonard to bid Alice a last good-bye.

"Take care of them, Uncle." She threw her arms around Leonard's neck and hugged him. "I know you're the Red King, but you'll always be Uncle Leonard to me as well."

Leonard hugged her back, tears glimmering in his eyes. "The honor is mine, dear Alice. You are the daughter I never had. I shall miss you, but who knows? Perhaps someday I'll return for a visit, or you'll come to Wonderland."

Alice didn't reply, but nodded and walked a few steps away, wiping her eyes with the backs of her hands. "Go on, now, before I start crying all over again."

Leonard held up his hand in a final farewell, and faced the mirror. Exchanging an anxious look with Hatter and Henry, he seemed to hold his breath as he stepped into the mirror and disappeared.

Hatter looked at Henry. "Together?"

Henry nodded, and reached for Hatter's hand, and together, they stepped into the mirror.

Chapter Sixteen

Once again, they passed through the thick, syrupy quasi-liquid that comprised the passage between worlds. It was uncomfortable but not painful, although Henry didn't look forward to going through it again on his way back home after their mission was completed.

He pushed through, and stepped out of the mirror, smack into Hatter's back. "Oomph. Hatter, move. Why are you standing there?"

"Shh. Don't move, don't talk," Hatter whispered, but didn't turn around.

Henry felt a shiver of fear, and dropped his voice to a hiss. "What is it? Is it the Red Guard?"

Hatter's head gave a minute shake. "If only it were the Guard! It's a pride of Bandersnatches. There are four of them blocking the exit. So far I don't think they've seen us, but—"

A shriek suddenly pierced the air, so shrill that Henry's hands flew to his ears as if to keep the knife-edged scream out of them. He'd never heard anything like it before. It sounded like a cross between Godzilla and a train whistle on steroids. Three other equally earsplitting screeches joined it, rising in a painful cacophony, made worse by an echo that repeated the excruciating sounds back.

"What are we going to do?" Henry slowly rose to his tiptoes and peered over Hatter's shoulder. He'd never seen a Bandersnatch, and if they couldn't figure their way past the creatures, might never have the opportunity to see one—or anything else for that matter—again.

They were all large creatures, although two of them were slightly smaller. A family perhaps, Henry thought. Dam, sire, and two offspring. Their bodies were stout, but segmented like an ant's, supported by six elephant-like legs, and ending in sinuous tails tipped with spikes. Their heads were long and narrow, mostly jaws filled with a frightening number of long, jagged teeth. He thought their necks were ridiculously short, almost nonexistent, until one of them shot out like a telescope, bringing those terrifying, snapping jaws almost within biting distance of Leonard.

One of the Bandersnatches began edging around the perimeter of the room, staying low to the ground. Another branched off the other way. They were trying to surround Henry, Hatter, and Leonard.

Hatter dug into his pocket, trying not to move too quickly or too much. He pulled out an object and tossed it at the Bandersnatches. It hit the floor and rolled, coming to stop at foot of one of the creatures. The Bandersnatch's head lowered, and it sniffed at the object. Then it opened its jaws and snapped it up, swallowing it. A long, black tongue snaked out and licked its chops.

"An apple? Are they poison to Bandersnatches?" Henry asked.

"No, damn it. I thought it was an exploding orb." Hatter's hand slipped back into his pocket.

The group of Bandersnatches howled again, their muscles bunching. They moved closer, their heads shooting out on their telescoping necks, jaws snapping. Their heavy legs, each foot tipped with long, sharp claws, ripped up the marble floor and trampled what bits and pieces of furniture they encountered into matchsticks. The Bandersnatches' tails cracked like bullwhips, carving deep fissures into the walls.

"Hatter, they're going to attack!" In his terror, Henry forgot to whisper. Not that it mattered—the Bandersnatch roars nearly drowned him out anyway.

"Wait!" Leonard slapped his forehead with the palm of his hand. "I'd nearly forgotten. How stupid of me!"

"What is it, Sire? Now would be a good time to share with the rest of the class." Hatter pulled a banana out of his pocket. "Damn it." He threw it at the nearest Bandersnatch, which, true to its name, snatched it up.

"How does one defeat the Bandersnatch? Think, Hatter. It's right there, in one of the greatest songs in our history. Remember?

'Beware the Jubjub bird, and shun the frumious Bandersnatch!' Shun is the answer."

Hatter barked a laugh. "Of course! It's quite obvious now, isn't it? You're a genius, Your Majesty."

Leonard's chest puffed out a bit. "Oh, well, I just paid attention in history class, that's all."

Henry looked between them, utterly confused. Had they forgotten they were being surrounded by the very frumious Bandersnatches in their stupid poem? Before he could say anything, both Leonard and Hatter turned their backs on the Bandersnatches.

"Turn around Henry. Quickly!" Leonard waved his hands at Henry, urged him to turn around. "Give them your back, and close your eyes."

"Shun them, Henry. Ignore them. They can't stand it. They live on fear and attention. Show them none, and they'll leave," Hatter explained.

Well, Henry reasoned, if it doesn't work, at least I wouldn't see the Bandersnatches biting my head off. He turned around, faced the wall, and squeezed his eyes shut.

The sounds around them intensified, the roars rising to a level that made Henry's ears ring. There were crashing sounds as well, as if the Bandersnatches were determined to bring the ruins of the White Castle down around their ears.

Then suddenly, blessedly, it all stopped and silence descended....

Henry felt a tap on his shoulder and nearly jumped out of his jeans. He cracked open his eyes to see Leonard and Hatter smiling at him.

"They're gone! We've won our first battle, but I think we should leave quickly before they decide to come back and give it another go," Leonard said. He led the way toward the door.

Hatter followed, with Henry trailing behind on shaky legs. Wherever the Bandersnatch family had disappeared to, it wasn't inside the castle ruins, at least not in sight of the areas the trio hurried through, unless they'd found a hidey-hole somewhere. Henry didn't see hide or scale of them on the way out of the White Castle, not that he was complaining. He'd be glad if he never saw one again. Out of all the crazy, frightening things he'd seen in Wonderland, he ranked the Bandersnatches as number one on the list. Still, he had to admit they were the easiest to defeat, once Leonard remembered how to do it. Like many bullies, Bandersnatches lost interest when no one paid attention to them. He did have the feeling, however, that the bite of the Bandersnatch would've been even worse than its deafening bark.

Once outside the castle, Leonard led them across a wide, rolling, flowery field beside which a lazy river wound. It caught Henry's eye, the way the water glimmered like silk, snaking from a gently splashing waterfall in the hills immediately north of the White Castle, and flowing south, thinning until it became no more than a silvery thread in the far distance.

The cool-looking, tranquil water seemed extremely inviting to Henry from the moment he saw it, as if it were beckoning him. Never had a river seemed so inviting. Out of nowhere came the thought: *I should go for swim. Best idea I've had all day.* He suddenly felt completely grungy and stinky. He couldn't stand the feel of his clothing against his skin, or the stench he seemed to be emitting like a fog. He turned and began hurrying toward the river. *A quick dip, then back on track, right? Sounds great to me.*

"Henry! Henry, no!" Hatter yelled at him, running in his direction.

Damn Hatter. A party pooper of cosmic proportions. "I need a bath, Hatter. It'll only take a minute." He hurried toward the water, pulling off his shirt and kicking off his shoes as he went.

"Henry, stop!" Leonard's voice reached him just a moment before Hatter's hand grabbed his arm. "You don't know what you're doing."

He tried to shake Hatter off. He had to get to the water. Had to. If he didn't, he'd die. He knew it. Felt it in his bones. He turned on Hatter, baring his teeth. "Let me go!"

"No! Henry, it's one of the River Witches. She's put a hex on you. If you go into the water, she'll pull you under and drown you before eating you. We'll be lucky to find a few of your bones washing ashore downstream when she's done." Hatter wrapped his arms around Henry, pulling him in close, holding him tight, refusing to let go no matter how hard Henry struggled.

"You're lying! You want me to die! Let me go. I have to get to the water!"

Leonard reached them, and wrapped his arms around Hatter and Henry both. They began slowly sidestepping away from the river toward the flowery fields. Henry fought them every step of the way, completely convinced that if he didn't dive into the river's silky waters, he would perish.

Slowly, as they put distance between Henry and the river, his compulsion to go swimming began to lessen, and finally disappeared altogether, leaving him wondering why he thought it was such a good idea to begin with. He sniffed his armpits. He didn't reek. Well, no more than usual, anyway. And it wasn't even very hot outside—there was a cool breeze blowing.

"I'm sorry, Henry." Leonard patted Henry on the shoulder. "I thought we were far enough from the river to be safe."

Henry smiled. "It's okay. What happened? What was that? I really felt like I was going to die if I didn't go into the river."

"It was one of the River Witches." Hatter took off his hat and fanned himself with it. It evidently had been a narrow escape. "There are several different types, none of them good. Not every river has one, but the White River has been home to a school of them for centuries. They cast out spells from the river like fishing nets, and once they snare someone, they convince him or her that it's death to remain dry. Unless restrained and removed from the spell's reach, the person will usually rush right into the water, where the witch will catch them, pull them under, drown them, and then eat them at its leisure."

"I guess I owe you my thanks. You saved my life, the both of you." Henry looked from Leonard to Hatter. "I keep forgetting how different things are here, and how much I don't know about anything in Wonderland."

Hatter grinned. "Just like I didn't know anything about your world. If you remember, I thought your cars were monsters with see-through bellies, who'd eaten people."

Henry had to admit, Hatter's admission made him feel a little better about being caught up in the River Witch's spell. He returned Hatter's smile.

"Did you think that, too, Hatter? So did I, at first. Nearly gave Alice a black eye the first time she tried to get me to go for a ride in her car. I thought she was trying to feed me to it." Leonard's laugh cleared the air of the last of the tension caused by their narrow escape. "Well, then. I think it best if we move on. I don't relish anything catching us out in the open once night falls, and I think we can find shelter not far from here. If memory serves, Tweedledee and Tweedledum keep a summer home just beyond those hills." He smiled, and elbowed Henry good-naturedly. "We'll be going to bed with the chickens, mark my words."

Chapter Seventeen

The hills in question were gently rolling ones, none attached to steeper points like the foothills of the Confection Mountains. The grass underfoot was thick, luxurious, and for Wonderland, surprisingly free of any type of hazard. It was an easy hike, and the trio cleared them just as the sun began painting purple and red streaks across the blue sky.

Leonard proved correct when, after clearing the last hill, they spotted a pair of cottages in the distance. As they neared them, they were revealed to be identical in every way, from the red and yellow color scheme and curlicue gingerbread trim, to the boxes of petunias and daisies underneath each window. Each had a small, carefully tended yard edged with a waist-high white picket fence, and a pathway laid with colored slate leading to the front stoop.

Henry started down the closest path, but Hatter quickly pulled him to a stop.

"Wait!" Hatter kept his hand on Henry's arm, and glanced at Leonard. "That would have been a terrible faux pas."

"What's a foe pah?" Henry asked, frowning.

"A faux pas is a mistake, a social blunder, and you nearly made a doozy." Hatter walked Henry back up the path to where Leonard waited. "Tweedledee and Tweedledum are the official Etiquette Ambassadors of Wonderland, so titled by the Red Queen before she went completely mad. They expect a certain degree of pomp and circumstance when folks come calling. Plus, they get highly insulted when one is favored above the other."

"That's correct," Leonard put in. "Ringing one's doorbell before the other's is a terrible error. They'd never allow us to stay if that happened."

"Allow us to stay?" Hatter laughed. "They'd have us charged with Breach of Etiquette. There's no worse crime as far as the twins are concerned. The punishment is tar and feathering. They use Jubjub feathers, and make the guilty pluck them straight from the bird. Believe you me, there's usually not enough left of the criminal to tar once the Jubjubs are through with them."

Henry looked confused. "So, what do we do, then?"

Hatter explained the protocol. "Easy. Two of us must each walk down one of the paths at the same time, and ring the bells at the same moment. Not a heartbeat sooner or later than the other, mind you! Then, when Tweedledum and Tweedledee answer the door, we introduce ourselves, and make polite conversation for a few moments."

Leonard placed a hand on Henry's shoulder, and picked up where Hatter left off. "Yes. Try to pick a subject of conversation interesting to whichever twin with whom you're speaking. Remember, the twins are identical, except when they're different."

"Yes. Dum likes to speak about the weather, in particular nice weather, clear skies, and sunny days," Hatter said. "Dee favors the weather as well, but prefers talk of rain and stormy nights, black skies split by lightning."

"Or pies," Leonard offered. "They both like pies and cakes. Of course, Dee prefers lemon chiffon, while Dum likes chocolate silk. They both enjoy apple, although Dum likes raisins in his apple pie, while Dee hates them, and neither is very fond of nutmeg, but love cinnamon."

"Oh! I nearly forgot, and it's very important," Hatter said. "One is never right if the other is always wrong. Have you got that?"

Henry looked rather dazed. His eyes held a funny sort of foggy, blank look that worried Hatter a bit. "Never mind, Henry. Perhaps Leonard and I should do this. You wait here."

Hatter and Leonard each stood in front of the one of the twin paths leading to the houses. Locking gazes with Leonard, Hatter counted off. "One... two... three!" They stepped off at three, each taking a nearly identical stride down their pathway.

"Step," Leonard said, and they both took one.

"Step," Hatter repeated, and they both took another one, and so forth, until they reached the front doors of the respective houses at the exact same time. "Finger on the doorbell. Push on three!" Hatter called. "One... two... three!"

Hatter heard loud chimes echo in the house before him, and a ghost of the same chiming coming at the same time from the house next door. The stomping of feet reached his ears—feet with some weight behind them from the sound of it, and knew Leonard was hearing the same.

The door opened, and he found himself facing Tweeddledee.

Or Dum.

He didn't know which. He always had trouble telling them apart. It wasn't really his fault—they were identical twins, after all. They were both nearly as wide as they were tall, bald as a Dodo egg, and wore matching red and yellow striped shirts under frayed and faded overalls. They went barefoot, summer and winter, and the soles of their feet were black with grime and shiny with calluses. Blue eyes squinted out from behind frameless spectacles, while hands the size of a holiday ham were planted on their wide hips.

"Yeth?" They both had a lisp, so that didn't help in identification, either.

"Tweedle! It's me, Hatter!" From across the way, he heard Leonard say the same thing to the other twin. "Good to see you, old boy! It's been an age, hasn't it?"

"Hatter?" Tweedledee (or Dum) looked thoughtful for a moment, before his face broke out in wide grin. The source of the Tweedle lisp was exposed in the wide gap caused by two missing front teeth. His twin, of course, had the same gap. Legend had it that one of them lost their teeth in a Bandersnatch attack, and the other was so grief-stricken at the marring of an otherwise perfect mirror image that he knocked out his own two teeth that very afternoon. "Come in, come in! Ith good to thee you."

"I appreciate the offer, Tweedle, but Leonard is visiting your brother, and we have an extra." He gestured toward Henry with his chin, and knew Leonard was going through the same routine with Twiddle's twin. "We know how you feel about third wheels, so perhaps we could visit outside, the lot of us."

Tweedledum (or Dee) wrung his ham-sized hands. "Oh, dear. Three ith a bad number. An awful, awful number. Sharp and pointy. Ith odd, you thee, and that makes it dangerous."

"Yes, I know, but do you remember Alice?"

"Queen Alith?"

"The one and only. Well, Henry there is Alice's brother. It's true! I swear on my life, and you know how precious I hold myself, Twiddle. He even looks like her. That makes him a duo, like you and your brother. So actually, there are six of us out there."

Tweedledee (or Dum) peered out the door at Henry. "He does look like Alith. All right. Make him come in. We'll have tea."

"No, no. If I did that, there would only be three of us in here!" He pointed to Tweedledum (or Dee), then to himself, then to Henry. "One, two, three. See? We need to meet outside for it to be a round number."

Tweedledee (or Dum) looked confused, slowly pointing to himself, then to Hatter, then to Henry, then back at himself again. "I... six, you thay?"

"Yeth. I mean, yes. Six. You, me, Leonard, your brother, Henry, and Alice."

"But Alith isn't here."

"Twiddle, I've explained this before. Henry is Alice's brother. Like you and your brother. That makes it six."

"You... he.... Alith...." Tweedledum (or Dee) so looked for a moment like his tremendous melon head might explode that Hatter considered whether or not he should rout out an umbrella from his pocket. But then Tweedledee (or Dum) seemed to come to a decision. "Okay. That theems logical."

Hatter hid the relieved sigh that tried to hiss its way past his lips, and smiled. "Very good. Shall we go?"

All four of them—Hatter, the two Tweedles, and Leonard— descended the stoop to the walkway, making their way toward Henry in a stately, precise procession. They stood in a loose circle, looking at one another for quite a few minutes before Hatter spoke again. "Henry, these are the Tweedles. Tweedles, this is Henry, Alice's brother."

"Printh Henry. Pleased to meet you." The Tweedles spoke in unison, beginning and ending at the same time. It was uncanny, or would have been, Hatter supposed, had it been anywhere but Wonderland.

"Um, Prince?" Henry glanced at Hatter.

Hatter gave a tiny nod. Best to let the Tweedles think what they wanted. After all, they'd be less likely to turn away royalty than they would peasants. "Yes, Prince Henry. It's all right. The Tweedles are loyal to Queen Alice." He turned to the Tweedles. "You are, aren't you?"

"Oh, yeth! Alith saved uth from the crow, you know!" Tweedledum (or Dee) exclaimed.

Tweedledee (or Dum) nodded vigorously in agreement. "We were going to have a battle because he"—he pointed to his twin— "broke my rattle."

"I did not! You keep thaying that, but I didn't!"

"Yeth, you did!"

"No, I didn't!" Tweedledum (or Dee) reached out and gave his brother a push.

"Take it back!" Tweedledee (or Dum) returned the favor, pushing hard enough to rock his brother on his feet.

"Boys!" Leonard's voice thundered, drowning out both Tweedles. "Enough!"

Both Tweedles looked contrite. "Thorry, Your Majesty."

"Anyway," Hatter said, once quiet descended again. "Prince Henry needs a place to spend the night."

"Oh, he can have my bed," Tweedledum (or Dee) said, grinning his broad, gap-toothed smile.

"No, he can have my bed," Tweedledee (or Dum) insisted. His smile matched his brother's.

"Boys, boys. Prince Henry can't stay in either of your houses. Remember? That would make three in each house. We went over this before. No, Prince Henry would like to spend the night in your barn." Hatter pointed to a large, red barn set off to the side of the houses.

"The barn?" Henry asked, looking at Hatter askance.

"Yes, the barn, your Highness. Remember?" Hatter winked at Henry.

"Oh! Oh, yes, the barn. May we?" Henry asked the Tweedles.

"Of courth, Printh Henry." The Tweedles answered at once, even though both still looked confused. "Our barn is your barn."

"Good. See you in the morning, then." Hatter took Henry's elbow, and followed by Leonard, led the way to the barn. They passed a lonely cow that blinked huge doe eyes at them, and lowed softly. "Shh, Bessie. There's room in there for you too, I'm sure."

The double barn doors were huge, nearly giant-sized, but there was a smaller, man-sized door in the middle of the right one. Hatter opened it and ushered Henry and Leonard inside.

Hatter chuckled at Henry's look of surprise when he fished a lantern out of his pocket and lit it. Half walls separated the barn into a dozen roomy stalls, each holding a large, fluffy bed covered over with a thick, patchwork quilt. A couple of cows occupied two of the stalls, the residents' horned heads resting on thick pillows. One mooed softly in its sleep and rolled over. Another stall held a dozen small beds, each holding a single fat hen, all fast asleep.

"Who puts beds in their barn for the livestock?" Henry asked.

"Everybody. Don't they do it the same way in your world? What do they do... let the animals sleep on the ground?" Leonard and Hatter laughed at the absurdity of it. "I told you we'd be going to bed with the chickens," Leonard replied. "What'd you think I meant? Come on, let's hit the hay."

The three of them each chose a stall and bedded down, undressing in the near dark and sliding under thick quilts. The beds were soft and the covers were warm, and they fell asleep almost instantly.

Suddenly Hatter was wide awake and staring open-eyed into the blackness. *The damn lantern must've gone out,* he thought. *I thought I heard something....* He sat quietly, listening, but hear nothing but Leonard's snoring and the cows' soft lowing. Every so often a chicken would cluck, but other than that, he heard nothing.

He was about to roll over and try to go back to sleep, when the noise that had startled him awake came again. It was a clanking sound, metal against metal. It wasn't the volume of the sound that woke him—the noise wasn't overly loud. It was the fact that it didn't belong in the barn. It was a strange noise, alien. Metal against metal. Like a sword sliding free from a sheath.

Hatter jumped out of bed and pulled his clothes on as he hopped awkwardly to Henry's stall. He shook Henry's shoulder until Henry's eyes blinked open. "Henry, wake up!"

He ran to Leonard's stall and woke the Red King. "Your Majesty, they're here. The Red Guard. They've found us."

Leonard woke and was dressed before Henry even got out of bed. Hatter went back into Henry's stall, and shook him again, then ripped the quilt off the bed. He grabbed Henry's clothes and pushed them into his arms. "Hurry!"

No sooner had they finished dressing than the barn's huge double doors banged open, revealing a dozen large figures backlit by the moonlight. The darkness ate the color red, but Hatter knew it would be there. Their coats, their pants, their armor, the color of their hair and skin would all be bright ruby red. It was the Queen's Red Guard, and she wouldn't have sent any but her best after them.

He wondered if she knew her husband was back in Wonderland. He could only hope she didn't. Their plans depended on it. Surprise was really their only weapon against her. He'd know in a few minutes, as soon as the Guard saw Leonard.

He wondered how she could know they were back, or where they were. *She must have had someone watching the White Castle,* he thought. *A Guard left behind to report if we came back. If she knew we came through the mirror, she would know the only place in the area to seek shelter would be at the Tweedles.* He swore softly, under his breath. *I wouldn't have credited her with being that smart. I'd do well to remember that. She's mad, not stupid.*

He and Henry stood shoulder-to-shoulder, facing the Guard. Hatter carried his lantern, and after fishing a matchbox from his pocket, slid a match out and flicked it against the sole of his shoe. The tiny flame flared, and he used it to light the lantern. It cast a soft yellow glow over them.

"Oy! You, Hatter! And you… er, Boy Alice. You are hereby under arrest by order of Her Majesty, the Red Queen." The largest Guard, a red giant, boomed. He took a step forward and produced a scroll. "You are charged with Duplicitous Despicableness and Insults of the First Degree. The punishment is death."

"Oh, dear," Hatter said. "Let me guess how… by beheading?"

The Red Guard sniffed. "As if there were any other sort of punishment."

Hatter shrugged. "Well, she could imprison us. She's done that before." He knew it only too well. His back ached, remembering the thin mattress covering the cot he'd slept on in his cell for so many years.

"No, your heads must roll. That's the sentence." The Guard looked thoughtful, and shifted his sword from hand to hand. "In fact, truth be told, beheading is the punishment now for every crime."

Hatter winced. It was worse than he'd thought. "You're a good man, very loyal to the Crown."

"Of course." The Guard glanced at the men behind him, and lowered his voice. "Doin' otherwise would mean my head would roll."

"I suppose that would be very inconvenient." Hatter nodded in sympathy.

"Indeed." The Guard agreed. "So, if you wouldn't mind, we should be moving along now. She's waiting, and you don't want to keep Her Majesty waiting any longer than you need to. Or at least I don't." He unconsciously touched his throat and swallowed hard, then pointed the sword toward Hatter and took a step forward.

"I command you to stand down," Leonard's voice bellowed from behind Hatter and Henry, echoing in the barn. "I said, 'Stand down!'"

The Guard squinted, looking past Hatter and Henry into the shadows. "Who's there? Who said that? Interfering with a Royal Arrest is a crime punishable by beheading. Come out here where I can see you!"

His head high and his shoulders back, his spine as straight as an arrow, Leonard walked into the light dressed in all his royal finery. His golden crown glinted in the lantern light.

"W-who are you?" The Red Guard held his sword in front of him, and took a step backward. "A-a ghost?"

"I assure you I am not a ghost. I am the Red King, and I demand your allegiance!" Leonard stepped up to the Guard, looking down his long nose.

He's very good at regal intimidation, Hatter thought, smiling to himself. He elbowed Henry and nodded toward Leonard. "See that? There's a talent only experience can give you. Look at him. He's got them cowed with only a single look."

Henry nodded without taking his eyes off Leonard and the guard.

"T-the Red King? But you're dead! The Red Queen said so." The Guard was obviously flummoxed. Should he believe or shouldn't he? His dilemma was obvious in his puzzled expression.

"He don't look dead. He's breathin', ain't he?" Another Guard, only slightly smaller than the first, put in. He sniffed, obviously proud of his deductive skills and fully confident no one could refute his conclusion.

"That don't mean nothing. Could be he's just fakin' breathing." The first Guard peered at Leonard. "Are you? Faking?"

"I assure you, I am not." Leonard folded his arms across his chest. "I am alive and well, and breathing quite nicely."

"Why should we believe you?" The second Guard refused to be swayed so easily. "Dead fellas might not want to tell the truth about bein' dead."

The first Guard nodded. "He's got a point there."

Hatter decided he'd had enough. "Perhaps, but it doesn't matter."

The Guards seemed shocked. "What? Of course, it matters!"

"Why?" Hatter asked. "Why does it matter whether he's dead or not, if he's standing right here in front of you?" He examined his fingernails, then buffed them against his lapel as he waited for the Guards to answer.

"Because... because...." The Guards looked at one another, their expressions twisting into twin looks of frustrated confusion.

"Alive or dead, it doesn't matter. All that does matter is that this is the Red King, and you are sworn to obey him." Hatter turned to Leonard. "Your Majesty. I believe these Guards may be guilty of treason by refusing to take your word on the matter of your being alive or not."

The second Guard was quicker to understand the implications than the first Guard was. He bowed low before Leonard. "Oh, Your Majesty, forgive me. I-I was only following his orders." He pointed to the first Guard. "He's the one who really didn't believe you. Perhaps his head should roll, but not mine. You can't put a man to the Axe just for followin' orders, can you?"

"He's lying!" The first Guard finally caught on that the second Guard was trying to throw him under the carriage. "I believed you all along. I was... I was testing him! That's it. Testing, and he failed!"

"Stop it, the two of you! Speak one more word on the subject, either of you, and I will send you both to the Axe. If you obey me from this moment on without hesitation, all shall be forgiven." He looked out at the troop of Guards and addressed them all. "As your King, I order you all to sheathe your weapons. Your allegiance was to my wife in my absence, but your King has returned. Hatter is my lieutenant, and Henry—Boy Alice—is my honored guest. You will obey Hatter and protect them both as you would me. Is that clear?"

The two Guards snapped a salute, and the rest of the Guard hesitantly, confusedly followed suit. "Yes, Your Majesty." They stood at stiff attention, awaiting Leonard's next order.

Hatter's grin escaped his control. He threw his arm around Henry's shoulders and nodded to Leonard. "Excellently done, Sire. Shall we march on the Red Castle now?"

Leonard returned his grin. "Oh, yes. Yes, we shall."

With Leonard in the lead, followed by Hatter, Henry, and the Red Guard, they began the trek toward the Red Castle.

Chapter Eighteen

The ease of the march took Henry quite by surprise. He'd been expecting more terrifying swamps, or backward-forwardness, or evil-tempered giants shooting candy cannons to block their way, but instead he found himself walking along a well-traveled path with no obstacles in sight. Lush vegetation lined both sides of the pathway, but nothing seemed threatening in any way. All he could see were trees, shrubs, flowers, and the occasional bee or rabbit of the non-waistcoat-wearing variety. Nothing seemed to have teeth or claws or to be otherwise dangerous.

It was rather unnerving. He kept waiting for something horrific to happen, so much so that when nothing did, he became even more anxious. Finally, he could take no more of the normalcy.

"Hatter?" Henry grabbed Hatter's elbow and pulled him to a stop. "What's going on here?"

Hatter blinked at him, and looked around. "Where? I don't see anything."

"That's just it. There's nothing here—no tree sharks, no gingerbread armies, no giant mushrooms and hookah-smoking caterpillars. It's just too damn quiet. I keep thinking something really bad is about to happen." Henry kept scanning the vegetation, as if waiting for something to pop out at him.

"Relax, Henry. This is the Neutral Wood. Nothing here is harmful… or beneficial, for that matter. There's nothing dangerous or gentle, nothing too loud or too soft, too high or too low. Everything is perfectly average, an absolute medium." He swept his arm in a broad gesture. "Look around! The tree leaves are neither dark green nor light green, but a shade precisely between the two. The berries on that bush over there are neither crimson nor pink, but a nice, midway shade of red. The grass underfoot is just soft enough, the temperature just warm enough, and the sky overhead just blue enough. Nothing here will hurt you. Nothing is capable of it."

Henry continued to look around him, but he knew Hatter was right. And that, Henry further realized, was exactly the problem. Everything here was neutral to the point of being boring. There was nothing to capture the imagination or spark curiosity. The only thing the forest had in abundance was a great, big, heaping helping of dullness. It was as unnatural as any of the other parts of Wonderland he'd visited.

He found himself forced into being dull. He tried to yell, but all he could manage was a monotone. He tried to run, but was unable to move at more than a leisurely pace. Even his word choice was tedious. He couldn't swear beyond a heartfelt "dang it," even though he repeatedly tried. It was unnerving. He didn't know what kind of magic was controlling him, or how it managed to do so, but it made him very uneasy.

"How big is this forest?" He asked Hatter. "Seems like we've been walking... er, a while. This place is, uh... okay." Wait. That wasn't what he'd meant to say! He wanted to complain about how long they'd been walking, hadn't he? About how dreary the forest was, and how boring it was here, but all that he'd been able to manage was "a while," and "okay."

Hatter nodded. "It's medium-sized, as forests go, I suppose. Not too big, not too small."

As if Henry had expected anything but a middling answer in this average place. He sighed and resigned himself to keeping their unhurried pace.

By noon, he realized the trees were thinning, until finally the path broadened into a wide meadow filled with brilliantly colored flowers. All of Henry's senses were assaulted at once, as if coming out of the Neutral Wood, the earth had dove headfirst into overly stimulating mode.

The colors were so bright he could barely look at them without his eyes tearing. Ditto for the sun; it shone so brightly he could feel his skin burning through his shirt, and he feared his hair might just burst into flame if he didn't find something to cover it with very soon. Although overly warm, the wind was brisk enough that he had to lean into it slightly to keep moving forward. The grass underfoot was stiff and scratchy; it clung to his pant legs like miniature cacti. Even the birdsong sounded wrong. It was loud, and jarring, and made Henry want to plug both ears with his fingers.

He planted both hands flat on his head to try to keep the sun from melting what few brains he retained, and turned to Hatter. "Where are we now?" He had to speak up to be heard over the wind.

"Plains of Excess." Hatter dug into his pocket and pulled out a flat cap, handing it to Henry. "Here, put this on before the sun bakes your brains into a tart."

Henry took the cap gratefully, and placed it on his head. "Thanks. Let me guess... everything here is too much, right? Too much sun, too much wind, too much crabgrass, too much *everything.* Right?"

"You're too right," Hatter replied, and chuckled. "Whatever you do, don't drink liquor here. I once made the mistake of having ale with the Cheshire Cat in a tavern located just over the western border of the Plains of Excess. I fell asleep halfway through, and didn't wake up for a week."

"I'll keep that in mind," Henry replied. He bent his head into the wind. "Is it far yet to the Red Castle?"

"No. It's just on the other side of the Plains of Excess. Some say that's why the Queen is so awful. They claim her bedroom faces the Plains, and the wind carries Excess Dust into it every night. Makes her excessively ornery."

"They need to explain her behavior, and it's as good a reason as any, I suppose," Leonard said. He'd been so quiet, Henry had nearly forgotten he was with them. "I like to believe our troubles started when she failed to conceive a child, but I know that isn't the truth. Many couples don't have offspring for a variety of reasons. Some can't have children, and some choose not to have them, but in either case, rarely does it result in uncontrolled beheadings. No, my wife was evil before that—I just refused to see it. I wanted her to be the woman of my dreams so badly that I overlooked or explained away warning signs. I made excuses for her behavior until it progressed to a point where even I couldn't remain blind to her faults anymore. That's when I left. I shouldn't have gone and left Wonderland unprotected from my wife's madness."

"Don't blame yourself, Your Majesty. You had it tough all those years. She took a lot of her aggression out on you," Hatter said.

"Men don't often like to admit they've been abused, do they? What I've come to understand is there's no disgrace in saying it," Leonard replied. "I've realized it doesn't make me less of a man. It took me a long time to be able to say it, though, and even longer before I believed it, and until just now to put it behind me and move on."

Henry's ears perked up at Leonard's confession. There'd been times when Henry had reason to think the same, times when Henry's father had been drinking and used his fists to talk. Henry had never told anyone, not even Alice. In fact, he flushed with shame remembering how he'd blamed Alice for their father's drinking and behavior. He'd had it all wrong. The only person to blame for it all was their father. "And now?"

Leonard offered Henry a weak smile. "And now I know the fault lies mostly with my wife. She was the aggressor. She took her anger out on me, both verbally and physically. Leaving her was the most difficult thing I'd ever done. It was frightening, but I thought it was the right thing to do. I'm not so sure now. Once I was gone, she took her frustration out on all of Wonderland. I do believe with all my heart that coming back now is the right thing though, the responsible thing for me to do."

It was as if Leonard confirmed Henry's thoughts, and it left Henry feeling lighter; a load he hadn't been aware he'd been carrying was gone. "I think you were right to leave when you did, Sire. You can't blame yourself for what the Red Queen has done to Wonderland."

"Yes," Hatter said. "Sire, you were too close to the situation before. You suffered at her hands, but didn't see how she was affecting your subjects. It took going away to put it all in perspective."

Leonard seemed to stand straighter, and his smile grew a bit bolder. "You're right. I can see that now. But I do owe you both a great deal. Thank you, both of you. If you hadn't come back to Alice's world, I may have convinced myself never to return to Wonderland."

"I don't believe that, Your Majesty." Hatter waved Leonard's confession away with a flip of his hand. "You would've come to the right decision eventually." He squinted into the distance, and smiled. "Ah, look! We're coming to the end of the Plains of Excess."

Henry was thrilled. He'd had just about enough excessive introspection to last a lifetime. It was bothersome and embarrassing, and left him feeling a bit weepy, something he definitely was not prone to being. He sniffed, and stepped the pace, eager to leave the Plains of Excess behind him.

They came to a split in the pathway. One way headed east, the other, west. Beyond the split stretched a dense, dark forest that didn't encourage exploration. Nothing about the woods looked inviting; not its dark colors, or spider-webbed branches, not the snufflings and howls of unseen beasts that seemed to come from its depths. Going through it would be dangerous at best and lethal at worst. They would need to take one path or the other.

A signpost held two placards shaped like arrows. The one pointing east read, "Success." The other, pointing west, read, "Ruin."

"Well, ordinarily I would think it obvious we should head east, but with this being Wonderland, I question whether that would be the wisest choice," Henry said.

Hatter grinned at him, and patted him on the back. "Now you're thinking like a true Wonderlander, my boy!" He gestured toward the road that led to Success. It was smooth, and lined with sweet-smelling flowers and graceful shade trees. "Success is never as easy a road to travel as it looks, and rarely as sweet as one expects. In Ruin, however, one can usually find something worthwhile, be it a lesson or something more tangible. Look at the ruins of the White Castle, for example. Everything was destroyed but the one thing we needed—the mirror."

"I never really thought about it like that before." Henry looked at the road to Ruin. Rocks studded it, and deep cracks rippled through it that would make walking treacherous. The vegetation bordering it was brown, withered, and rotting. The bent and twisted trees on either side of the path were leafless and blighted. Overall, it looked desolate and unforgiving. He couldn't see anyone voluntarily taking that fork.

Which, of course, was the whole point. The Red Queen had made certain no one she didn't want visiting the Red Castle would find it. Only those who figured out the secret of the paths would make it there.

"Clever, huh?" Hatter sighed, almost sounding admiring of the Queen's shrewdness. "Clever, but mad. Mustn't forget that." He grabbed Henry's hand, and started down the path to Ruin.

Chapter Nineteen

The pathway was every bit as difficult to navigate as its name had promised. Hatter tripped over rocks and stepped in potholes, losing his balance on more than one occasion. It was quite distressing. He found it ridiculously embarrassing to appear so incredibly ungraceful, particularly in front of Henry. It really wasn't like him at all. Usually, he was quite light on his feet. Indeed, he was known to perform the *Gallumphing Gyre* as well as Nobody, which of course was saying quite a bit since Nobody was a better dancer than Hatter.

It helped somewhat, that everyone else was having the same trouble as Hatter. The Red Guard, for example, never the most graceful of creatures to begin with, were falling all over one another. Even Leonard had to pick his way slowly and carefully over the path to avoid ending up in an undignified, red-velvet-and-ermine-trimmed heap. The trouble was that the path kept changing with little or no warning. Looking ahead at it to see where you were going did you no good, because by the time your feet reached the part of the path your eyes had seen, the road altered itself. Potholes appeared and disappeared; stones moved, rocking and rolling beneath your feet, throwing you off balance.

Henry, however, seemed to be rather enjoying himself. He stepped from one craggy rock to another, lithely jumping over the deeper cracks in the earth like a blond gazelle. Even when a stone or pothole threw him off-center and he staggered, he grinned and went on. Hatter smiled to himself, admiring Henry's energetic moves, and his slender but clearly well-muscled form... particularly the latter.

Henry's body wasn't overly bulky, like those of the Red Guard, but slim and wiry, yet Hatter knew the strength that lay in Henry's trim physique. He'd felt those hard muscles surround him in a hug, and felt the whole of Henry's body press up against his own.

He'd never been gladder than when Henry agreed to accompany them back to Wonderland. It wasn't because Hatter felt their cause a lost one without Henry's aid—although Hatter was glad for help—but because he didn't want to say good-bye to Henry. He wanted more time with Henry, more opportunities to ponder how he felt about Henry and vice versa, and why it was so difficult to comprehend them never being together again.

Hatter was an intelligent, experienced man, and he had an inkling of an idea, outrageous though it might be. He suspected he wasn't just *attracted* to Henry, but that somewhere during their travels together he'd actually begun to fall in *love* with Boy Alice.

At least, he *thought* it might be love. For all he knew, what he was feeling *could* be the onset of some strange and lethal swamp fever, something picked up during their sloggy trek through the Neverglades.

Is this what being in love feels like? Hatter wondered. He really had no experience in the matter, nothing to gauge it by. Did love make one feel like he had a warm blanket wrapped around him on a cold winter's day, or like being filled from his toes to his hairline with bubbly juice, tickly and effervescent? Did being in love make one feel as though his very next breath depended on the person he loved being near them?

Moreover, was it even *possible* for him to love? Could it be true? Him, the Mad Hatter of Wonderland, Master Magician, Cursed by Time, Tea Pourer Extraordinaire, and most recently Right Hand to the Red King? Could it be possible he'd actually, finally fallen in love? He never had before, he was quite sure of it. Then why now? Why Henry?

Equally importantly, if not more so, was the question of whether Henry had developed feelings for Hatter in return?

Hatter suddenly gasped, and stepped into an especially deep pothole, nearly falling over as another question occurred to him. *If Henry doesn't love me back, what then? What if what I suspect I feel for Henry is only one-sided?* Hatter chewed his bottom lip as a feeling much like ice-cold pain gripped his heart. *What will I do then?*

The mere thought of living without Henry made his stomach feel as though it had taken a long, fast fall with a sudden stop at the end. There were options, of course, but none of them were the least bit appealing. Love potions were available if one knew where to inquire, but they were notoriously unreliable. He'd hate to use one and end up being the love interest of a Jubjub bird or Walrus, or some other, equally appalling creature.

Anyway, he didn't much like the feeling of forcing Henry to love him. *It would be as if I were obliged to eat an entire bakery full of cakes,* he mused. *Oh, the first few bites might be sweet, but by the end, it's likely I'd be barfing chocolate treacle cheesecake on my shoes.*

What should he do? What should he say? Should he risk confessing his feelings to Henry, or keep them to himself? They were fast approaching the last leg of their journey together. Soon they'd be at the Red Castle and, for better or worse, a showdown with the Red Queen. If the confrontation ended favorably for them, and their heads didn't roll, what then? What if Henry wanted to return to his own world?

Hatter's eyes opened wide at the next thought to enter his mind, close on the heels of the last. *What if Henry left me behind in Wonderland, and I was never to know if what I feel really is love, or if Henry returns those feelings in kind?*

Hatter supposed he could follow Henry back to Alice's house through the looking glass, but what then? If Henry didn't want Hatter, he'd be no better off than he was here. Worse, for he'd be in a strange world he didn't understand, all alone. *I might as well allow one of those rolling automobile monsters to gobble me up and be done with it, then.* He swallowed hard, not relishing a future spent rolling around in the belly of a metal beast.

It was at times like this he wished his life were a book just so he could flip to the last page to see how it all turned out.

The road to Ruin soon showed how it had earned its name, and as it turned out, rocks and potholes were the least of it.

The vegetation lining both sides of the path began to thin, replaced by structures of all kinds, built with a variety of materials. Henry spotted quaint cottages more suited to a seashore community than a trail in the middle of nowhere, gabled Victorians dripping with gingerbread trim, squat, unpainted cinderblock rectangles with casement windows, and tall, multi-floor high-rises. The spaces between them were filled with rough log cabins, tiny clapboard schoolhouses, wigwams, igloos, thatched huts, and some for which Henry had no name. The buildings were as different from one another as snowflakes, with one element alone in common—they were, to a one, utterly destroyed.

No window was intact. Instead, jagged pieces of glass glinted like shiny daggers in the sun. No painted surface was unscratched or defaced by graffiti. One particularly colorful tag read "Time Flies or Dies but Never Sits Still." Henry glanced at Hatter sideways, wondering if Hatter had a hand in painting that one.

Henry didn't see a single door that wasn't hanging crookedly on its hinges, or missing entirely. Walls boasted large and small holes; front stoops sagged and were missing steps. The roofs, both flat and pitched, boasted bald spots where shingles or tiles had been ripped away, and large holes had been punched through them. The landscaping around the structures was either wild and unkempt or browning and half dead, often growing into broken windows or gaping doorways, as if the earth were trying to move in, the newest tenant in a dying village.

As they passed, Henry could see small, faded signs in front of some of the buildings, most with letters scratched out. Dish and Spoon Bak ry. Jack Sprat's Restaur nt. Miss Muffet's Millinery. Mother Hubbard's Bed and Breakf st. Thr e Bl nd Mice Bookstore. Mary Contrary's Dairy.

"Welcome to Ruin," Hatter said. He gestured toward the crumbling buildings. "Horribly depressing place, and they serve an amazingly good fig pudding."

Henry gaped slack jawed at him. "Do you mean to tell me people *live* here? By *choice?* Why don't they fix the place up?"

"Fix it up!" Hatter looked shocked. "For goodness sakes, why would they want to do that after they'd spent all their time and funds fixing it down so nicely?"

Henry turned back toward the ruins. "You mean they did this on purpose? They like it this way?"

"Of course. Ruin has the best wreckage in Wonderland. You won't find better anywhere, I promise. Why, they were voted 'Best Rubble' by *The Wonderland Architect* for twenty years straight." Hatter buffed his fingernails against his lapel and grinned. "I, of course, have had the pleasure of experiencing the awful ambiance several times. Not everyone can say that, eh?"

"Hatter is right, Henry. Only the best people vacation in the worst spot in Wonderland," Leonard put in. "I haven't even stayed there." He sighed. "Perhaps one day, when our present tribulations are at an end and I can manage a holiday."

Henry didn't understand it all, but shrugged and chalked it up to something only a native from Wonderland could appreciate. It didn't really bother him all that much. After all, he didn't half understand anything else in this weird world, either. Wonderland almost seemed *designed* to be strange. If so, it succeeded splendidly, in his opinion.

As they continued down the path, he noticed each ruin was consistently dilapidated and in appropriate states of distress. Henry also spotted people moving between the buildings. He wasn't surprised at all to discover the residents of Ruin looked just as seedy and neglected as their homes. Everyone was dressed in shades of dusty gray, their pants, coats, dresses, and aprons suitably shabby and patched, shoes scuffed and worn. No one smiled or laughed; everyone seemed to wear identical forlorn expressions on their faces, even the children.

Ruin seemed exactly as wretched a place to live in as its appearance implied. He wondered why anyone would choose to live in Ruin, then realized that perhaps their residence wasn't by choice. The Queen, by reputation, was a ruthless sort. Was it possible she forced these people to live here?

Henry was more impressed by Ruin than he'd expected to be. It seemed as if it took a great deal of dedication for an entire village to be so diverse, yet so decrepit. As he thought about it, he wondered if he could stand living there. Certainly not for any prolonged length of time. Think of it! It would require a tremendous amount of work to maintain such a place. All the buildings, the tall, the short, the long, and the squat, must be tended carefully, making sure all surfaces were well spread with dust, and spider webs artfully draped in each corner. Each one must be architecturally sound so as not to collapse on their residents' heads, yet appear as fragile as a sheet of tissue paper in a windstorm. Every garden would need to be planted each season with crab grass and bindii prickles, and carefully pruned of any pretty wildflowers that might take root. Trees must be festooned with dripping shrouds of Spanish moss and swathed with kudzu vines. Any newly unfurling leaf must be plucked and discarded.

And that was only to keep up the outward appearance of the city. The inhabitants would require every bit as much work.

All new clothes would need to be beaten and pounded, washed and rewashed until they were suitably faded and frayed. Each pair of new shoes and boots, scuffed until the shine wore off, and new tennis shoes beaten until the canvas split and shredded.

Personal hygiene required constant attention as well, he supposed. Hair must never be uniformly trimmed, but left to grow wild and unkempt no matter how much the wind whipped it into greasy tangles. Beards and mustaches must be allowed to grow out, no matter how much they itched. Fingernails would either grow wild or be bitten, and must be consistently dirty at all times. Smiles must never be white, but yellowed and preferably missing a tooth here and there.

It really was exhausting just thinking about it, not to mention wholly depressing.

Henry tugged on Hatter's elbow. "Why do these people live here? They look positively miserable."

Hatter glanced at the town, and nodded. "I suppose they are. I know people who are born in Ruin often fail to leave it, and some who aren't born to Ruin sometimes end up living there. There are those who claim Ruin is necessary so other parts of Wonderland can flourish. Their thinking is, without the wretched poor, how can there be the privileged others? Who would they compare themselves to without those who live in Ruin?"

Henry frowned, thinking about it. It didn't sound right to him. "Do you believe that?"

Hatter seemed to ponder a moment before answering. "I think the ones who *say* it believe it. Trouble is, those who believe it are among the rich and powerful, like the Red Queen, and we know how difficult it is to oppose *her*."

As Henry pondered Hatter's words, wondering whether Ruin might benefit if they succeeded in overthrowing the Queen, the road took them past the city limits. Forest again took possession of the sides of the road as they left the city behind. As they walked, he feared he must have nodded off on his feet, because something interesting—and slightly disturbing—had happened without his notice.

Everything, from the trees to the birds that flitted between them, from the shrubs to the shy forest creatures peeking out from beneath their branches, *everything* had turned to a single color.

Red. Everything was red. Even the sky and clouds had taken on a pinkish cast. It was as if some mad artist had painted the entire world in shades of crimson.

They had reached the Red Queen's territory, and rising in the distance, past a few gently rolling red hills, blood-red against the pink sky, stood the formidable silhouette of the Red Castle.

Chapter Twenty

Leonard held his hand up, signaling the rest of them to stop. The rear Red Guard didn't get the memo soon enough. He bumped into the Guard in front of him, and that Guard fell forward onto the next, until the entire squadron tumbled like dominoes. Their chain mail and armor seemed to tangle, cementing them together. Leonard sighed and rolled his eyes.

"We need to go over our plan before advancing on the Red Castle." He turned to Hatter. "What's the plan?"

Hatter blinked, and looked from side to side, his expression puzzled. He finally pointed hesitantly to himself. "Me? I don't have a plan. I thought *you* had a plan."

"Me?" Leonard's eyes flashed open wide, shock glinting in their depths. "I'm the King."

Hatter nodded and shrugged, as if Leonard had merely agreed with him. He took his hat off, and dusted the brim with the cuff of his sleeve. "Exactly."

"No, no, you misunderstand. I'm the Red King. I have people who do things for me, like polishing my crown, and fluffing my pillows, and drawing up plans and such."

"I don't have a plan," Hatter said, looking slightly confused. He turned to Henry. "Do you have a plan?"

Henry shook his head. "I don't have a plan. I wouldn't know how to begin to make one."

Leonard scowled at them. "Well, *someone* has to have a plan. Hatter, I command you to formulate one immediately."

"Me? You can't just... I...." Hatter stuttered, looking back and forth between Henry and Leonard, and finally tamped his hat back on and swore. "Well, of all the slurvish scut shukm!" He began to pace, pausing every so often to shoot Leonard a look so black and foul it caused several flies unintentionally buzzing in its path to drop like tiny stones, dead. "Fine. Let's think about this. We can't very well storm the front gates, now can we?" He jerked his thumb toward the Red Guard, all of whom were still trying to disentangle themselves and stand up. "Not with this lot."

"Is there another way into the Castle? One the Queen might not have heavily guarded?" Henry asked.

Hatter grinned at him. "You've read my mind, Henry. There is only one place that fits the bill. The dungeon."

Henry looked at Hatter with surprise, the smile he'd just finished forming sliding away. "The *dungeon?* I would think that would be crawling with Guards!"

"Certainly, but they'll be looking for people trying to break *out*, not *in*. It's perfect!" Hatter rubbed his white-gloved hands together. "Now, here's what I propose…."

They gathered around Hatter, leaning in as he whispered his plan. The Head Red Guard pulled himself forward on his elbows, dragging the rest of the Guard behind him, so he could hear what Hatter had to say.

Henry didn't know if Hatter's plan would work, but glancing down at the Red Guard, lying on their bellies looking very much like a lobster parade, he thought maybe, just maybe, it might.

They crouched behind a low wall fashioned of fieldstones, peeking over the top at the entrance to the Red Castle. The immense wooden double doors, both painted scarlet, were tall enough for a giant to pass through without needing to duck, and were closed, no doubt barricaded from the inside.

The doors, however, were the least of their problems. Getting to the doors was going to be far more difficult than opening them once Hatter and his friends got there. *If* they got there.

"Beg pardon, Your Majesty," The Head Red Guard began, making a small bow to Leonard, a feat made far more awkward by the fact that the Guard was already crouching behind a wall. "What do we do now?"

Leonard cleared his throat, and took another look over the wall. "Well, er... I suppose we should go inside."

"Yes sir," said the Guard. "But, um, how?"

"By ordinary means, I should think. Through the doors." Leonard motioned the Guard forward. "You first, then. Go on. We'll be right behind you."

The Guard began to get up, but then paused and sank even lower than he'd been before. "I think you should lead us, Your Majesty. Seeing you up front would give the men heart."

Hatter rolled his eyes. "Your Majesty, it appears obvious we must think of a different tactic than merely waltzing in through the front doors as if we're calling on the Queen for tea."

"Why not?" Henry asked. "Isn't that what she'd least expect us to do?"

"I should think she believes us dead, actually. She certainly wouldn't have set the Guard to watch for our return by the mirror in the White Castle if she didn't think they'd kill us. The problem, Henry, is the moat." Hatter pointed to the small drawbridge leading to the castle doors. It was up, prohibiting safe travel across it to the castle. Beneath it, muddy waters churned with red-tinted foam. "It's filled with hungry crocodiles."

"How do you know they're hungry?" Henry asked.

"Because crocodiles are *always* hungry. They're mostly just teeth and stomach, you know. Takes a lot to fill them up." Hatter sat down and leaned his back against the wall. "Even if we managed to cross the moat, the front doors are patrolled by a Jabberwock, and that's our biggest problem."

Henry huffed, and scowled at Hatter. "Wait a minute. Alice told me a boy slew the Jabberwock with a... a vocal sword."

"*Vorpal*. He slew it with a Vorpal sword." Hatter patted Henry's arm. "Good try, though. And it's true, but this is a different Jabberwock, a hatchling of the old one, raised and fed by the hand of the Queen, or so it's said, and therefore especially vile."

"It's true." Leonard's voice sounded weary, and his expression was one of disgust. "She kept the damnable thing on a leash when it was little. Took it everywhere, fed it chicken fingers and toes, and tried to let it sleep in our bed until it became apparent Jabberwocks cannot be housebroken. There's nothing worse, I tell you, than rolling over in your sleep face-first into a pile of Jabberwock droppings. She had a small house built for the beast then, and made sure it ate the best parts of whoever met the Axe that day. When heads rolled, they rolled right into the Jabberwock's mouth!"

"And the only thing that can kill it is a Vorpal sword?"

"As far as anyone knows, it is. It's something in the way the blade is fashioned, you see," Leonard explained. "The process makes it especially sharp and nearly unbreakable. The Vorpal blade is the strongest known in Wonderland. Anything else would just snap against the Jabberwock's armor-like hide."

Henry sighed and sat next to Hatter. "I don't suppose you have a Vorpal sword in your pocket, huh?"

Hatter chuckled. "No. It's been on my mind for some time to find one, but so far I've haven't had any luck. I have a Vorpal letter opener, and a full set of Vorpal steak knives, but Vorpal swords are few and far between." He patted Henry on the leg. "However, being my wonderfully inventive and incredibly resourceful self, I have a plan. We'll simply go in the out."

"In the out?" Henry cocked an eyebrow. "What does that mean? Please tell me it doesn't have anything to do with Drawrof! I really hated that place."

"No, no, of course not. If it did, I'd be speaking backwards, wouldn't I? Then I would have said, 'we'll go out the in,' which wouldn't make a bit of sense." Hatter thunked Henry on the forehead with his index finger. "Silly, silly boy. No, we shall go in the out, meaning through the back door, which is ordinarily only used for exiting the castle. It's located near the dungeon, where I had the unfortunate luck to be incarcerated for quite some time."

A wide smile slowly creased Leonard's cheeks. "A most brilliant plan, Hatter! She'd never consider anyone trying to break *into* the dungeon, now would she? Not when so very many people spend all their time trying to break out of it!"

"Exactly!" Hatter tried not to sound so very full of himself, but he simply couldn't help it. When he had moments of genius like this, he just couldn't keep all of himself inside his skin where he belonged. It was unavoidable that some of him would slip out. "Now, everyone keep your heads down. We'll follow this wall around to the rear of the castle." Hatter bent his body in half, trying to keep his upper half lower than the wall and his lower half higher than the ground. It wasn't as easy as it seemed.

Henry tapped Hatter on the back. "Hatter, doesn't the moat go all the way around?"

"What? Oh, yes. The moat. Of course it does. Otherwise it wouldn't be a moat. It would merely be a muddy, crocodile-infested pond." Hatter put his hand on the top of his hat to keep it from falling forward over his eyes.

Again Henry tapped Hatter, knocking his hat askew. "Well, aren't there crocodiles in the back half of the moat as well?"

Hatter sighed. "Yes, but there's only one Jabberwock, and it's chained up at the front of the castle."

Once again, Henry's finger poked Hatter. His hat tipped down over his eyes again. It was really becoming quite annoying. "But Hatter, don't we still have to figure out a way past the crocodiles?"

Hatter stopped, sat down, and took off his hat. He rummaged in his pocket for a moment before pulling out a large roll of bright yellow tape. Measuring off a length, he put his hat on and used the tape to secure it to his head by looping the length over the top of the hat and under his chin. "Are you made up entirely of questions, Henry? Seriously, I begin to think there's nothing inside you except questions and more questions, all waiting for the slightest opening of your mouth to escape." He tested his hat, and made a slight adjustment until he was sure it would stay put. "We'll deal with the crocodiles when we get there. At least we won't have the Jabberwock to contend with, which was far more than half the battle if we went in through the front. Therefore, logic tells us we've already won more than half the battle, and here you are, worried about a few crocodiles."

Henry blinked, and still looked confused, but at least his questions had ceased... for the moment. Considering it was Henry, Hatter had no doubt the respite would only be momentary. He grunted and gathered his feet under him, then continued his half-bent shuffle, following the wall around to the back of the castle.

It was quite a long walk, much longer than Hatter remembered it, and he wondered if the distance had grown longer in his absence. Perhaps the castle had had a growth spurt. By the time they rounded the far corner of the castle, Hatter's back was in a foul mood from crouching for so long. In fact, it was screaming at him. Not with words, mind you, but with great, jagged jolts of pain that were perhaps even more effective than actual speech and left him feeling quite mimsy. He wasn't as young as he used to be. Or as limber, it seemed.

He sneaked a quick peek over the wall to make sure there were no Red Guards patrolling the rear of the castle, which, of course, there weren't. He hadn't expected there to be any. As Leonard remarked earlier, no one ever tried to break *into* the dungeon, only out of it. Standing up, he winced as his spine loudly realigned itself. It sounded like a handful of pebbles dropped onto a china dinner plate.

"Now what?" Henry asked. He was bending backward, his hands on the small of his back, as if trying to keep his lower vertebrae from escaping.

Hatter carefully removed the tape that had held his hat to his head. Balling the used tape up, he dropped it into his pocket before tamping his hat back on. "Now, we cross the moat and enter the castle."

"And how are we going to do that? I hate to point this out, but there's no drawbridge on this side." Henry gestured toward the moat. "I doubt if swimming is an option." Even from the distance of the wall, the ridged backs of the crocodiles floating in the muddy, red-tinted water were obvious.

"Swim? How ridiculous! Of course we can't swim," Hatter said. He chuckled and shook his head. "Really, Henry, what could you possibly be thinking?" He placed a hand on top of the low fieldstone wall and hopped over to the other side. "We're going to walk over."

Henry's eyes flashed open and he sputtered a bit. "Walk! How?"

"Most people use their feet to accomplish the task. Like this. Watch closely." Hatter pointed to his boots, and placed one foot in front of the other. "See how it's done?" He snickered at the frumious expression clouding Henry's face. Henry, Hatter decided, was positively adorable when sputtering. He grinned and crooked a finger at Henry to follow as he set off toward the moat.

Henry caught up to him. "I know how to walk!"

"I can see that. Very talented, you are."

"You're starting to really piss me off, Hatter."

Hatter grinned, and noticed when Henry's eyes sparked with fury they turned the most interesting shade of blue-green. "My apologies. I never intended to suggest you lacked the fundamentals of locomotion. I merely answered your question. You asked how we were going to walk across the moat, and I answered."

"You know very well I meant how we were going to walk on water, since there's no bridge!"

"Walk on water? Can you do that in your world? It's impossible here, unless you've a spell, which I haven't, or are a deity of some sort, which I'm not." Leonard injected himself into the conversation, his expression one of deep interest.

Henry turned to Leonard. "No, we can't walk on water in my world! That's ridiculous!"

"Then why suggest it?" Hatter asked. He shook his head. "Really, Henry, sometimes you make no sense at all." He pointed toward the moat. "We'll use the stepping stones, of course."

Henry peered in the direction Hatter indicated. "Are you crazy? Those aren't stepping stones—they're the crocodiles!"

"Of course they are. What do you make stepping stones out of in your world?" Hatter asked.

Henry threw his hands up in the air. "Out of... stones. What else?"

Leonard and Hatter, and a few of the Red Guard close enough overhear the conversation, laughed.

"Stones!" Hatter elbowed Leonard. He turned back to Henry. "What good would rocks do you? They'd only sink to the bottom of the water!" He jerked his thumb at the moat. "The crocodiles float."

"Yeah, they float, and bite, if you've forgotten," Henry pointed out. "They'll eat you if you step on them."

"Eat me? The Red King? Don't be silly, Henry." Leonard's eyes streamed tears from laughing, and he wiped them with a corner of his red velvet cape. "Do I look the sort who'd set crocodiles loose in his moat without spelling them to protect him and those in his charge?"

"Uh, no, I guess not." Henry looked embarrassed and awkwardly scratched the back of his neck. "I keep forgetting everything is different here. You'd think I'd have learned by now."

Hatter threw his arm around Henry's shoulders and gave him a squeeze. "That's okay, Henry. You'll learn, and if you don't you've got me here to remind you." He decided he would've faced a hundred hungry crocodiles for the smile Henry gave him in return.

Leonard led them to the moat. The great crocodiles, some upward of twenty feet in length, floated like deadly logs in the murky red water. Their jaws opened, showing mouthfuls of long, sharp, glistening, white teeth. "Now, let me think. What was the tune that turns the spell on?" He whistled a few notes. "No, that's not it." He tapped his chin with one finger, then smiled and snapped his fingers. "Oh, yes! I remember now. You'll have to excuse me," he said to Henry and Hatter. "It's been a while since I've had to use the back door." He whistled again, low, then high, and then somehow sideways.

The crocodiles' yawning jaws snapped closed like a dozen doors slamming shut, and their massive bodies maneuvered into a makeshift path leading from the riverbank to a small dock at the rear of the castle courtyard. Their mouths remained closed, but their eyes rolled, watching Leonard and the rest of the party.

"Very good, men, er... crocodiles. You shall allow me and my guests to pass unharmed." Leonard's voice was loud and commanding. He wagged a finger at one of the biggest crocodiles in the bunch. "That goes for you too, Peabody. Take one nip out of anyone, and I'll have you made into a pair of boots. See if I don't."

The crocodile rolled its eyes and huffed, but its mouth remained closed up tight.

Leonard glanced at Henry and Hatter. "He ate a Red Guard the last time we came through. Only a small one, it's true, but really, I can't have my stepping stones eating my Guards regardless of how big they are." He patted Henry on the shoulder. "Oh, don't look so terrified, Henry. I've strengthened the spell since then, too. Now, off we go, before my wife finds out we're here."

Sweeping the bottom of his cape up over the crook of his arm, Leonard gingerly stepped on the back of the closest crocodile, then lightly hopped to the next, and so forth, until he at last reached the dock. He turned and beckoned to Hatter and Henry. "Come on, stop dawdling!"

Hatter grabbed Henry's hand. "Ready?"

"Not really," Henry said, glancing down at the toothy crocodiles. "But I suppose we have no choice."

"It'll be fine. Trust me," Hatter said. "Have I steered you wrong yet?"

Henry pulled his hand away. "Seriously? You almost got me stung to death on Stinging Hill, blown up in the Confection Mountains, eaten by tree sharks in the Neverglades, and let's not even talk about—"

"Tut, tut," Hatter said, placing a finger over Henry's lips, effectively silencing him. "Almost only counts in unicorn jousting and Bandersnatch baiting. You're standing here all in one piece, none the worse for the wear, aren't you?"

Henry snorted, which made Hatter pull his hand away, wiping his fingers on the front of his coat. "Ew. I would do nicely without a fistful of your snot, Henry, thank you very much."

"Then don't put your hand under my nose." Henry shrugged and grinned, his eyes twinkling.

Hatter couldn't help but return Henry's smile. "It's a good thing I like you."

"Yeah, well, I like you, too."

Hatter wondered why those words made him feel as if he could fly across the moat. A small voice in his head whispered, *Because you're glad he likes you, since you're beginning to feel more for him than mere friendship.*

He smiled wider, and didn't bother to pretend to disagree with himself.

Holding hands, they hopped across the crocodiles' backs and reached the other side without either of them getting so much as a dirty look from any of the crocs.

The Guard followed them, one by one. Peabody behaved himself right up until the very last Guard was crossing over. Then he lifted his great head out of the water and snapped at the Guard's right boot.

Hatter could swear Peabody was laughing when the Guard let out a bloodcurdling shriek and lost his balance. Pinwheeling his arms, the Guard fell backward into the water. Amid much splashing and cursing, the Guard managed to swim to the dock and his fellow Guards pulled him out of the water.

Leonard shook his finger at Peabody again, but was laughing too hard to admonish the crocodile. Instead, he tried to control his snickering as he walked up to the castle's door.

It was a small door as such things go, unlike the giant, ornately carved doors at the front of the castle. They were for show; this one was purely for ordinary use. It was locked, but clicked open at the sound of the Red King's voice.

Opening it, Leonard ushered them all inside the Red Palace.

Now, nothing stood between them and the Red Queen. It was time for a showdown.

Chapter Twenty-One

Once inside, the group found themselves in the Red Castle dungeon. It looked every bit as grim, dirty, and hopeless as Henry imagined dungeons would be. Nothing was clean; not the floors, the walls, the bars, the cells, nor the few prisoners they spotted in the dim recesses of the dank, narrow cubicles. The smell was positively noxious, thick with the stench of moldy hay, rancid food, and other odors best left unidentified. Most of the inmates looked as bad as the cells, and judging from the lengths of their beards, as if they'd been in there a long, long time. Henry even remarked on it to Hatter.

Hatter shook his head. "Oh, I can't say they've been here for very long. Those are Furfaces, from a village in the northeast. Funny group of folks. Everyone in their tribe has a beard, even the women and children, except for the youngest babies. They use their beards as currency. Need to purchase a new pair of boots? Lop off an inch or two of your chin whiskers to pay for them. The seller braids that bit of hair into his own beard, making it longer and fuller, and therefore wealthier. Besides, during my unfortunate incarceration here, I was the only prisoner. They must've come in after I left. Funny, that. The Queen usually doesn't bother with troublesome prison sentences when a quick head-rolling will do."

One of the gaunt, hairy prisoners came up to the bars of his cell, peering intently at them. "Bless my beard! Can it be? Is that really… it is!" He turned his head and hissed at his fellow inmates. "Take a knee and show some respect for our King!" He dipped down on one knee, bowing his head. His long, full beard brushed the floor, collecting bits of dust like a mop. "Your Majesty! We all thought you dead!"

Leonard stepped up, and nodded formally to the bearded man. "Please stand. As you can see, I am still among the living. I've been on sabbatical these past few years, studying subjects of, er, great importance and relevance to the whole of Wonderland." Leonard shot Hatter a cautionary look as if warning him not to say anything to the contrary. For once Hatter took the hint and remained silent. "Tell me, how did men of the Furface Tribe come to be in my dungeon?

The first hairy man spoke. "I am Neckbeard, Tribal Elder. Beg pardon, Sire, but it was your wife who put us here. The Queen found us guilty of treason and sentenced us to the Axe. The Axe, however, was dull from its recent overuse, and we were put here until it was sufficiently sharp again."

Leonard's bushy white eyebrows shot up. "I have never known the Furface Tribe to be the cause of difficulties before. What did you do to be found guilty of such a heinous crime?"

"She...." Neckbeard's face—what little could be seen peeking from under his facial hair—paled, and tears came to his eyes. "Oh, it was horrible, Your Majesty! She ordered us, the Furface People of the North, to... to shave!"

The men behind him moaned aloud as if in pain, and gathered up their beards, holding them protectively in their hands.

"Great heavens!" Leonard gasped, and put a hand to his chest. "What was she thinking? It would be easier to get the Cheshire Cat to change his stripes than convince a Furface to shave his beard! They're part of who you are, like the color of your eyes, or the shape of your ears. How dare she condemn you for the simple act of being as Nature intended you to be?" He turned to Hatter and Henry. "That seals it. I can no longer doubt my wife's incompetence. She is a threat and danger to everyone in Wonderland that I cannot and *will* not tolerate a moment longer."

"Oh, Your Majesty! I knew you wouldn't forsake your people!" Neckbeard plucked out a nice-sized patch of chin hair, wincing as he did so. "Please accept this small token of our appreciation." He held it out to Leonard, who graciously accepted the curl of silver hair and stuffed it into a pocket.

"Your gift is generous, as is your spirit." Leonard touched the lock on the cell door, which immediately clicked open. "By order of the Red King, you and your men are free, Neckbeard. Go in peace, and know your tribe will be safe from any and all shears, and held in high esteem by the Throne." He turned back to Hatter and Henry. "I'm going to tell the crocodiles to allow Neckbeard and his men to safely cross the moat. Then we're going to find my wife and settle this nonsense once and for all!"

Henry watched the Furfaces as they followed Leonard out the back door, and absently rubbed the peach fuzz on his own chin. Imagine, condemning someone for simply refusing to shave! It didn't make sense to him. What skin was it off the Red Queen's nose if the Furfaces had beards? No one was telling her *she* had to grow one.

Personally, he was a little jealous of the Furfaces. According to Hatter, even the kids of the tribe had beards. He'd always thought he might like to grow one, a goatee, maybe, or at least a nice, full mustache. Unfortunately, it was difficult for him to grow anything more than a sparse dusting on his cheeks, and when he did, it was such a light blondish-red it was barely noticeable. He shaved more for the sake of shaving than any real need, although he'd never admit it. His lack of facial hair was a sore point with him, and he was more than envious of the Furfaces' thick beards.

Even Hatter had dark, sexy stubble shadowing his jaw. It wasn't thick enough for Henry to call it a beard, but it wasn't spotty or scraggly, either. Actually, now that Henry thought about it, Hatter's stubble suited him perfectly, and made Hatter seem just a tiny bit dangerous and wild.

"How long were you in the dungeon for, Hatter?" he asked as a way of distracting himself from the very tempting notion to touch Hatter's cheeks and feel that scratchy stubble against his palm. He was almost sorry he asked when Hatter's smile dropped away, and a frown puckered his brow.

"Too long." He seemed to consider the question for a bit. "How many years has Alice been back in her world after her second trip to Wonderland?"

Henry thought for a moment. "She was seven and half or so then, I think, and she's twenty-two now. That's fourteen and a half years. I was only two and a half when she came back. I grew up hearing her stories of Wonderland."

Hatter's voice was very soft. "Fourteen and a half years? It felt like much longer."

Henry turned to him, his mouth hanging open in shock. "You were locked up here for that long? Alice said you were already grown when she met you at the Tea Party. How old *are* you?"

A small, sad smile lifted Hatter's lips. "Older than yesterday, and younger than tomorrow."

"Come on, Hatter. I need a better answer than that."

"Do you?" Hatter sighed. "I suppose you're right. The truth is I don't know. I was twenty when the Queen found me guilty of murdering Time, and Time cursed me into the never-ending Tea Party. I really don't know how long I was in there, but when I escaped, everyone I knew seemed so much older to me, and we know fourteen and a half years have passed since Alice's last visit. Trouble is, I haven't aged at all. I can't. Even though I escaped the Tea Party, Time hasn't lifted its curse. I'll be twenty years old forever."

"Well, that's kind of cool, isn't it? Never to grow old?"

"You'd think so, wouldn't you? I thought so too, in the beginning. I've had time to consider the matter, though, and don't find the proposition so very wonderful after all. Henry, there's a reason it's called a curse. I won't change, but eventually, everyone I know and love will grow old and die, and I'll be left here all alone. I'll meet new people, I suppose, and grow to love them, perhaps, but then I'll lose them to Time and death, too, again and again, forever."

The true scope of Hatter's curse hit Henry like a punch to the gut, and he gasped. He spontaneously threw his arms around Hatter, patting his back, although he didn't know if he was comforting Hatter or himself. He couldn't help it. Hatter looked so incredibly sad, he was sorry he'd brought the subject up at all. How awful, to watch everyone you love grow old and die! Hatter would never find anyone to grow old with because Hatter would never age. "I'm sorry, Hatter."

Hatter leaned into him for a minute, resting his cheek on Henry's shoulder before pulling away. "Never you mind. It's all right. I've nearly grown used to the idea." The smile he tried to summon was so cheerless and resigned it only made Henry feel worse, though.

Hatter pointed at the third cell on their left. "That one was mine. Gah! I'd hoped never to see it again." He chuckled, but Henry didn't think he sounded very amused.

Leonard came back from seeing the Furfaces out, and stood waiting by a stone archway. "Come on, cheer up now, Hatter. You're free, and I'll make certain you never see the inside of a cell again."

Leonard disappeared through the archway, and they hurried to catch up. "Thank you, Your Majesty," Hatter said. "That comes as a relief."

"I should say so," Henry added. He shivered, thinking of himself forced to spend any length of time at all in one of the cramped, filthy cells. He doubted prisons in his own world were much better, and promised himself that when he got back—if he got back—he wouldn't break the law. Not so much as jaywalk. There was no way he was going to jail if he could help it, not in his own world and definitely not in this one

They found themselves standing in a narrow corridor. The walls were soaring hedges, grown to many feet above the tallest Red Guard's head. They were thick, impenetrable walls of green, filled with many long, sharp thorns. Gazing up, Henry realized he could see the sky. The hedges were grown in some sort of open courtyard within the Red Castle walls.

"Ah, the Great Hedge Maze. I always loved taking long walks in there. So peaceful," Leonard whispered. "I once got lost in there for over a week. It was the best seven days of my marriage in recent memory."

"Never fear," Hatter said. He rummaged in his pocket, pulling out several items—a mug, a photo frame, and the umbrella Henry remembered from their escape from the Red Anthill—and handing them to Henry to hold, before pulling out a folded piece of paper. The paper looked old, creased and browned with age. He carefully unfolded it, holding it out in front of him.

Henry juggled the items Hatter had handed him as he leaned in to see what the paper was. It was a map.

"I always knew this would come in handy." Hatter pointed to an arrow on the map, which boasted large white letters that read *You Are Here.* "We just need to follow this map to get through the Maze."

"What if we aren't here, where the arrow is pointing?" Henry asked, tapping the spot on the map with his finger. "What if we're somewhere else?"

"Nonsense. Think about it. No matter *where* we were, we'd be *there*, which of course, would make it *here* for us, now wouldn't it?" Hatter clucked his tongue. "Really, Henry, I'd have thought you'd understand Wonderland a bit better by now."

He was right, of course. Henry should've known better than to ask. It was much easier in Wonderland to just go with the flow and not examine things too closely. In fact, now that he thought about it, he thought that might be what made all magic work—you had to *believe* the magician was really pulling a rabbit out of an empty hat. Without belief, it was just a crazy guy with a top hat and a pet bunny.

Was that what made Ruin a reality? People believing that someone needed to live in Ruin so others could enjoy more? If it was, he didn't think it was right. It sounded like something the Red Queen might've come up with, a plan that wasn't a plan at all but another way to punish people and keep them under her heel. What about the people in Ruin? Why did they stay? Did they believe it too?

He filed the question away to ponder on sometime later, and turned his attention to the Maze itself. His gaze wandered up the leafy sides, and he saw sharp thorns studding the soaring green walls of thick shrubbery. It reminded Henry greatly of the Caterpillar's Lair. Perhaps the seeds from Caterpillar's hedge had sowed the ones forming the Maze, or vice versa. In either case, there was no chance of him burrowing a shortcut through the walls without skewering himself.

He realized the group was already marching through, and hurried to catch up to Hatter. The twists and turns inside the Maze as Hatter boldly led them through it, following the course marked on the map, soon had Henry's head spinning. He tried to keep track, but quickly became so lost he had no idea where he was or how to retrace his steps if need be. Trusting in Hatter's map to see them through was all he could do, and he hoped his belief was strong enough, and that his faith wasn't misplaced, especially when he spied a dusty, gray skull sitting atop a roughly man-shaped pile of bones in a corner of the Maze.

Not everyone who went into the Maze, evidently, got out again. He had to wonder how many others met their deaths wandering the narrow corridors of verdant green, and said a silent prayer he wouldn't be among them.

His fear proved to be needless soon enough as, after rounding yet another corner in a seemingly never-ending line of zigs and zags, he a saw an arch carved into the center of a tall green wall. Beyond it, all he could see was blessedly wide, flat landscape.

They filed out of the Maze, and all of them breathed a sigh of relief, even Hatter, whom later confided to Henry he hadn't been as confident in his map as he professed to be. "The map, after all," Hatter explained, "was drawn by an elf that was far less than trustworthy than most people and far more inebriated than some. For all I knew, it might've not been a map to the maze at all, but one detailing the inner ear canal of a hippopotamus."

Henry was very glad Hatter's confession came *after* they'd left the Maze.

Leonard stepped past them and smiled. "I always loved this part of the garden. A rousing game of chess was just the thing I needed on days when my wife busied herself making my life miserable."

Henry looked down at the giant, alternating red and white squares painted on the grass, then around at the life-sized chess pieces that stood in two stately lines on each side of the board. Each piece was a topiary—a bush, carefully trimmed and snipped into shapes—the Kings and Queens, the Bishops, the Knights on their Horses, the Rooks, and the Pawns. All sat in absolute stillness, with no hint of life about them. They all looked so massive and heavy, the shortest Pawn standing far taller than Henry did, that he wondered how anyone could maneuver them across the field-sized chessboard. He decided to ask, then immediately gave himself a mental kick to the head as soon as the words passed his lips, since he really should have known better. The answer was the same as he always received when he asked ridiculous questions, but by then it was too late. He could no more pull the words back into his mouth than rescind a fart once let loose.

"How else?" Hatter replied with a shrug. "Magic."

"Of course. How stupid of me." Henry sighed, plucked a leaf from a Knight topiary, and held it up before his eyes, examining it. It looked like an ordinary leaf, green and shaped like an arrowhead. It smelled green, too, or *would* smell like green, he imagined, if colors had odors. Green would smell like this, like a warm, lazy, summer day.

This particular leaf was identical to any one of a million leaves he'd seen on trees in his own world, completely unremarkable, except he truly believed this one was imbued with some sort of mystical, unknowable magic that would allow it to move when a player gave it an order. Why shouldn't he believe it? It was no stranger than anything else he'd seen in Wonderland. "Knight to F3," he mumbled, tossing the leaf aside.

There was a rumble under his feet reminiscent of a slight earthquake, and a rustling sounded in the air as if a strong wind were blowing through trees. Then the Knight topiary beside him lurched forward. The Knight's horse leapt into the air, the horse's hooves trailing long, scraggly roots, sailing over the head of a pawn and landed exactly where Henry told it to, on the F3 square of the board.

"Henry!" Leonard clucked his tongue. "Really, we've no time to play games. Now, put the Knight back, and let's get moving."

Henry gaped at the Knight for a moment—which looked stoically ahead, unmoving, as if made of stone instead of shrubbery—and then grinned. *Belief it is*, he concluded. *I believed the piece would move and it did! That's the secret to Wonderland. Believing. It's what fuels magic.* He felt very satisfied with himself, and smug, as if he'd discovered a great secret.

Perhaps he had. He certainly felt more comfortable in Wonderland now that he believed than he had before, when he'd spent all his time questioning and doubting everything around him. His smile was still on his face when he passed the Knight and said "Knight to G1." He barely even noticed the Knight leaping back over the same Pawn to its original square, as if giant hopping topiaries were as common as houseflies.

There really was no more time to ruminate on magic, or belief, on the nature of Ruin or any one of a number of other questions rumbling around in Henry's mind after his newfound discovery clicked into place. The entire group, Hatter, Leonard, Henry, and the Red Guard, had all come to a complete standstill once they'd passed the far side of the chessboard.

Before them was a long swatch of lawn, not especially wide, but quite lush and studded with croquet wickets. At the far end, a flock of bright pink flamingos lounged, each bird resting comfortably on long, spindly black legs. Their lengthy, graceful necks curled over their backs, with their heads tucked neatly under their wings.

A slight noise woke them, and they looked up as Henry, Hatter, Leonard and the Guards approached, but quickly went back to their naps when it became apparent no one favored a game of croquet.

Hatter pulled away from the group and ran to a nearby planting of shrubs. Henry frowned as he watched Hatter drop to his knees and begin rooting among the roots under the bushes.

"Yes! I've found you!" Hatter stood up, cradling something long and thin in his arms. "I thought you were lost forever!"

Henry saw a shiny blue orb glint on one end of the item. "What is it, Hatter?"

"My cane!" Hatter grinned and held it up. It was carved from a dark, oily wood, and topped with a sparkling blue diamond as big as Henry's fist.

"Well... good. I'm glad." Henry blinked.

"Indeed!" Hatter seemed to be in a much more buoyant mood. He strutted back to Henry, and hefted the cane like a drum major leading a parade. "Onward!"

Just on the other side of the croquet lawn, the open courtyard area ended. In the castle's red wall, they spotted another door.

Henry tapped Hatter's arm. "Where does this door lead to? Another dungeon? The kitchen?"

"No, I'm afraid not." Hatter reached for Henry's hand and gave it a squeeze. "This is it, Henry. The end of our journey. Beyond that door is a hallway that leads to the throne room."

Henry hadn't thought he'd be especially frightened or nervous when they reached their ultimate destination, not when they'd been walking such a long road with so many dangerous diversions, they made his head spin. Now that they'd arrived at the Red Castle and their quarry waited within, he felt his heartbeat speed up and a cold sweat dampen his forehead. This was it! Another moment or two and he'd be face-to-face with the Red Queen. After hearing all the stories about her, in his mind he was convinced she was the most sinister, despicable, dangerous creature ever to draw breath, and their imminent meeting in the flesh had him weak in the knees. The Red Queen was a woman who sentenced people to die as easily as others swatted bothersome flies. Would he be able to make a stand against her with Hatter and Leonard, or would he disgrace himself by running away?

Chapter Twenty-Two

Leonard signaled one of the Red Guard to open and hold the door so he and the rest of the party could enter the Castle proper. It was dimmer inside than the sunny, open courtyard, although many burning candles set in wall sconces cast the hallway with adequate light. Even so, they could barely make out the shapes of two huge men standing in front of them as their eyes adjusted.

Two immense Red Guard blocked their way, their swords drawn. "Halt! Who goes there?"

"Who goes where?" Hatter asked. "There or here? We're all quite here, but the two of you are there. You really must be more specific."

The Guards looked at one another. "Uh, there. Right there." He pointed his sword at Hatter's feet.

"Right here?" Hatter asked, and pointed to the same spot. "That's not there. That's here. Are you purposely trying to confuse us?"

The first Red Guard thought it over. Watching him try to make sense of it was positively painful. Finally, he seemed to come up with a solution. "All right then, who goes *here?* Is that better?"

Hatter shrugged. "If by 'here' you mean over there where you are, then no. Conversely, if by 'here' you mean over here where we are, then yes, it is better. To answer your question, we go here."

"Who *are* you?" The Red Guard sputtered. He seemed well past confused and halfway to bewildered, and kept turning to the second Red Guard for help. The second didn't seem to understand what Hatter was talking about either, so was of absolutely no value to the first.

"I'm afraid 'Who' isn't my name. In fact, I don't know anyone named 'Who.'" Hatter turned to Henry. "Do you know anyone named Who?" He turned back to the Guard. "There's no Who here."

"Oh, Hatter, do desist in confusing my Guard." Leonard chuckled as he pushed past Hatter and stood in front of the two Guards. "It is I, the Red King."

Perhaps the two Guards were loyal to Leonard, or else they were just so relieved not to have to try to figure out Hatter's doubletalk anymore that they dropped to one knee and bowed their heads. "Sire! We thought you dead!"

"Yes, that seems to be a popular misconception. I'm not, as you can see. Not even a little bit. Never have been." Leonard motioned for them to rise. "I'm here to dethrone my wife."

The two Guards let out a horrified gasp in perfect, two-part harmony. "Are you sure, Your Majesty? You seem to be doing so well with not being dead, and still having your head attached to your shoulders and all. It'd be a shame for you to turn toes up now."

Leonard shook his head. "I appreciate your concern, but I've made up my mind. The Red Queen's reign of terror must end. Come along, now. Fall in behind the others." He gestured toward the Guards who'd been with them since the White Castle.

The two new Guards looked at their fellows, then at each other. "Is that an order, Sire?"

Leonard folded his arms across his chest. "Yes. It's an order."

They seemed disinclined to believe Leonard was commanding them, or, more likely, hoped it wasn't the case. "Is that an official order, Sire, or is it more like a request?"

Leonard scowled at the Guard. "It's an official order. A command." He sighed and rolled his eyes when the Guard still hesitated. "Do it *now.*"

"Yes, Sire." Neither of the Guard seemed particularly enthusiastic about joining Leonard's party, but they eventually did as Leonard instructed, taking up spots at the rear. Maybe they remembered to whom they owed their loyalty, or perhaps they simply consoled themselves with the fact that Leonard, Hatter, Henry, and the other Guards formed a nice, thick, fleshy barrier between them and the wrath of the Red Queen.

Henry leaned over and whispered to Hatter. "Um, do you have any sort of weapon in your pocket? I feel a little useless here. I think I'd feel better if I had something to defend us with when we go into the throne room."

"Hmm. Weapons, eh?" Hatter stuck his arm into his pocket up to the elbow, rummaging around. "I hadn't thought of weapons before. I'm not sure what I have.... Ah, yes! Here you are. Not the most efficient weapon, I suppose, but it will do in a pinch." He pulled out his umbrella and offered it to Henry.

"Hatter, this is an umbrella. The only thing it'll be good for is if I get attacked by a sudden rain shower."

"I know! Those sudden showers are particularly troublesome. They sneak up on you, and then before you know it, you're soaked to the skin, coughing, feverish, and dying of some despicable rain-borne illness. With this in hand, you don't need to worry about any of that. You're welcome."

"Ha! If I lose my head, I won't need to worry about it, either." He made a practice jab with the closed umbrella, and wondered if it was possible to poke someone to death.

Hatter either didn't hear Henry, or more likely chose to ignore the sarcastic comment. Instead, he rooted around in his pocket again, before withdrawing a very long, very slender drinking straw. He held it up and smiled.

"A straw? Suddenly, I don't feel so bad about my umbrella," Henry said. "What good is that going to do you unless you're attacked by a giant carbonated beverage?"

Hatter shot him a dark look. "Soda Pop attacks are nothing to laugh about, Henry. First of all, they rarely attack alone. Soda Pops always bring their Soda Moms, along with their Soda Sons, Daughters, Nephews, Nieces, Aunts, Uncles, and Next-Door Neighbors with them. A Mass Soda Attack is a serious thing." He brandished his straw. "This is no ordinary drinking straw. It's a Soul Sucker. With this, I can suck the soul out of anything. Not for long, mind you. Souls are notoriously territorial, and will flee back to their original vessels after only a short time, but in the meanwhile, their owners are left frozen, giving the user time to destroy the vessel or escape the vicinity."

Henry arched an eyebrow and examined the straw. It didn't look any different from any you'd find in a gas station that sold oversized cold drinks, yet he didn't doubt it would do just as Hatter claimed. He'd seen too many strange and bizarre things in Wonderland to question it.

They continued following Leonard down the long, red-carpeted hallway. Henry gazed round-eyed at the portraits of Kings and Queens hanging on both sides, and noticed the crowns in each painting which grew larger and larger as they progressed toward the throne room. He whispered to Hatter, feeling uncomfortable with raising his voice this close to the room where they suspected the Red Queen waited. "Why do they each need bigger and bigger crowns?"

"Bigger heads. Seems with every generation, their noggins swell a bit more. It's the ever-thickening vanity in their blood. Conceit is a bloated, nasty thing, and takes up quite a bit of room inside the skull. Each new Red Prince or Princess seems to have more of it than their parents did. I should know. Once upon a time, I was the Royal Hatter." Pride shone in Hatter's eyes. "The Queen's father would wear no hat that didn't come from my shop."

"It's true," Leonard said. "My wife's grandfather wore a size 8, and her father, a size 8 1/2. Her own head couldn't fit a hat smaller than 9, although she'll swear she's only a 6 1/2. The new Royal Hatter—he wasn't nearly as talented as you, Hatter—made the mistake of putting her actual size on the inside label of one of her winter hats. I suppose you can guess what she had done to him." He made a rude noise and sliced a finger across his throat. "Her vanity is outdone only by her viciousness."

"I wonder if her head has swelled any more since last I saw her. I always thought it if got any bigger, it would pop like a balloon and save us all a lot of trouble," Hatter said as they reached the end of the hallway. A pair of immense intricately carved double doors stood between them and the throne room. "I don't suppose she'd be so accommodating as to self-explode, would she?"

"Not likely," Leonard replied. "One can always hope, of course." He gestured toward two of the Red Guard. "Open the doors to the throne room, please."

Neither looked very anxious to obey, and both made sure to stay safely hidden behind the doors as they slowly pulled them open.

"What is this? Who's there?" The Queen's voice, high-pitched and as sharp as broken glass, echoed in the throne room. "Rabbit! Find out who dares enter my throne room without a formal announcement. It's rude. Off with their heads!"

"Erm, should their heads be removed before or after I find out who it is, Your Majesty?" Rabbit's voice was much more timid than the Queen's, although still audible. The acoustics in the throne room were excellent for that purpose.

A different voice answered for the Red Queen. "I should think asking *after* their heads roll would result in a less than satisfactory answer."

Hatter recognized the Cheshire Cat's voice, and frowned. He'd hoped the damned Cat would be gone by now. Cat tended to make everything more complicated and confuzzling than it needed to be.

Leonard pushed past the doors and boldly stalked up the aisle toward the dais on which the royal thrones sat. Well, *one* throne sat there, anyway… he noticed his own throne tossed to one side of the room, lying on its side, covered in cobwebs and a fat layer of dust. "No need, Rabbit. No heads will roll today. It is I, the Red King, come back to claim my throne!"

Rabbit gasped and wheezed, and clutched his heart, then seemed to decide against dying from a heart attack and took a knee instead, bowing his head. "Your Majesty!"

Hatter, Henry, and the Red Guard had followed Leonard into the throne room. Everything looked just as Hatter recalled it from his last visit. The Red Queen was sitting on her throne, having a full-fledged tantrum. Her enormous royal crown hung over her head, suspended from the ceiling by a wire. Nearby, the Cheshire Cat floated in the air, grinning his mischievous smile.

Hatter had to admit Leonard struck quite an imposing figure, and he couldn't help but admire him. Leonard stood tall, his expression regal and proud, his eyes glowing like blue flame. Even Hatter was tempted to take a knee, although he talked himself out of it soon enough.

The Cheshire Cat fell silent, a condition Hatter had never before seen the Cat in. Hatter decided he rather liked it, and hoped it would continue for the foreseeable future.

There was no such luck with the Red Queen, though. Staring at Leonard, for a moment her tongue seemed to refuse to function properly. Her eyes grew very big and very round, bulging out of her head in a most unattractive manner and her mouth grew very small and puckered, as if she'd just sucked on a lemon. The shock of seeing her husband standing in her throne room, alive and breathing, seemed to pass quickly, though, because she drew in a great lungful of air, and let out a howling screech that shattered two of the Red Guards' eardrums and six panes of window glass. "You! What are *you* doing here? I sent my Guard to the ruins of the White Castle to make sure you never returned from the mirror. You're supposed to be good and gone!"

Leonard gestured toward himself. "As you can see, I am not even a little bit gone. I am fully here."

The Queen gnashed her teeth and gripped the arms of her throne so tightly, her nails bit into the wood. "Well, then I sentence you to the Axe. Off with your head! I command it!"

Leonard leaned forward a bit. He didn't scream, didn't yell, didn't even raise his voice at all, but the word echoed through the room anyway, bringing a collective gasp from everyone, perhaps simply because no one had ever heard the word said in the Queen's presence before.

"No."

The Queen set loose a scream unlike any heard before in all of Wonderland. It ripped through the throne room, cracking the remaining windowpanes, every wineglass in the room, and Rabbit's pair of spectacles. It bounced off the walls like a living thing, overturning chairs, knocking the stuffing out of all the royal cushions, and causing the gigantic crown hanging above the Queen's head to sway. "WHAT DID YOU SAY?"

Leonard seemed completely unmoved and unafraid in the face of her fury. Perhaps, since he was married to the Queen for so many years, the effect of her terrible temper had worn off on him. He shrugged, as if unconcerned. "I said, 'no.'"

"AXE! Come in here now! Off with his head!" The Queen bounced furiously on her throne, banging her fists and kicking her feet. "Off with his head!"

The side door, which led out to the courtyard, creaked open and the Axe entered the throne room at the Queen's call. The Axe was just that—a huge, double-bladed Axe, animated by powerful magic, and spelled to do the Queen's bidding. Its razor-sharp edge gleamed bright as it swung through the air in massive arcs.

Every head turned to stare at the Axe, hands immediately flying to their throats as if they could protect their necks from the Axe's blade.

Every head, that is, except Leonard's. He hurried up the few steps to the dais, and stood next to the throne. He ignored the Axe, and smiled smugly at his wife, as if he knew something she did not. As it turned out, he did. "You ruled all those years because I was too weak or too indifferent to do my duty. That is my sin, and I shall live with it forever. No more will I shirk my responsibility. You may be royal by blood, while I am merely royal by marriage, but you, my dear, are a *terrible* monarch and a *dreadful* human being. I hereby declare a coup, relieving you of your crown."

The Red Queen screamed again and stood up on her throne, glowering at Leonard. She clenched her hands in tight fists, and her face flushed as red as her hair. Veins stood out on her forehead like fat, angry worms. "You dare speak to me this way? Off with your head! Off, I say! Here he is, Axe. Hurry!"

The Axe, enchanted to obey her as always, swung.

Leonard, however, did something unexpected. He refused to stand still and have his head lopped off properly. When the Axe sliced through the air aiming for Leonard's neck, he ducked.

Instead of cutting through Leonard's flesh, the Axe passed over his head and cut through the wire holding the enormous crown up over the Queen's head.

The heavy, solid gold crown fell straight down with a dull, ringing *thung*, completely covering the Queen from head to foot. It toppled off the throne with the same *thunging* sound, and rolled a few feet across the floor before coming to a stop. All anyone could see of the Queen were the tips of her red shoes.

The Axe fell to the floor, clattering loudly, before falling still. It lay there looking very disenchanted, like an ordinary, everyday, giant-sized axe. Hatter tentatively toed it with the tip of his shoe.

Silence fell on the throne room.

"Well," Hatter said, "that was unexpected."

Henry's hand slipped into his. "Is she… is she dead?" His face was pale, but his grip was warm and firm.

Hatter gave his hand a squeeze. "Look at the Axe. Its magic is gone. It was enchanted to obey the Red Queen only, so I'd say the odds are she's gone toes up. I can't say I'm sorry, and I don't think anyone else is, either. She didn't exactly endear herself to anyone, what with lopping off people's heads left and right."

Leonard brushed off the velvet cushion of the throne, and sat down. "I hereby reclaim my throne, and right to rule over Wonderland. Does anyone challenge my right to do so?"

No one stepped forward. Hatter didn't think anyone would. It was a lot of work, running a kingdom the size of Wonderland. At least, it was when it was done right, and the monarch didn't spend all her time ordering heads to roll. There were lots of details to tend to—squabbles to referee, property disputes to settle, magic to dispense or dispel as needed. Certainly, there was too much work and not enough benefits as far as Hatter was concerned. With great power came great responsibility and even greater headaches. Leonard was welcome to it. Everyone else, Henry, the Red Guard, Rabbit, and the Cheshire Cat, all seemed to agree, since no one volunteered.

Leonard smiled. He tossed a pointed glance at the giant crown and the tips of his former wife's shoes. "Well, then. That's settled. I suppose I'll need to commission a new crown. Nothing heavy, and metal, even gold, is too damn uncomfortable to wear. I'm thinking of something in a nice derby, perhaps. Think you can manage to create one for me, Hatter?"

"Of course, Your Majesty. It would be my pleasure." Hatter grinned.

The Cheshire Cat floated nearer to the throne, still grinning. "It's very good to have you back, Your Majesty."

Leonard returned Cat's smile. "Thank you, Cat. You did well. Remind me to reward you later. I happen to know where there is a rather substantial quantity of catnip of an excellent year stored."

"Wait… what?" Hatter shook his head, then stuck his fingers in his ears, wiggling them as if to clean them out. "You knew about Leonard being in Alice's World?"

Cat yawned, and began grooming himself. "Of course I did. Someone had to be left behind to make sure the Queen didn't completely destroy Wonderland."

Hatter turned to Leonard in disbelief. "You told Cat you were leaving, but not me? The Queen nearly had me killed!"

"Nonsense. I had everything under control at all times," Cat said. "I got her to send you after Henry, didn't I?"

Hatter sputtered, not quite able to decide whether he wanted to strangle Cat or thank him. He decided, in the interest of fairness, to do neither.

Leonard nodded, and turned to Henry. "Henry, my boy, I want to thank you for returning here to support me. I suppose it's obvious I'll not be returning to your world, but what about you?"

Henry bit his lip and glanced at Hatter. "I'm not sure. Do I have to decide right now?"

"Of course not." Leonard winked at him. "You're welcome to stay in Wonderland for as long as you wish. I'm sure Hatter wouldn't mind putting you up. The Royal Hatter's Suite is quite spacious."

That was enough to take Hatter's mind off Cat as he realized he had far sweeter things to consider. Things like Henry, and their kiss, and whether there would any more kisses like it in their future. He grinned and squeezed Henry's hand again. "I'd be most happy for Henry to stay with me. For as long as he wants to remain here."

He felt warmth flush him from his hairline to his toes when Henry smiled and squeezed his hand back. "I think I'd like that, Uncle Leonard... er, Your Majesty."

Hatter couldn't contain himself any more. Joy bubbled up from the vicinity of his heart and overflowed. Reaching out, he pulled Henry into a fiery kiss that sent sparks sizzling through the air around them. One lit on Cat's tail, causing Cat to hiss at them, and everyone else to chuckle.

"Finally," Leonard said. A broad smile lit his face. "Alice was right, then. She said you two were made for each other. It was one of the reasons she and I conspired to send you to Wonderland in the first place, Henry. Well, that, and because we both felt it was the only way to convince you she'd been telling the truth all those years."

Hatter seemed to have kissed Henry silly, since a loopy grin remained on Henry's face and he failed to challenge Leonard's confession. Hatter wasn't even sure Henry had heard it. "Well, I, for one, think Wonderland just got a little bit more wonderful when Henry arrived. Now, if you don't mind, Your Majesty, I think you've got some cleaning up to do. Then you'll have announcements to make, messengers sent out to the rest of Wonderland, so forth and so on. Henry and I have some things to talk over as well, so we'll retire to the Royal Hatter Suite until you need us again."

Leonard waved his hand, and nodded, dismissing them. As Hatter led Henry out of the throne room, he could hear Leonard begin issuing kingly orders. "Well, we might as well make it official. I hereby find the Red Queen guilty of crimes against Wonderland and its people. Take that ridiculous crown and the Queen to the Royal Physician. It simply wouldn't do to bury her unless she's truly dead. The ghosts in the Royal Crypt would have fits. If the Royal Physician finds her to be alive, then she can have Hatter's old cell. In the meantime, I suppose I'll need the Royal Scribe so I can put forth a few announcements and proclamations, that sort of thing."

Cat addressed Leonard. "Sorry, Your Majesty, but the position of Royal Scribe is currently open. The Queen sent the last one to the Axe."

"Why am I not surprised? I suppose I'll have to replace nearly *all* the staff, hmm? Well, first things first. I need a new Royal Scribe. My penmanship is like chicken scratch." Leonard said. "Rabbit, how is *your* handwriting?"

Rabbit's nervous gulp was audible. "M-me, Sire?"

"No, the invisible rabbit standing next to you. Yes, you."

"Oh, dear. I... I'm afraid I'm very late for an appointment, Your Majesty. Yes, indeed, I'm running out of time. I must—"

Leonard scowled down at Rabbit. "The only thing you should be running after is a quill and parchment. *Now,* Rabbit, before I get a sudden craving for Rabbit stew."

Rabbit gave a little squeak. "Immediately, Sire. Just what I had in mind. Back in a jiffy. A quill. Where would one find a quill?" Rabbit scurried about, checking all the nooks and crannies in the throne room, although he gave the Queen-filled crown a wide berth. The longer he went without finding one, the more upset he seemed to become. No doubt he was picturing himself stewing in the Royal Pot.

"Don't let him suffer, Hatter," Henry whispered. "Don't you have a pen or something in that pocket of yours?"

Hatter sniffed. "Hmph. Help him? He worked for the Queen! Tried to haul us back to the castle, remember?"

"Sure, I remember. I also remember you worked for the Queen, at least when we first met. Or did you think I'd forgotten?" Henry frowned at Hatter, but a small smile played at his lips.

Hatter cringed. "I said I was sorry. Very well." He dug into his pocket and withdrew a large, feathery white quill, a small pot of ink, and a rolled piece of parchment tied with a red bow. He handed them to Rabbit. "Don't say I never gave you anything."

Rabbit snatched them out of Hatter's hands. "Well, it's about time. Imagine, letting me run about like a crazy person while you had a quill, ink, and parchment in your possession all the while! I'm the new Royal Scribe, in case you haven't heard. I've got the King's ear. I ought to bring you up on charges with him. In fact, I believe there's still an outstanding warrant for you that the Queen issued." Rabbit huffed, lifting his little pink nose in the air.

Leonard's voice thundered, causing Rabbit to squeak and leave a few tiny brown pellets on the floor. "Rabbit! Stop pooping on my throne room floor before I order you put in diapers. I'm waiting to proclaim things. Let's get on with it."

"Right away, Your Majesty!" Rabbit blushed an unattractive shade of pink, turned and raced for the dais, already unrolling the parchment and readying his pot of ink and quill.

Leonard looked over Rabbit's head. "Hatter? Henry? What are you still doing here?"

Hatter and Henry shrugged and chuckled as they made their way out of the room and down the hall.

Epilogue

Three months later....

Henry folded a shirt and set it neatly on the small pile of others in his new suitcase. A satchel, Hatter called it. It was brown leather, and had straps to hold it closed. It was extremely old fashioned, but all he could find in the shops outside of the Red Castle.

He went to the narrow chest of drawers and removed two pairs of pants, but when he turned back to the suitcase, it was empty. He turned to see Hatter replacing his shirts in a dresser drawer.

Grabbing the shirts out of the drawer, he held them behind his back so Hatter couldn't reclaim them. "Hatter! I keep packing, and you keep unpacking. I'm never going to get done this way."

"That's the whole point. Besides, you don't need to pack. You're not *really* leaving."

Henry sighed, and sat down on the foot of his bed. "Hatter, it's been three months. I have to go back now."

"Why? You like it here, don't you? You like me, don't you?

Henry's lips lifted in a soft, sad smile. "Of course I do. But I still have to go back home."

Hatter sat next to him, looking like someone had just killed his puppy. "Why, Henry? Why not stay here with me? This is your home, too."

"I have to go back because Alice deserves to know what happened, and that I'm okay. Plus, she, Phillip, and the kids are all the family I have left in the world besides my dad. And my dad... he needs help, and I need to see that he gets it."

Hatter sniffed, and turned away, but Henry saw a tear glisten in his dark eyes. "I know."

"I'd stay if I could," Henry said. He placed a hand on Hatter's arm. "These three months have been great, and I loved all the places you've taken me. Diamond Falls, the Jubjub hatchery, the

Fiery Ice Cave...." He shook his head, and fought back tears of his own. "Just being with *you* has been an adventure I'll never forget."

Hatter leaned his elbows on his knees, and stared at the floor. "I don't want you to leave, Henry. I'm going to miss you too much."

"Then come with me."

"What?" Hatter looked up in surprise.

Henry grinned. "Come with me! There are so many places in my world I want to show you. New York City. The Grand Canyon. The Atlantic and Pacific oceans."

"And pizza?" Mischief glinted in Hatter's eyes.

Henry laughed. "All the pizza you can eat."

Hatter's smile faded, and his expression darkened. "No, I couldn't, Henry. You know, it's funny. Before I met you, I wouldn't have given a fig for responsibility. I came and went as I pleased, did what I wanted. My only concern was saving my own hide. I messed up more often that I care to remember, and lost everything I had. But being with you has made me grow up, and realize what's really important.

"I'm the Royal Hatter again. Leonard gave me a fresh start. I can't abandon him now that he's just getting settled in. He depends on me for all his hat needs, you know. Party hats. Diplomatic hats. Royal Audience hats. Court hats. Sun hats and Night caps, bowlers, fedoras, boaters, panamas... the list goes on and on."

"Can't he make do with the hats you've already made him for a while?"

"Oh, I don't know. A King needs to keep up appearances. It wouldn't do for people to see him in the same hat too often. People would begin to talk. They'd say his Royal Hatter is insufficiently sufficient in providing Royal haberdashery. Besides, it's not really about the hats, Henry. It's about responsibility, and honoring my word."

Henry sighed. "I understand. I guess I have to go back alone." He returned the shirts to his suitcase and closed the lid, securing the straps, then looked up at Hatter. "I'm going to miss you something awful." He reached for a hug, and they stood there for a long time, leaning against one another as if both could draw strength from the other. Tipping his head back, he placed a soft kiss on Hatter's lips, then pulled away and picked up his suitcase. "I'd better get going. It's a long way back to the White Castle. I'd like to reach Tweedledee and Tweedledum's before dark."

"Bye, Henry." Hatter's voice cracked with emotion.

Henry didn't trust his own voice to answer at all. He just nodded, and left the room without looking back again.

Leonard insisted on providing Henry with a Red Guard escort for his own safety, even though Henry tried to refuse. He didn't want anyone around him while he traveled back to the White Castle and the magic mirror. He wasn't in the mood for company or small talk. Even though he believed with his whole heart that he needed to go back to his own world, leaving Hatter behind had been one of the hardest things he'd had to do in his life.

As hard as it was, having Hatter choose his responsibility to Leonard over going with Henry was even worse. He'd thought he'd meant more to Hatter than that. Finding out he was wrong was like a knife to the heart that kept pushing in deeper and twisting every time he thought about it.

He swiped at an angry tear with the back of his hand. He'd be home soon—he could see the broken turrets of the White Castle in the distance—and he'd work to forget all about Hatter and Wonderland. In his world, there were other people, people more like himself. He'd find someone else to love.

Someone who didn't speak in double-talk all the time. Someone who didn't pull all manner of crazy stuff from a magic pocket. Someone who knew what a combustion engine was, and who didn't believe saddling a dragon was the fastest mode of transportation available.

Someone who wasn't Hatter.

Because there is nobody like Hatter, he thought morosely, his head hanging low as he walked. *Not in my world, or in Wonderland.*

"Henry! Henry!"

Henry smirked. *I can almost hear his voice. I wonder how long it'll take before I forget what he sounds like? Forget what he looks like? Or how his kisses made me feel?*

"Henry! For the love of shiny Jabberwock balls, wait up!"

Henry blinked and picked his head up. He spun around, scanning the path behind him. A figure was running toward him, one hand on top of its head, as if trying to keep a hat from flying off. After a moment, a face came into focus.

"Hatter? What are you doing here?" Henry felt a tentative finger of excitement tickle his belly. "Have you been following me all this time?"

Hatter reached him, and bent over at the waist, gasping for air while still holding his hat to his head. It took him a moment to regain enough breath to speak. "I almost caught up with you after you'd passed Ruin, but I found myself unable to hurry in the Neutral Wood. It made me slow my pace to a mere crawl, as if I had all the time and not a care in the world."

"Why were you following me? We said our good-byes." Henry felt his cheeks burn and looked away. "You made it perfectly clear your responsibility to Leonard was what mattered."

Hatter grabbed Henry by the shoulders, and forced Henry to look him in the eye. "Listen to me. I am a very stupid man. My duty to Leonard is important, and I can't just forget about it, but you're important to me, too. More important than any royal appointment or any hat I could possibly be called upon to make for the King. I thought Leonard was going to resurrect the Axe when he heard I'd sent you on alone. He told me to catch up to you even if I had to run the whole way. Ordered me to, in fact, and told me I'm not to return until you were sick and tired of having me around." He smiled and pulled Henry close, into a bear hug. "So you see, I have to go with you. If I don't, I'll be in direct violation of a royal order."

Henry's smile burgeoned into a wide, delighted grin. "Well, we can't have that, now can we?"

"No, we certainly cannot." Hatter placed his hands on Henry's cheeks, and kissed him good, long, and hard. So long and hard, in fact, that the Red Guard began clearing their throats and coughing to remind them they weren't alone.

Henry chuckled, and stepped away from Hatter. He reached for Hatter's hand, and held it. "Then I suppose we should go. We don't want to be accused of wasting Time."

Hatter gave a mock shudder. "No, indeed! Time, as I'm sure I've mentioned once or twice, has no sense of humor."

Time must not have been offended because it flew by as they chatted and laughed, climbing the hill to the White Castle, and making their way up to the room where the magic mirror waited.

"Ready?" Henry asked Hatter.

"Together," Hatter replied, holding up their linked hands.

Grinning at one another, they stepped through to the other side to their future in Henry's world.